CW00731878

The
CODE
BREAKER
GIRL

BOOKS BY GOSIA NEALON

Gosia Nealon

The CODE BREAKER GIRL

bookouture

Published by Bookouture in 2024

An imprint of Storyfire Ltd.
Carmelite House
50 Victoria Embankment
London EC4Y 0DZ

www.bookouture.com

Copyright © Gosia Nealon, 2024

Gosia Nealon has asserted her right to be identified as the author of this work.

All rights reserved. No part of this publication may be reproduced, stored in any retrieval system, or transmitted, in any form or by any means, electronic, mechanical, photocopying, recording or otherwise, without the prior written permission of the publishers.

ISBN: 978-1-83525-559-9
eBook ISBN: 978-1-83525-558-2

This book is a work of fiction. Names, characters, businesses, organizations, places and events other than those clearly in the public domain, are either the product of the author's imagination or are used fictitiously. Any resemblance to actual persons, living or dead, events or locales is entirely coincidental.

To my husband Jim and my sons Jacob, Jack and Jordan.
You're my everything.

PART 1

THE ENIGMA CIPHER MACHINE

PROLOGUE

BEATA

December 1932, Cipher Bureau of the Polish Armed Forces, Saski Palace, Warsaw

"Are you telling me that you cracked the Enigma codes, Mr. Rejewski?" A strong voice sounds through a wall. Kneeling in a tiny storage space, I freeze holding folders in my hands. I thought there wasn't anyone in the colonel's office...

It's my first day at a new job, and Czesława, a gray-haired secretary who's in charge of training me, announced earlier that the colonel phoned and ordered us to call it a day. Before she ran out to catch her bus, she instructed me to leave within minutes.

Nervous about not doing my job right, I ignored her request and stayed a little longer to finish sorting out the files, especially given that the colonel wasn't in today. This job is so important to me as it's my first decent employment since I got kicked out from my orphanage after turning eighteen a year ago. I found it thanks to my fluency in foreign languages, and I must do every-thing to keep it.

I worked so hard to be hired for a wonderful position like

this. I studied English, German and French whenever I could, keeping my studies secret from the orphanage caregivers. I spent endless nights working by the dim light of a tiny candle. I knew that it was my only chance to make my life better, far away from the homelessness of the streets.

But now, I'm afraid to even budge. I've disobeyed his order and if the colonel finds out he will fire me. I haven't met him yet, so I don't know what to expect. But I know for sure he will be strict.

I wipe sweat from my forehead and stay still, ignoring the air rich with dust. The walls between the storage space and the colonel's office are thin; I hear their voices so clearly.

"To be precise, sir, I solved the internal wiring in the German cipher machine." Mr. Rejewski speaks in a low voice, but I'm still able to hear him well enough. What exactly does he mean by this? It's all so new to me. I push aside my thoughts and listen, hungry for his next words.

"The next step would be to work on methods for finding daily keys and cracking real codes as quickly as possible. And we can do it now when we have the pattern of wiring inside the three rotors and the reflector in the military Enigma."

I've no idea what he's talking about, but I sense these must be high-priority matters, as we were ordered to leave the office promptly. They didn't want any witnesses, nor any eaves-droppers.

"This is incredible." Excitement spoils the colonel's stable voice. "Could you elaborate some more?"

"Of course, sir. Actually, there is far too much information to share right now but it's worth mentioning that I took a mathe-matical approach and used my knowledge of permutation theory. I also detected some weaknesses in their code enci-pherment."

For a moment, there is the clapping together of hands. "Mr. Rejewski," the colonel says, "you've managed to accomplish something that the entire world, including the British and French, has deemed impossible."

"Kudos to the French. The code books they provided for October and November turned out to be very useful."

A moment of silence stretches out before the colonel says, "I knew that our dearest Captain Bertrand's *gifts* would be helpful, but only your genius could use them in the right way."

"Thank you, sir."

"Please, tell me more about the weaknesses in their code encipherment that you mentioned."

"As you know, sir, I made a careful study of the Enigma ciphers. I focused on the first six letters of messages sent on a single day and I found something very interesting. The German weakness is to repeat a three-letter setting chosen by an operator in the enciphered six-letter indicator. The first and fourth letters are the same, the second and fifth are the same, and the third and sixth are the same. Those relations helped me break into the cipher. Are you following thus far, sir?"

"I am indeed. Do they encrypt each message with different starting positions then?"

"Yes, with a three-letter setting, but to convey it, they use a six-letter indicator which is formed using the Enigma machine with its rotors set to the particular setting for that day and shared by all operators. There are trillions of possible coding settings."

I hear the colonel breathe out deeply. "So," he says, "we need to build replicas as soon as possible."

"That would be the best approach."

"Using your instructions, engineer Palluth and his electronics firm AVA will begin producing parts for replicas of the German military Enigma machines. We will assemble them here at our Cipher Bureau to ensure the work is top secret. Then you will use it to decrypt German messages."

"Understood, sir."

"Your peers, Jerzy Różycki and Henryk Zygalski, will join you immediately to work on methods and equipment to decode Enigma ciphers consistently. We can't count on Captain Bertrand to keep supplying us with the monthly key-sheets."

Then, at the sound of screeching chairs, I swallow hard, back off out of the storage space and walk purposefully out of the office and Saski Palace. My heart is thumping at the complexity of the information I have just absorbed. The colonel and Czesława cannot know that I disobeyed their order and overheard this conversation. It was not intended for my ears, or indeed for any ears outside of the Cipher Bureau's top brass.

The rush of crisp air swaddles me, so I pull up my fur collar to my face and stroll through Piłsudski Square, which was named after the late Marshal of Poland. I pass the arcade housing the Tomb of the Unknown Soldier and the statue of Prince Poniatowski on his horse.

I don't take the tram but walk down the streets trying to put my thoughts in order. It's so much to take on. That man named Rejewski was claiming to have solved the German cipher machine; whatever that means, it sounds like a serious accomplishment.

ONE

BEATA

July 1939, Warsaw

Growing up in the orphanage wasn't a fairy tale, but it prepared me for life's sourness and unexpected twists. Or at least that's what I always thought until Gabriel, the man I trusted with all my heart, made a fool out of me. While we were still engaged, I caught him in bed with another woman.

I shake away my thoughts before entering the orphanage's dirty-gray tenement. As pathetic as it may sound, it's the only childhood home I ever had. I never felt truly loved or understood in here, but at least the caregivers treated me in a civil way. I was never hungry, always had a functional pair of shoes and a decent coat for winter.

I like to visit whenever I can because I feel for the children in here, especially for my sweet Felka who's turning sixteen today. I promised her a trip to the cinema.

The orphanage is small; there are only nineteen children, from toddlers to teenagers. I share my chocolate with them and urge Felka to get ready for our outing.

"Miss Beata, can you tell us a story?" says a blond boy named Ignaś, his angelic mouth caked in chocolate.

"Of course, sunshine. I would love to."

He jumps up and flaps his hands. "It's story time, everyone, get closer," he urges.

"I have a special one for you today," I say in a whispery voice. "Only the chosen children get to listen to it as it's a very old tale."

"What's it about?" Antosia, a seven-year-old girl with freckles asks, her voice laden with concern.

I go on telling them the legend of the Warsaw mermaid; how she decided to rest on the Vistula shore during her trip to the Baltic Sea; how the rich merchant trapped and imprisoned her; how the fishermen taken by the beauty of her singing rescued her; how she promised to always protect our city, armed with a sword and a shield.

"Miss Beata," Antosia asks, "does the mermaid live in the Vistula now?"

"I think so. It's why we will be always safe."

"Will she protect us too when Germans attack our city?" the little girl says, making me speechless. Even the youngest ones hear about the threat of war.

"Mr. Ficek said that there will be no war," Ignaś says while bouncing up and down. "I heard the story of the mermaid before but it was different," he adds, gazing at me with wonder.

I can't suppress my smile and wag my finger at him and the rest of the children. "There're different legends around but mine tells the truth."

For a moment, he seems to consider my words, but soon his mouth spreads in a contagious smile. "I believe you, Miss Beata. You never lie to us because you grew up here too."

❧

After the story, I stroll with Felka through the crowded streets of Warsaw. She looks pretty in a yellow summer dress I found for her in one of the boutiques in the Old Town. It was hard to convince Mrs. Kalencka, the orphanage director, to allow her to accompany me for the evening film, but it was all worth it.

Felka swirls around. "This is the most gorgeous gown I've ever worn," she says with her usual exaltation as her infectious smile reaches her turquoise eyes. "I feel like Cinderella going to the ball."

It warms my heart seeing her this happy. "You deserve it, sweetheart."

She stops all of a sudden and her alarmed gaze meets mine. "Oh, Miss Beata, what if there are no available seats at the cinema? It's already so late."

I playfully nudge her arm and smile. "Honey, I promised you will see a film today—you will see a film today." I understand her so well. Orphanage children often need a little extra reassurance, because good things always seem out of reach for them. I still struggle with the same insecurities at the age of twenty-six.

The Napoleon Cinema located in Three Cross Square has its name glowing in neon on the building's façade. Once inside, we settle in the armchairs upholstered in purple velvet, each decorated with the letter N in gold.

"I'm so excited," Felka whispers with wonder in her face as she claps her hands. "It's exactly how I've imagined my first time at the cinema."

I have no heart to tell her that normally cinemas are not as luxurious as this one. I picked this place as I wanted to make her birthday so much more special. With the world being on the brink of war, who knows what fate holds in store for us? But I keep my thoughts to myself, because that sweet girl doesn't deserve to be showered by worries. After all, I might be wrong; it might be that Germany will not attack us.

Vagabonds turns out to be a perfect film for Felka. It's the story of a young girl who becomes an orphan after her father's death. She refuses to live with her cold, rich grandmother and, with the help of two friends, Szczepko and Tonko, she escapes. Eventually she finds love and there is a happy ending.

Felka laughs, cries, and understands the orphaned girl so well. When Szczepko and Tonko sing *Only in Lviv*, Felka adores it so much that she squeezes my hand, bringing a surge of warmth to my heart. The two men skip past market stalls laden with flowers and vegetables as they sing about the charm of their beloved Lviv, exposing its folklore and humor.

We leave the cinema giggling, and recall funny and romantic scenes on our walk back to the orphanage. The dreamy look on Felka's face convinces me that I gave her a memorable experience tonight.

By the time we arrive at the orphanage it's already nine o'clock. I wait until the door closes behind her before turning to walk home. Words can't describe how much I love this girl—the same way any caring mother loves her child. I swear deep in my heart to always watch out for her.

TWO

BEATA

July 1939, cryptology bunker in the woods near Pyry, a village outside of Warsaw

An iron gate opens, and a navy-blue minibus, which I boarded only minutes ago, cruises through a forest road. We are leaving behind a bunker in the deep woods, which stores a top-secret codebreaking mission. In 1937, the German section of the Cipher Bureau at Saski Palace in Warsaw was moved here.

All day, security at the Cipher Bureau has been on the highest alert, as there was a suspicion of a spy within our team. It's because the Germans made a significant change to their military Enigma cipher machine. Our command started suspecting that one of us might be working for the enemy by supplying them with details in regards to our breakthrough with the Enigma, and it's why the Germans decided to modify it. In the end, it turned out that these were false accusations.

I close my eyes to quieten down my spinning thoughts. I must try to relax a little after this terrible turmoil at work.

Shortly after Marian Rejewski's breakthrough with the Enigma's internal wirings in December 1932, our genius team of three cryptologists cracked daily codes, enabling us to read German messages. Throughout the years, the Germans have kept changing their procedures and systems to preserve the security of their precious Enigma. They have no reason to suspect that we can read their messages. After all, the entire world deems it impossible, and we Poles keep our secret very well; beside the team in the bunker in Pyry, only very few high-ranking officers know about it.

For the last seven years, Marian, Henryk and Jerzy not only kept pace with all the changes, but also invented new machines to automate the process of codebreaking. Now we need more equipment but there are no funds for it. That's a huge obstacle.

I can't help but sigh. My tired brain can't handle it right now, so I push all the thoughts aside. Tomorrow will bring better news. I've learned from the years of working at the Cipher Bureau that things change rapidly.

After going through extensive training seven years ago at the Saski Palace, I ended up working as a clerk in the Cipher Bureau's German section. I'm in the team that decrypts messages after the three cryptologists crack the daily codes and pass them to us. I'm also summoned whenever the Cipher Bureau needs me for translations.

Now, I get off the bus at Teatralny Square and head toward Piłsudski Square where merchants are selling their goods, including fresh fruit and vegetables.

Memories rush over me—when I was still with my ex-fiancé Gabriel, we loved spending time here. Back then, I thought he was an honest man, so these were happy moments. The only emotion left now is disgust.

"Miss Beata." A cheerful voice breaks my reverie and I realize that I've been staring at a wooden box filled with ripe apples.

"What are you doing here, Felka?" I hug her.

She points at an elderly lady in a long, shabby apron with a large wicker basket at her feet, who's talking to a group of women. "I'm helping Mrs. Agata sell her homemade cheese." She reaches to her skirt pocket and takes out a red beaded bracelet. "Isn't this pretty, Miss Beata?" Her rosy cheeks add to the excitement reflected in her eyes.

I wish I was more like her during my years in the orphanage. I worked hard, especially at secretly learning other languages, but I had no happiness in me. This teenage girl brings light everywhere she goes. I always look forward to seeing her: she is a breath of fresh air in this gloomy world.

"It's gorgeous," I say. "Let's make something special this Sunday at the orphanage."

After we say our goodbyes, I go to my flat in the Old Town, which I share with my friend Joanna.

Besides my work, I only have her and Felka. As a baby, I was left in a basket on the steps of St. Martin's Church in the Old Town. No note. No belongings. I have no family.

THREE

BEATA

July 1939, Hotel Bristol, Warsaw city center

"We have news." These words play in my mind like a broken record. A couple of weeks ago, I was asked to translate a telegram sent to Major Gustave Bertrand into French. I think that a decision has been made to share our methods of cracking the Enigma codes with the French and British. Why else would Lieutenant Colonel Langer need me tomorrow as a translator at the station in Pyry?

Something big is going on, but my department is being kept in the dark. Still, it isn't hard to put two and two together and guess the reason for tomorrow's visit. Could there be any better time to take the next step than now, when Hitler is showing more and more aggression?

"Would you care to have something to drink, miss?" a lanky waiter with a pencil mustache says after approaching my table in the Hotel Bristol's café.

"A glass of Grodziskie, please." The air simmers with aromas of savory food and wine, but I'm in the mood for beer today.

Joanna will be joining me for dinner. Her shift ended at seven o'clock, so she should be here soon. She helps her aunt Marta clean the Bristol's rooms. It's our routine to meet here every last Tuesday of the month.

For a moment, I listen to Ignacy Jan Paderewski's dynamic composition, "The Polish Fantasy", which reminds me a lot of our folk music. Paderewski often played it during his concerts, before Poland gained back its independence in 1918. By doing so, he kept reminding the world that even though Poland didn't exist on maps, it was always in the hearts of its people.

I sigh. And now Hitler could attack at any moment, or at least that's how it feels due to the tense political atmosphere.

A conversation in English between two men at the nearby table disturbs my thoughts. The blond one raves about how delicious and flirtatious Polish women appear to be. They talk about us in their British accents like we're merchandise on a market stall, easily accessible commodities.

I wrinkle my nose but ignore them and their nonsense. No point wasting my time. Before I look away, the other man, with shiny dark hair and wide shoulders, meets my gaze, a hint of curiosity in it... or judgment?

Without betraying any emotion or the fact I understand English, I move my gaze away. These men in expensive suits think they are above an ordinary woman like me.

Growing up in orphanage, I got used to people looking at me with pity, but this man knows nothing about me. Yet the way he scrutinized me reignited my old insecurities.

"Here you are, my friend," Joanna says and drops to the chair. The fact that she has on one of her prettiest ivory deep-necked evening dresses tells me that she's made an effort to look stunning today. That usually brings trouble. What a far cry from my simple black skirt suit.

"It seems there is more commotion in here today than normal," I say before taking another sip of my beer.

She lights a cigarette and after exhaling clouds of smoke, she says, "It's because so many foreigners have checked in. Have you already decided on your meal?"

When the waiter arrives, we both order veal cutlet in crayfish sauce with mashed potatoes and cucumber salad.

"Is everything all right?" Joanna asks, her eyes narrowing as she searches my face. "You seem quiet today."

"I'm worried about what's going to happen to Felka and the children in the orphanage once the war begins."

She slouches against her chair. "If that's what truly concerns you, then you need not fret." As she speaks, her eyes stay fixed on mine. "There will be no war."

"What makes you so sure?" I can't comprehend that so many people still stay blind to the threats from Germany. "I wonder if the people of Czechoslovakia were calm like you before Hitler's assault." I tilt my head and pause for a longer moment. "And what's the name of that port in Lithuania that he seized?"

She waves me off. "Adolf Hitler has a bigger fish to be concerned with than us." A smile edges her mouth. "Anyway, I hate talking politics on such a lovely evening. Especially, when we are about to enjoy this delicious meal."

A sudden exhaustion washes over me. Continuing the subject of war is pointless. I adore my friend, but her priorities are a far cry from mine. "You're right. Let's not ruin the evening," I say and return her smile.

"By the way, do you happen to know the handsome gentleman to our left?" she says, twirling her fingers through her black curls.

I shake my head. "Why?" I don't bother to look in the direction she just indicated, as I suspect she's implying that broad-shouldered British man.

She leans forward and whispers, "He keeps glancing at you."

There is an edge to my laughter. "I don't know the man."

Joanna leans forward and touches my arm. "He likes you." She beams. "What a handsome devil that man is."

"That's ridiculous. He doesn't even know me. Besides, the gentlemen at that table have a terrible notion of women."

It's time to change the subject, otherwise Joanna will do something that will embarrass both of us. "When does your vacation start?" I ask before taking a sip of my beer; Grodziskie is my favorite, and some call it Polish Champagne because of its high carbonation. As always, it tastes light and crisp, but it also has a strong flavor of oak-smoked wheat malt. It complements my meal.

"Next week," she says and leans toward me again. "They seem nice and I'm in the mood for dancing today."

I shake my head, but before I can stop her, she walks over to the British men.

I sigh and close my eyes. Why is she always doing this? Why, just for once, can't she ignore any men that are in the same room as us? Usually, it ends up with her spending the night with one of them while I get back home by myself. I'm not interested in one-night stands.

She treats the blond man in his black suit to her angelic smile and asks, "I was wondering if you could help me?" She lifts her hand; her fingers are holding an unlit cigarette.

The man reads her gesture and nods, takes out a box of matches and lights her cigarette while winking at the other man, the one with wide shoulders, his face sardonic.

Joanna exhales clouds of smoke and folds her mouth in another provocative smile.

"What's your name, beauty?" he asks in a scornfully mocking voice.

Joanna's face reflects an instant surprise, most likely at the fact that he spoke to her in English, but she smiles even wider and bats her lashes at him. It's not the first time she would be spending the night with a foreigner without knowing his language.

Something snaps in me. I can't watch this exchange without feeling humiliated, so I stand up and walk out of the restaurant.

Outside, a surge of hot, stagnant air batters my skin, making me wince. The night sky is filled by twinkling stars, like the restaurant with its chatting customers.

As I walk further away from the hotel, I pass a kissing couple and two men arguing about politics. How is it that some know how to drink up every moment and cherish happiness, while others are always braced against the absurdity of this world?

Where's my place in all of this? I have a job that I enjoy. I have Joanna and Felka, and I adore both, though the first one knows how to hit my nerves. I couldn't be true to myself and stay in that room. Next thing, she would be asking me to act as a translator.

I sigh as a nauseating odor from the trash at the side of the street hits my nostrils. Every beauty has its ugliness.

"Miss," someone shouts behind me in English. "You forgot your purse."

I swirl around to bump into a tall figure, who holds my arms for balance. It's only thanks to his quick reaction that I avoided collapsing.

When I lift my head, deep-set, dark gray eyes look down at me. I quickly recognize the broad-shouldered man from the restaurant, which brings a sour taste to my mouth.

He extends his hand with my purse, and I take it. "Thank you, sir," I say in English. "I truly appreciate it." I make an effort to fold my lips in a polite smile.

"Please call me Harry." He crinkles a smile back at me. "And my pleasure. Your friend seemed distressed that you forgot it."

Great. Joanna probably gave a nice show but she didn't even

bother to bring it to me on her own. How's she even communicating with them?

For a brief moment, an awkward silence stretches.

"Well, thank you again, sir. I mean Harry. Enjoy your meal," I say and turn to walk away, not caring to tell him my name.

"Would you mind if I keep you company on your walk home? The streets might not be so safe at this time of the night."

I freeze at first, but then I turn back to face him. Why is he doing this? To find a one-night stand, since his friend obviously got lucky with Joanna?

He holds his hands up. "Please don't look at me like that. I promise to safely walk you to your door and go straight back to the hotel. I have no sinister intentions."

He reads me well. "Please yourself," I say and start walking in the hope he gets discouraged by my aloofness, but he's right beside me. Why would I trust him? Why would I trust anyone? Just to be made a fool of, again? Gabriel taught me a valuable lesson: to fully trust only myself.

"Have you ever visited England? Your English is impressive," he says.

"Thank you, and no, I haven't, but I would love to. Though, considering Adolf Hitler's activities, I doubt I'll have an opportunity any time soon." I make sure to walk swiftly, so we don't have to talk for too long.

"You make a valid point there," he says but stops his brisk trot. His laugh rings out, sounding so healthy and vital that I pause. I'm not sure what to think of his behavior.

"Are you trying to race me," he asks, "or does your house happen to be on fire?"

"Well, if you don't enjoy the walk, you're free to go back," I say as I cross my arms over my chest.

"It's a gallop, not a walk, so it's impossible to have a civil conversation. Can we slow down a little? Please."

His matter-of-fact attitude irritates me. I know I should apologize and comply with his request, but who is this man to tell me how to walk? He's the first one to point out how flirtatious Polish women are, but then he acts like a jerk.

"And you're rude," I say. "If you keep following me, I will call the authorities." Without further ado, I turn and scamper away. It's not like I'm going to see him again anyway. Plus, it's fun to play with his male ego.

FOUR

BEATA

July 1939, cryptology bunker in the woods near Pyry, a village outside of Warsaw

By the time Lieutenant Colonel Langer and Major Ciężki arrive with the French and British delegations at the bunker, we are ready for them. In addition to our white and red flag, we decorated the main room with the French and British ones. It's a powerful message that together we can do more.

We were informed ahead of time that Major Gustave Bertrand, recently promoted, and the cryptologist Henri Braquenie will represent the French side. When it comes to the British guests, we are expecting the cryptologist Alfred Dillwyn Knox and commanders Alastair Denniston and Humphrey Sandwith.

This is an impressive list of guests, so just at the thought of it, I feel nervous. My duty is to provide translation services as needed in all three languages.

"These are new," the French Major Bertrand says. He points to the black replicas of Enigma that are smaller than typewriters, a friendly smile on his face. I remember him from previous visits as a vibrant man full of enthusiasm.

"These are our replicas of the German military Enigma machines," Langer says and tilts his strong nose, his eyes gleaming. He waits till I'm done translating, and continues, "Thanks to our genius cryptologists, our specialists were able to build it. And now, when times are not stable and peace not guaranteed, we believe it's the right moment to share our breakthrough with our French and British friends."

Never before have I witnessed so many faces bearing a stunned look at the same time. None of them believes what they just heard. Well, with the exception of Bertrand, whose face beams. He already knows just how important all of this is when comes to the approaching war. I'm afraid Adolf Hitler will not wait much longer before starting one.

The meeting starts with Major Ciężki giving a lecture about Polish struggles with Enigma and the procedures for breaking it.

After the speech, a skinny man walks toward one of the machines and opens its lid. "You say this is the military Enigma?" he asks in disbelief, his face sour, even scornful.

I relay his question into Polish and French, then wait for Langer's response.

"Yes, indeed, Mr. Knox." Langer's voice bears this familiar note of forced patience. He knows his ground and will not let anyone underestimate him.

As I translate his speech, I realize that a broad-shouldered guest from the British delegation is Harry, the man I met last night. The realization makes me dizzy, to the point I almost fumble. How is it possible that he is here? He wasn't on the list of guests.

His intense gray eyes meet mine, causing my heart to skip while his lips quirk. He nods my way, but says nothing.

I nod back then, not knowing where to look, I gaze past him making sure not to show any hint of the confusion inside me.

It's not like I care about his presence anyway. He was rude to me. Well, I suppose I wasn't that pleasant either...

By now, the entire room has grown silent, and all eyes are on me. As I realize they're expecting something to be translated, my knees feel weak and heat rushes to my face.

I clear my throat and say, "I apologize, gentlemen, my attention wasn't at the right place. This won't happen again." Then I look at my colleague, Marian Rejewski. "Would you repeat it for me?" When he does, I make sure to carefully, immaculately translate his words.

I can't be slipping like this; it's extremely unprofessional, and so unlike me. I resolve to erase Harry from my thoughts for the rest of the meeting, and I focus on my task like never before.

It turns out that Marian was in the middle of explaining how the Enigma machine works, demonstrating it on one of the black replicas while our guests encircle him. "And here is a lamp board with a set of twenty-six stenciled letters with tiny lightbulbs behind, which connects to letters on a keyboard." He fixes his wire-rimmed glasses and glances around as if checking if all the men follow. His broad forehead and deep-set eyes reflect his lofty intelligence.

He waits for my translations, and points to the next element of the machine. "And here we have a plugboard. It's extremely important to mention that the commercial Enigma machines, which we're all familiar with, do not have this part."

A nervous silence hangs thick in the air as faces betray concentration mixed with wonder at every word.

Then, step after step, Marian continues to explain the remaining parts of our Enigma machine, including its three rotating wheels.

"To encipher a message, Germans set the Enigma's rotating wheels to a certain starting position. In order for the recipients to read it, they must know the chosen key setting. It's changed every day."

"Does this machine have the same internal wiring as the military Enigma used by the Germans?" Harry asks, not taking his eyes from my face, while pointing at the replica.

"Yes, indeed, Mr. Smith," Marian says after I relay his words. I take note of Harry's family name, though I can't think why. "Once we solved the internal wiring, we were able to build our replicas and focus on methods of cracking daily codes. It's important to mention that, unlike the commercial machine, in the military Enigma the keys are wired to the entry drum in alphabetical order, instead of the German 'QWERTZU'. Many cryptologists dismissed that option as too obvious. My intuition and awareness of the German love for order helped me guess it correctly."

I look around the room and see that everyone's eyes are wide open. It's as if they are in a state of uncertainty about whether what I just converted into both languages could in fact be the truth.

"Unbelievable," someone whispers in English before I can see who it was.

"You must know that there are trillions of potential coding settings which are combinations of plugboard and rotating wheels positions," our other brilliant cryptologist, Jerzy Różycki says, his short dark-blond hair and gentle features making him look much younger than his thirty years of age. I smile at him while I convey his input. I like Jerzy and value him as a colleague. "If someone wished to check one possible setting each minute, it would take a great deal longer than the life of the universe to do it. It's exactly why Germans are so certain no one can break their system." After I translate these words, Jerzy winks at me, a gesture that brings warmth to my heart.

Marian nods and turns on the machine. "What made Enigma extremely hard to solve is that the inner connections always change as the rotating wheels move. When I press the letter 'a', the letter 't' illuminates on the lamp board. If I press 'a' again, now 'w' pops up. As you see, typing the same letter on the keyboard brings a different result on the lamp board—every time."

His explanations are so clear, I have no problem relaying them in other languages.

He takes a piece of paper then types something on the keyboard. Every time a new letter flashes on the lamp board, he writes it down. Then he shows it to everyone.

"This is the enciphered version of my message. If someone wanted to read it, they would have to begin decryption at the same setting *and* know the key that I'd used on this machine."

"I would like to know if you are currently able to read any ciphered messages from Germany?" Knox asks.

As I translate, I wonder about the tension in the room. I'm sure it's because of the impending war, but there is something else I can't grasp at.

"Since 1933, we have been able to read almost all of their military cryptograms," Langer says in a quiet voice and then nods at me, to continue a moment later. "But the Germans keep introducing new improvements to their machine. In December of last year, they added two extra rotors."

"So your machine is ineffective," Knox says in a cool voice.

FIVE

BEATA

Marian shakes his head while staying calm. "You couldn't be further from the truth, Mr. Knox." I make sure to emphasize his stable tone of voice. "It's not the first time we have had to deal with German advancements and changes. It's been a constant fight. In addition, this time, we've already solved the internal wiring pattern for the two new rotors."

Langer adds, "Through the years, we've automated the system of codebreaking with special machines that are effective, and which speed up the process, like Jerzy Różycki's clock or Henryk Zygalski's sheets." After I translate his words, he gestures to the next room. "Please let me introduce you to my genius cryptologist, Henryk Zygalski. He will explain the way our newest— and greatest—invention by Marian Rejewski, which we have called 'Bomba', works."

Everyone follows Langer to the adjacent room where the tall, dark-haired Henryk in a pristine white apron greets the guests with a polite smile. He speaks English well, so I only have to translate his words into French.

After introductions, Langer says, "In September 1938, Germans implemented user-chosen ground-settings which differ from one message to message. This change complicated our lives to the point that our cryptologists invented this machine." Langer motions to Henryk to continue while I translate.

"This electrical aggregate called Bomba was built of six Enigma machines. Its function is to crack the daily keys by finding the rotor settings of German messages with repeats in their beginning part." As Henryk goes on explaining and demonstrating how Bomba works, everyone listens without even the slightest motion.

"At the end of 1938, the Germans changed from three rotors in their machines to five. Because of this, right now we would need sixty Bombas to decipher intercepted messages at the same rate as before." He gazes at Langer who patiently awaits my translations.

"With the six Bombas we have in our possession, we can read only ten percent of messages right now," Langer says in a monotone. "It's our biggest challenge; building an additional fifty-four machines isn't something our Cipher Bureau can afford. Instead, we use a manual method of perforated sheets invented by our own Henryk Zygalski."

Henryk leads us to a table with thick cardboard sheets marked with letters, points and squares. After explaining in detail how his sheets work in narrowing down the daily settings of the Enigma, he says, "As you see, this method requires a tremendous amount of labor and time to be effective in doing the work of the additional Bombas that we don't have. We require a massive production of these sheets, but instead we're facing a huge shortage."

Now Langer claps his hands together. "Please, gentlemen, ask any questions you may have before we continue to show you in more detail all our methods and equipment. My team of cryptologists is at your disposal."

Everyone nods even before my voice rings out.

So far, throughout the entire meeting, I've got the impression that our guests are making substantial efforts to hide their admiration for our achievements, and thus the tension in the room is apparent. The only people who openly show their admiration are Bertrand and Harry.

The latter now leans toward the Bomba machine and says, "Simply genius." I can't help but like him a bit in this very moment. But only a tiny bit. The fact that he hasn't made any reference to yesterday puts me at ease. Obviously, Joanna spent the night with one of them as she came back home in the morning, disheveled and flushed, right before I left for work. I had no time to talk to her.

Bertrand tilts his head slightly to the side. "Polish cryptologists," he says cheerfully, "in my opinion have accomplished something unbelievable. There is no other country in the world with such genius and determination. Even my best spy couldn't obtain much information about the German military Enigma. And here, we were just shown an internal wiring of the machine. Whatever I was able to get from my spy, I gave to the British and others, but only Poles cracked the Enigma. I salute them."

When all eyes turn my way, I translate, not trying to hide my delight. These words highlight everything we've worked on for so many years. This clever man knows how important all of this is in regard to the dark clouds from Germany. I suspect they all know, but only Bertrand fully expresses it.

"We would need to send our specialists over here, so they can check everything and inspect your machines." Knox waves a hand in the air. "Is this possible?"

Langer gives knowing glances to Ciężki and Bertrand. "Besides all of us here, no one else will ever enter this building," he says in a firm voice but a second later he smiles. "It's unnecessary anyway, as we will gift two of our replicas to Major

Bertrand, and one of them our dearest Major will personally deliver to Colonel Menzies in London."

Everyone becomes still while their eyes widen, then a friendly and stout English commander, by the name of Denniston, who's been mostly quiet throughout the meeting, says, "Very well, then. We're thankful for this."

At least one voice of reason from the British delegation— well, besides Mr. Smith, but it seems he has the least say.

"But on one condition," Langer continues, as all eyes in the room swivel back to him. "And that is that once the Enigma is no longer a secret, the French and British will inform the public that they received the pioneer replicas of the Enigma machine from us, the Poles, near our capital Warsaw." He pauses. "You will tell your people that our cryptologists cracked the codes first."

After both sides eagerly assure him of their compliance with this condition, Langer says, "Of course, everything you hear and see here during your visit today and tomorrow is top secret. The Germans cannot—*must* not—realize that we are reading them."

When Langer announces a short break, I head into my favorite spot at the edge of the woods. I need a moment for myself. My brain is spinning from perpetually switching between three languages.

For the first five minutes, I lean against a birch tree and close my eyes. I inhale pine needle scents; I let the sun caress my face. The sound of singing birds is heaven to my ears. Only nature can calm life's turmoil, and lately the atmosphere inside that bunker is so tense that I live in constant anxiety.

"I owe you an apology for being rude yesterday." A now-familiar voice makes me open my eyes.

At first, I am upset that this man has chosen to ruin my moment alone, but I remember his positive attitude during the meeting.

"Apology accepted," I say with a smile. "I should be more hospitable too."

He disregards my remark, saying instead, "You navigate between all those languages like a champ."

I laugh. "I'm trying my best."

"It's all very technical, so I'm truly impressed with your fluency." He gives me a meaningful look. "I'm being honest."

"Well, I'm not just a translator," I admit. "I also work in the decrypting department, so none of this is new to me. But, as you know, we should not discuss details outside of the building."

"That's true. I'm sorry for intruding on you again. It seems it's all I do lately, at least on this trip." His lips form an apologetic smile.

"The world is small here," I say. I hope I don't come across as flirtatious, but there is something irresistible about this man that makes me put all my weapons away. He seems so different from how I judged him at the café yesterday.

"I still do not know your name," he says. "Unless it's another top priority secret?"

I can't suppress a chuckle. "My name is Beata Koszyczek."

SIX

HARRY

July 1939, London

Dearest Mother,

As I promised, I'm writing to tell you about my trip to Poland. The few days I was there were filled with work, so no time for sightseeing. But just the thought of staying in your beloved Warsaw brought me a good amount of peace. It also made me realize how rusty my Polish is. I understood it but couldn't say a word. After all, last time I spoke it, I was only eleven, only minutes before you departed this world. Never again since then. Through the years, I simply had no one to speak this language to, and now I don't know how.

Please, forgive my grumpy mood today, Mother. The whole stay over there exhausted me, but it was worth it. We learned something that is going to impact the world in a significant way, or at least, that's what I believe.

Do you remember my thoughts about the secret cipher machine? Well, I'm sure you do, as you know how passionately I feel about it. We've been getting nowhere in our attempts to crack it. I thought that the rest of the world deemed it unbreakable as well, but how wrong I have been in this matter.

You can be proud, Mother. One of the biggest secrets hasn't been a secret to Poles for a while now. Three men from your own nation accomplished the impossible. The cipher machine was first cracked by Marian Rejewski. He's worked with Jerzy Różycki and Henryk Zygalski on breaking daily codes and inventing methods to speed up the process. These genius mathematicians and cryptologists deserve an honorable place in history books. They made me feel like a complete fool during our meetings.

I do not want to bore you with this any further. Just know that this is a significant breakthrough, and I couldn't feel happier being a part of this as it moves forward. We will use their knowledge wisely. It's not like I can discuss this with anyone else beside you, Mother, as I'm bound to keep it top secret. And I'm making sure that no one is able to access my journal.

There is something else I want to share with you, even though it might sound silly. I don't even know myself what to think of it, but I can't get it out of my mind.

Tell me, Mother, is it possible to love someone from first sight? Can you look at someone and feel in your heart that this person would be right for you? The most logical answer would be "no".

I saw her the first time at the Bristol's café in Warsaw and felt hypnotized to the point I couldn't take my eyes off her. She sat alone at a table, deep in her thoughts, as if there was no world around her. But when my friend spoke not so respectfully about women, her face twitched. That's when I knew she understood English.

When her gaze met mine, I detected only anger, yet she controlled herself and ignored us. I wanted to grab that idiot Stuart and drag him out. We'd bumped into each other that evening and he convinced me to have a drink with him. I couldn't believe his arrogant statements about women and can't stand the way he watches them, like a vulture.

Then, later that same evening, she accused me of being rude, and just when I thought I would never see her again, it turned out that she works for the Polish Cipher Bureau. In the end, we parted on friendly terms.

She intrigues me. The golden gloss of her hair and her blue eyes remind me of you, Mother. There is this freshness about her despite the sadness of her eyes. The guarded look makes her inapproachable, but how tempting too.

There is not a chance that I'll meet her again, but I can't get her out of my mind.

Mother, rest assured that I will write to you soon.

I love you forever,

Your Harry

I've had this weakness of writing notes to my mother since I turned eleven. Since she died. My father eventually remarried. I, on the other hand, didn't know how to deal with my emotions, so I started writing letters to her, even though I knew she would never read them. It somehow made me feel closer to her.

The habit has stayed with me. Now, at thirty, I still write although rarely—only when something important happens and there is this need in me to share it with her. Writing it down on paper brings some satisfaction. But who knows, maybe she can read my letters after all. Maybe this life, the love between us, doesn't end when our bodies die. I like to think so.

SEVEN

BEATA

September 1939, Warsaw

"Hello, hello! This is Warsaw and all Polish radio stations. This morning at forty minutes past five o'clock, German troops crossed the Polish border, breaking the non-aggression pact."

I sit up in my bed, my mind frozen.

Joanna charges into my room without knocking. "Did you just hear this?" She points to the radio set and stares at me with disbelief in her eyes.

I lift a finger to my lips.

"This means war," says a strong voice from the radio. The rest of the message states that now we are all soldiers and must fight until our shared victory.

Joanna clears her throat. "I can't believe this. Everything you were afraid of is actually happening."

"We must be strong now, more than ever."

The shriek of air-raid sirens chokes up my words. We sit a moment longer in sad silence before getting on with the day. Joanna's shift at the hotel starts at noon, so she decides to organize the kitchen cabinets. It's her usual way of dealing with distress.

I take a few sips of my black coffee and put on a charcoal, knee-length dress, the one I always wear when I'm feeling sad. I could not stomach any food right now, so I leave for work earlier than usual.

Things seem normal outside, but people's faces show nervousness mixed with disbelief. The reality of the war hasn't truly sunk in yet. But now more civilians are working on digging anti-aircraft ditches. Men in military uniforms rush wherever they are summoned to by the Polish army.

Halfway to my bus stop, the rumble of large planes makes me cease walking. I lift my gaze to the sky, before I run along with other people into the nearest gateway for shelter. A huge explosion in the distance has me covering my ears. The sky is inflamed by explosions from anti-aircraft guns; crowds of pigeons fly from the rooftops.

Soon the sirens announce the all-clear, so people emerge once more. It feels so hard to accept this as our new reality.

At the cryptology center in Pyry, the atmosphere is heavier than normal, but everyone keeps busy. Our three cryptologists are now expected to work day and night on breaking the codes despite the equipment shortage. Before today, we hoped there would be no war and convinced ourselves that the Germans made changes to their Enigma machine only for security reasons. Now we know exactly why they did it, and this knowledge makes me sick to my stomach.

We learn that Germany started the assault against Poland by attacking Westerplatte, our munition base on the Baltic Sea. Then their Luftwaffe planes lost no time in heading to Warsaw where they hit the Okęcie airport and tenements in the Rakowiec and Koło districts. These are the first victims of this awful war. I still can't grasp the fact that this is happening.

My day goes by fast and by the time I board the minibus to

go home, I struggle to keep my headache at bay. It seems there are more soldiers guarding the grounds of the cryptology center. This doesn't come as a surprise since it's imperative that the Germans don't find out that we can read them. Their spies could be anywhere.

I get off at Teatralny Square determined to visit the orphanage. Felka and the other children have been on my mind all day.

But I decide to stay a bit longer at the bus stop, my eyes glued to a poster with President Mościcki's proclamation: "*Last night our old enemy invaded Poland, which I state in front of God and history...*"

Then our president called on all of us to help give a worthy response to our German attacker, so we can stride to victory.

I fail to stop my chin from trembling. We are in this fight for good. But I can't even comprehend how everything is going to change. Still, German troops aren't in Warsaw yet and I know that our soldiers will do everything to stop them. Once I assure myself of this, I feel a little better. I tell myself it's important to be positive, that now it's time to go and console the children.

"Beata." Joanna's voice brings me back to reality. "I was hoping to find you before you reached..." she says and takes time to stabilize her breathing. "I need to tell you something." There is this haunted look in her eyes while she stares at me. She's clearly having a hard time processing news of the war.

I touch her arm. "I know it's been a long day." I sigh. "Actually, for all of us." It's always been hard not to be able to talk with her about my job. But it's the most vital part of my work agreement, that I keep it confidential.

"Would you like to join me on my brief visit to the orphanage? We can talk on the way there. I'm dying to know all the war news from the city," I say. Working at the Hotel Bristol, Joanna stays on top of the city's gossip and news, unlike myself; I am surrounded by woods, away from Warsaw.

She lays a hand against her chest. "There is something else," she says, her voice weak.

My throat constricts. Something is very wrong. "What is it?" I ask, not taking my eyes from hers.

"One of the bombs hit the orphanage this morning," she says, her voice utterly empty.

Every fiber of my body is taut with terror. "Which orphanage?" I wait for her to name one of the many in Warsaw, but the sorrow in her eyes betrays the awful truth. "Are the children all right?" I insist.

"Six children and two caregivers didn't survive."

A hand of fear clutches at my heart. I know every child in the orphanage. Unable to blink, I ask what I must, "Do you know who?"

Her gaze drops to the sidewalk... and stays there. "I do."

My mouth goes dry as we stand without a word for a minute that seems like eternity, but she finally says with a catch in her voice, "One of them is your Felka."

The entire world spins before me, then there is nothing.

EIGHT

BEATA

September 1939, Warsaw

When I was little, I often imagined how it would be to have family. Mother, father, siblings, grandparents... I desperately wanted to belong to someone, to be loved.

I thought I had found it in Gabriel until he broke my heart. Afterwards, I felt lonely and I was determined to never trust anyone, but I still had this lovely girl who lived in the orphanage. She'd run away from an alcoholic father who'd abused her after her mother died. Beaten by him, she appeared stricken; still, when I saw her for the first time, she had the warmest smile on her face.

My Felka was a diamond among ordinary stones. Her inner beauty shone through life's ugliness and her happiness was infectious. She became so dear to me that I knew I'd always watch over her. And now she's gone.

I wipe away my tears. I must be strong, especially now that we are about to leave Warsaw. My flat is so quiet since Joanna moved out and traveled south to her childhood town where her parents live, not far from Kraków. Without Felka, I have no reason to stay here, so I've agreed to travel with the Cipher Bureau team to England where we can continue our work on breaking ciphers.

Our city brims with chaos as there are refugees arriving from the west while crowds of Varsovians escape east. It seems like Hitler's troops are unstoppable in their relentless advance toward Warsaw.

During our last days there, we burned all documentation in the Cipher Bureau, and today we torched the bunker in Pyry with almost all the Enigma equipment inside. We are more determined than ever that the Germans do not learn about our breakthrough on their Enigma cipher machine, and that we've been able to read their enciphered messages. Whatever wasn't destroyed, we will be taking with us on the train.

With a heavy heart, I lock the door to my flat and pick up my suitcase. It's impossible to pack your entire life into one bag, so without thinking much, I grabbed only a few necessary things.

We board the evening train to the town of Brześć on the Bug River and for the coming days we're paralyzed by frequent air bombing raids that set the towns around us ablaze. We deal with track clearances and derailed trains, but on the third day we arrive in Brześć. From there we continue by car to the Romanian border, which we cross more than a week later. But that's when things get complicated because the Romanian authorities split us into two groups: civilians and the military. Each group is designated a different refugee camp to report at.

When they tell the three cryptologists and me to head to a camp near the Bacau train station, I have an idea.

"Why don't we try taking the first train to Bucharest instead?" I say while we walk to Bacau. "That way we can go to the British embassy and tell them about our cooperation with their Cipher Bureau."

It turns out that the others in my group have been thinking the same, so that's what we end up doing, but there is a significant commotion at the British embassy. They're overwhelmed with staff arriving from their embassy in Warsaw. Even though the ambassador assures us that he will contact London for permissions regarding our situation, we know it will take a while for progress to be made, so we decide to go to the French. We must leave Bucharest before we're tracked down by the Abwehr agents. We suspect that they are already looking for us.

At the French embassy we immediately receive passports, visas and train tickets to Paris. We don't think twice before accepting their hospitality; the more time spent here, the higher the risk of being caught by the German spies, who we know are everywhere. Especially given right now we should be in the Romanian refugee camp, where any spies would easily root out our cryptologists. In France we will be safe and able to resume our work, so we board the train as soon as we can.

Four days later, we arrive in Paris at midnight. The whole journey, millions of thoughts crowd my mind. It feels like so long since we left Warsaw. I can't help but wonder if I made the right decision by leaving my homeland. Before the war, I thought that when Hitler attacked, we all should stand firm and fight for freedom. But losing Felka changed everything for me. Then my beloved city reminded me too much of my sweet girl, to the point I couldn't function, so leaving seemed the only sensible option.

Now I'm on this foreign soil and feel so lonely. I like and value my colleagues here, but the only connection between us is our shared mission. Without Felka and Joanna, it's like I live with only one half of my heart.

It's time to give everything to my work; it's how I can contribute to this war, so that one day we can return to a Poland free from German occupation. My loneliness doesn't matter anymore. There are far more important matters. I will get used to this life that fate threw at me.

In October the rest of the team joins us, thanks to Major Bertrand who manages to secure their release from the Romanian camps.

Paris stuns me with its imposing monuments and the Eiffel Tower. There is something uplifting in the air here that touches my soul. Maybe the city's culture and history create that unique feeling, or maybe it's just the knowledge that we are free here, unlike in our own country.

On the twentieth day of October, Bertrand moves us to a castle outside of Paris where we hope to be able to continue our mission of decoding and decrypting Enigma messages.

NINE

BEATA

November 1939, Chateau de Vignolles near Gretz, France

The two-story Chateau de Vignolles is surrounded by an enchanted park, now marked with autumn colors of gold and red. I enjoy my walks here as the surroundings remind me of the village near Kraków where I often visited Joanna's parents. Except, they live in a wooden shack, not a castle like this one. But the freshness and beauty of Mother Nature is the same.

There isn't much codebreaking so far as we don't have our Bomba or Zygalski's sheets. We do have the two replicas of the Enigma machine we brought with us, and our knowledge.

"Listen to this," I say to Jerzy, Marian and Henryk, while pointing to the radio set broadcasting one of the French stations. We are in the quiet of the castle's attic where we find the perfect solitude needed for work. "They just mentioned Warsaw." I'm unable to contain the excitement in my voice.

"On the twenty-fifth day of September, German aircraft dropped many tons of bombs on Warsaw, the Polish capital and Poland's largest city. The air bombardment turned out to be the

heaviest in the history of the city. The deadly raid continued for several hours and killed around ten thousand people and wounded another thirty-five thousand. This day will be forever written on the cards of history as a Black Monday."

Speechless, for a moment I forget that my friends don't understand what the French radio announcer just declared. We've been waiting for news for months. But their inquiring gazes bring me back to reality and with a heavy heart I repeat it all to them in Polish.

"The whole time we knew nothing about it." Marian's voice is quiet and regretful.

I understand him so well. In moments like this, it's hard not to wish to be there with loved ones, to make sure they are safe. I've no family but Warsaw is my city and the people who live there are innocent. So many have died because of this cruel bombing raid.

"You would know if your family didn't survive this," I say trying to sound convincing. "You know how well-informed Bertrand is."

He nods but agonized pain twists his face. I imagine all our faces look like this. "I got a letter from my wife written after that terrible day. Though she didn't mention a word to me about it."

The other men keep silent as if the thoughts that run through their minds are ones that can't be tamed into words. Only silence can express the deepest soreness that mingles in our souls. Thousands of people dead. What else don't we know that has happened since our departure from Poland? What else will my beloved city and country go through?

We sit without speaking for a long time, our work forgotten. I feel drained. The fact that we are shielded from the brutality of Hitler's troops stains my conscience. We enjoy good food and wine here, and we work in peace while our brothers and sisters suffer. Something tells me that it will get even worse over there.

"I will ask Bertrand to keep his ears open for any news from Poland. He has connections and can find out a lot," I say, breaking the empty silence.

TEN

HARRY

January 1940, France

Dearest Mother,

Tomorrow will be nineteen years since your departure from this world...

I'm sorry I haven't written to you in the last six months. A lot has happened and now we are caught up in the war with Germany. Adolf Hitler started it by assaulting Poland. I wish I got to fight with a weapon in my hand but there are other ways of fighting too.

We've been busy working at Bletchley on implementing Polish methods in codebreaking but we are still not where we want to be. Anyway, that's why I'm writing to you from the little chateau in France. I accompanied the young Alan Turing who has some questions for the Polish cryptologists. I am instructed to stay here for the next couple of months and send regular reports to Bletchley.

Commander Denniston attempted more than once to have the Polish team transferred to Bletchley, but Bertrand insists on keeping them here, at this castle where he created his cryptology center. Too bad, as they would have more opportunities at Bletchley than here.

We brought with us some copies of perforated sheets for the Polish team, the same ones they showed us how to make back in Poland. Shortly after we handed them in, the Polish cryptologists cracked the Enigma cipher for the first time during the war. This left me speechless and confirmed that their codebreaking methods are valid, something I'd begun to doubt. I must mention that our own attempts at Bletchley to use their sheets in breaking the Enigma cipher failed.

I've done it once more, Mother—I'm talking about my work. But you see, I have no more private life, everything turns around my job. It gives me the necessary purpose in life. During war, there is no time for pleasantries. Besides, thanks to my work, I don't remember my loneliness. I felt so lonely before the war, while I was surrounded by so many people in London. The irony.

Oh, dearest Mother, how I miss you. There has not been a day in those nineteen years that you weren't on my mind. I was just thinking how much I would appreciate some of your cheesecake, how you loved using Grandma's recipe. Too bad that during those years, I didn't get to go back to see my grandparents and the rest of your side of the family.

Do you remember when I told you about the Polish woman whose name is Beata? The one with blonde hair and blue eyes? Well, she is here with the Polish cryptologists. It was hard to believe it at first, but she truly is here.

I'm curious about her. Will my initial infatuation diminish once I get to know her more?

I must get some shut eye now as tomorrow it will be busy again. I love you and miss you every day.

Your Harry

ELEVEN
BEATA

January 1940, Chateau de Vignolles near Gretz, France

Harry chuckles at something that Bertrand explains to him while we all sit at a long table. I hadn't expected to see him ever again, yet he is here, once more stirring my inside with that weird feeling I can't even define.

"*Na zdrowie*, cheers, to this young lady." Langer lifts his glass and smiles at me, and the others follow suit.

"*Na zdrowie*," they all chant.

Heat rushes to my cheeks at his unexpected gesture. How does he even know that it's my birthday today? I was hoping to keep it a secret. With Felka gone, I've no heart to celebrate.

I smile at Langer and everyone else, thanking them. At the thought of Felka, a flow of tears emerges, but I blink them away and swallow a painful lump. To my relief, people soon get back to eating and chatting. I'm thankful that no one saw my weakness. My grief must stay in silence because there aren't words to reflect it.

After excusing myself to Henryk, with whom I've been conversing, I walk to the other part of the room where there is a stone chimney. Standing with my back to the others, I pretend to stir the fire with a stick, but in truth I'm allowing the tears to flow. I could not hold them any longer. Since Felka's passing, they come every time I allow my mind drift to the memory of my sweet girl.

"What is it?" I hear a soft voice right behind me. Alarmed, I wipe my tears. I don't know who it is, but obviously someone has noticed my distress.

I compose a smile and whirl around to meet a set of dark gray and steady eyes. Harry Smith.

"It's nothing," I say. "Just a little homesick." For a moment I'm taken aback by the pure strength in his rugged face.

His jaws tighten. "I can see it's more than that." This man has no problem saying what he thinks.

Despite everything, a sudden need to share my pain with someone overtakes me. Why not? Maybe it will bring me some comfort.

"I lost someone dearest to me on the first day of the war." By saying it, it feels like I'm dropping a bomb from my chest. I don't care right now to hide my sorrow.

I expect him to give me his condolences and then turn to walk away. I got that a lot in Warsaw in the days after Felka's death. People don't know what to say and how to talk to those who are immersed in grief. I was one of those people once too.

He doesn't ask about anything but instead he takes my hand and kisses it. "Your loved one lives in your heart," he says, and his strong gaze confronts the sadness in my eyes. "Until you meet again."

I can feel he truly believes in what he just told me. In this quiet moment, while our eyes swim in mutual understanding, something changes between us. He is no more a stranger.

"You believe that?" I say and wipe my tears.

He clears his throat. "I do." He looks away but swiftly gazes back at me. Now his face shows pain. "Today is the anniversary of my mother's passing. It still hurts like hell despite the nine-teen years."

Without thinking, I hug him. I don't care what he thinks, or what others think. My heart tells me he needs that hug as much as I do.

The initial stiffness in his muscles dissolves in seconds and his arms envelop me. Without another word, I rest my face on his shoulder, too exhausted to say anything else, wondering why his touch feels so right and brings such a sense of feeling at home when we are so far adrift in the world.

"Thank you," he whispers. "I needed this today more than ever."

"I think I might have the wrong impression of you," I say and step back. Feeling awkward, I pick up a stick, turn away and resume stirring logs in the fire.

"I'm afraid to inquire for more details."

The intimate moment that connected us before is gone now. "It's nothing. You probably don't even remember me that much from Poland."

"I remember you well." His voice is quiet.

When I swirl back to face him, I'm confronted by a curious gaze, the quirk of his lips. Despite the time that has passed, I still remember our first encounter at the café. There was some-thing in the way he looked at me, that made me feel something new. Now, all I feel is confusion because I'm sure there is no trace of judgment in his eyes.

"You seem to think that Polish women are easy and flirta-tious," I challenge him.

"I apologize for my friend Stuart," he says, giving me a meaningful look. "Though your friend Joanna seemed to appre-ciate his advances." His eyes focus intently on my face.

At first, I don't know how to react to his words and if I should get upset on behalf of Joanna. He's stated the truth—she went over to their table to flirt with the man. Later, she talked about it with delight, telling me her night was filled with passion and unforgettable moments.

At the thought of Joanna's account of her night with the other British man, I feel heat creeping up my cheeks. Then, the hilarity of the entire situation strikes me like a bolt of electricity. I can't restrain myself from laughing out loud.

"I think they had a good time together," I manage, unable to stop laughing. "Who am I to judge?"

His shoulders lift in a shrug, then he grins. "Well, Stuart couldn't stop gushing about your friend."

When we grow serious again, he takes my hand in his. "I respect women no less than men. Please, believe me."

When I think about it now, I only remember his curious gaze on me, his friend was the one who said the inappropriate words. "Well, I didn't hear you arguing with Stuart."

"My grandpa once told me that you can't explain to the fool, and the wise man doesn't need any explanations." He smirks at me. "That's the case with Stuart, I'm afraid."

"Your grandpa nailed it."

This time his laughter rings out, bringing more light to the darkness in me. I like this man.

TWELVE
BEATA

February 1940, Chateau de Vignolles near Gretz, France

I stroll through the castle's park, scraps of snow still hugging the ground. I needed to get out to refresh my tired mind and inhale the crisp air. Sometimes the smallest things can give more than any wealth ever could.

It's been almost four months since Bertrand brought us to this place, one kilometer away from a town called Gretz, where he runs his radio intelligence. Here, our Polish team—fifteen of us—is responsible for decoding and decrypting intercepted messages from German radiographs.

I've been wandering through the fenced-in grounds of the castle for over an hour now. The guard at the gate must be thinking I'm a lunatic, or perhaps wondering if I'm a spy.

I pass a small brick building where Spanish cryptographers, refugees from Franco's regime, reside, and I resolve to walk in the direction of a pond a little further away, where I can stay for the remainder of my break.

On 28 October, Jerzy Różycki figured out the Enigma's modifications that the Germans applied in July, and now, given that we have the Zygalski sheets that Harry and the other Brits brought last month, our three cryptologists are able to crack the Enigma codes again and we can read the enemy's messages.

The Germans change their daily keys every day at midnight, and we are especially interested in the first messages that they send out. There is a very important pattern about the nature of those first keys that speeds up the codebreaking process. But I have no energy to even think of it now. I must forget for a moment about my job and my duties.

However, I do have a passion for what I do. I find a sweet satisfaction every time I decrypt a new message. We are short-handed, so the three cryptologists also help us read messages even though their hands are full when it comes to breaking the daily codes. Bertrand plans to have his French workers go through the series of trainings, and hopefully we will then have the necessary help.

Right now, we've an agreement with the team at Bletchley that whoever breaks any codes first will send them to the other. We supply them with the intercepted telegraphs from the Kriegsmarine and Luftwaffe, and they keep gifting us with the Zygalski perforated sheets.

The pond, which has a sliding gate, brims with croaking frogs and birds that trill through, splashing water. Despite it still being February, the temperatures have risen, causing waters to unfreeze. In Poland it will be so much colder now.

But I'm not the only one here. Harry stands at a muddy bank strewn with rocks, his gaze on the water. I know that he and Captain MacFarlan are expected to stay here with us for a couple of months, whereas the other cryptologist, Alan Turing, has already gone back to England after receiving training from our cryptologists.

Since our encounter on my birthday, we've only spoken a few words here and there. At first, I felt uncomfortable knowing I'd hugged him, but his warm and respectful attitude toward me melted my worries. We both needed a sliver of comfort that day, but now we're back to normal.

I see him differently now. He's not that arrogant man I thought when I met him at Hotel Bristol. Still, other than that he's smart at mathematics, I know little to nothing about him. We do have one thing in common: the loss of someone very dear to us. This fact makes me want to know him better, to spend time with him and feel his understanding gaze on me more often.

"Hello," I say and stop beside him. "I see we have the same idea of resting."

I expect surprise, maybe even annoyance at me for interfering, but his eyes sparkle with something undefined the moment they rest on me, bringing a surge of warmth to my cheeks.

For a moment, he smiles. "It's good to get away at least once a day."

"It smells like wet earth here," I say and laugh. "Much better than the stagnant air of the castle."

He grins. "I won't argue with you on that."

Wind rustles the branches of the nearby trees. "Hopefully spring is just around the corner. Do you have the same weather in England?"

He nods. "Only more rain."

For a moment we stay in silence while watching the swirling waters of the pond. He keeps glancing my way. Maybe he's as curious about me as I am about him? Never before have I felt like this about a man. Not even Gabriel. I'm sure it's because of my loneliness in this castle crowded by men. Since that private moment between us on my birthday, I feel understood by him.

"I prefer working here than at Bletchley," he says, folding his arms behind his head and stretching.

"Why?"

"It rains way too often over there. Here is much more pleasant," he says.

"I didn't know about that pessimistic side of you." I playfully nudge his arm.

"I have my moments," he says, as a sudden sigh escapes from his lips. "But who doesn't in today's world?"

"I often wonder how my life would look if not for this stupid war." I wipe a single tear that emerges against my will. "My Felka would be here." I fight to stop more tears. I don't want to cry; I don't want his pity. This state of mind is so new to me, this feeling so vulnerable, and I'm unable to control my emotions. Even at the orphanage, I rarely wept as a child, and never during my adolescent years. After Gabriel broke my heart, I was upset but never cried as I knew he'd proved himself to be undeserving of me.

Now, I'm at a loss for words when it comes to my emotional state. It's easier when I'm busy focusing on my duties and maintaining a professional attitude toward my coworkers. The moment I find myself alone, tears never fail to emerge at the first thought of Felka. Yet, I want to think of her, to remember her, to honor her.

There is also something in Harry that awakens those painful emotions within me, not to mention I have this weird need for his touch. For God's sake, I reprimand myself, I don't even know the man, so why do I feel the way I do?

As if sensing my state of mind, he puts his arm around me and brings me closer. His intimate touch isn't offensive; in truth, it brings the comfort I think he anticipates. Besides Gabriel, I've never let any other man touch me like this, but again, there is something about Harry that silences my restraint, and also my shyness.

We stay like this for a moment longer, until I regain my composure. It strikes me that he doesn't ask about Felka at all.

"I'm sorry," I say and pull away from him. "You probably think that I'm overly emotional."

"I don't judge people if I don't know them."

"Would you like to know me more then?" I don't know why I say this, but the moment I do, I regret it. He may get the impression that I'm trying to flirt with him.

When he answers, his voice is quiet. "I would." His eyes gain a darker shade now while he seems to softly study every feature of my face.

Another bliss of warmth creeps up my cheeks, but I don't tell him how much I yearn to get to know him too. I don't understand this yearning at all.

"Are you going to attend the dinner in the town tomorrow?" he says, gently. "Marian, Henryk and Jerzy are going to join me."

I wasn't planning to, since it's Sunday and I hoped to rest after church, but I nod. When I am with this man, I seem to be constantly surprising myself.

THIRTEEN

HARRY

February 1940, France

Dearest Mother,

I still don't know if it's possible to fall in love with someone you know so little.

I have no idea what her favorite food is, or what color she likes best. The only thing I know of her is that she lost someone dear to her, and that she struggles to accept it. I know the feeling so well, so I don't force her to talk about it. I trust that she will tell me more when she's ready.

Every time her ocean-blue eyes look at me, my heart makes a strange lurch. Her encounters with the rest of the team are professional and friendly, yet every time she talks to me in private, she has tears in her eyes.

I will do everything to put a smile on her face tomorrow. I know that you would like her. There is this inner warmth in this girl that makes her irresistible.

I wish I could call Heaven and speak to you, Mother. I

would give everything to hear your voice, see your smile, enjoy your vibrant laugh. We would have tea together, something you enjoyed very much.

I miss you today more than ever,

Your Harry

FOURTEEN
BEATA

February 1940, Bar de Margot, Gretz

We all enjoy the *pot-au-feu* that consists of two courses: broth, and beef with vegetables. It's so warm and delicious, and it reminds me of dinners that Joanna prepared every Sunday. Then, we finish the meal with rum cake, or in French, *baba au rhum*.

Harry orders a bottle of Château Margaux, which we split between the five of us. The red wine is smooth with a hint of soft fruit, maybe cherry or raspberry.

By now, the tavern is crowded, overtaken by the cigarette smoke and buzz of loud conversations. People dance to lively yet melancholic French folk music.

Marian, Jerzy and Henryk move on to a strong spirit called Pastis, while Harry and I stay with wine. Our moods are sour as we talk about Poland and the war, and the alcohol gives a lethargic feel to everything. They all worry about their families left behind, especially Marian and Jerzy, who talk about their wives and children. I can't help but think about Joanna.

At the first chords of Edith Piaf's song, "Elle fréquentait la

Rue Pigalle", I sigh. "It's so depressing to sit here with you, gentlemen," I say and roll my eyes. "I need a dancing partner." I don't look at Harry, but hope he volunteers.

"My wife would not approve," Marian says. "But Henryk is free like a bird." He gives a brief laugh and turns to the empty chair to his right where Henryk sat just a minute ago. "Never mind," he adds and lifts his glass to his lips.

I shrug and laugh, but then a tall and muscular man with blond shoulder-length hair bows before me. "Can I have this dance?"

Before I realize it, my mouth falls open. Why would this Frenchman ask me to dance when there are so many beautiful women here?

I touch my throat, deciding how to reject his offer. Dancing with him would feel awkward. I've seen tonight the way he rules the dance floor with stunning women in his arms. The last thing I want is to embarrass myself.

"This dance is already mine," Harry says in English, a note of firmness in his voice, and I remember to breathe again.

The man's gaze moves back from Harry to me, and his eyebrows squish together.

I clear my throat. "My friend just explained to you, sir, that I already promised him this dance." I smile as I say it. "Perhaps, another time."

He has a pinched expression now, but he bows again and walks away.

A moment later, Harry holds me in his arms as we dance to Edith Piaf's song.

"Thank you for saving me," I say, wondering about his motives. "I didn't know how to reject him without causing trouble." To me, the Frenchman had this Casanova look about him. Joanna likes to date men like him, one-night stands. At the thought of her, a wave of warmth settles in my heart. I miss my silly, impetuous friend so much. I didn't realize how important she was in my life.

"I judged correctly then." A teasing smile crosses his face.

Edith Piaf's song turns out to be perfect for my dancing abilities, not so fast, not so slow. I enjoy the warm touch of Harry's hands, his closeness, and I notice how good he smells. The citrus scent of his cologne is clean and refreshing. I know that my inner loneliness is making my senses feel so alert. I should not show it because I don't want to give him the wrong idea. Besides, he only acted to save me from that gigolo; he's not trying to seduce me. I'm sure there is a pretty girl waiting for him in England. Good-looking and cultured men like him change women like gloves, or at least that's what Joanna has told me at least a million times.

"How do you like the song?" I ask, trying to sound neutral but friendly.

"It's a little downbeat," he says. "Maybe if I could fully understand the lyrics, my perception of it would be different, but she sings so fast."

"Well, if I was to translate the title into English, it would be like this: *She frequented the rue Pigalle*. It tells the story of a woman who led a sinful life, but one day she meets a man who saw only beauty in her. He took her with him to a better life, telling her that her past doesn't matter, only her beauty. Just when she thought she could be happy, all of a sudden, the man changed. Her past started bothering him and her beauty didn't matter any longer. He told her that it would be better if she went back to her previous life, as he didn't want her anymore. From that moment on, sadness never left her big blue eyes, and she returned to her sins."

Harry doesn't respond right away, but when he does his voice is laden with emotion. "So, it is a sad story, indeed."

I like that he doesn't judge the woman right away. "Yes. It always makes me think how much harder we women have it than you men. Through the centuries, women have had no say, or often no choice."

"Would you do the same—return to a past sinful life after being rejected by a man who once saw more in you than just your beauty?"

At first, his question surprises me. It's hard to read his somber face in the immediacy of this moment, so I'm not sure where he is going with his question. "Depends."

A hint of curiosity sparkles in his eyes. "Depends on what?"

"It depends if I were living centuries ago or now, and on my social status. If I was in the past, I'd never judge or be sure of what my decisions might be. I'd need to find myself in the situation to know my behavior. But if it was now, in the twentieth century, I'd take things in my own hands. I would never be interested in building a relationship based on looks."

He doesn't get a chance to respond because the music stops, and we head back to our table. During the dance, Jerzy came over to let us know that they were leaving to get an hour or two of sleep as they had to be up at midnight. Harry assured him that he would keep me safe.

I yawn and say, "I would like to get back too. It's going to be a long day tomorrow."

I bury my face into my scarf, as we walk through the windy night. He insists I take his arm because of the harsh conditions. I obey, thanking him as I do so.

When we get closer to the castle, the wind quietens down a little. "I always wondered what a great thing God did by inventing trees," Harry says. "Even now, thanks to them it's so much easier to walk in this wind."

"We shouldn't underestimate Mother Nature." I lift my face from the scarf and smile at him.

"True. You know what happened to Napoleon's troops in Russia?" The corners of his mouth lift in a teasing smile.

"Yes, the extreme weather conditions defeated them. Let's hope that Hitler commits the same mistake one day."

He shrugs. "I wish. It seems it's not going to be so simple when it comes to this war."

"It's like the wind," I say. "At some point, the war must end. I just hope the outcome will not be fatal for us."

"Another question is when that point will be. None of us knows how long this war will last." He pauses and lifts his gaze to the sky. "Look, the moon watches over our castle."

The chateau basks in the moonlight like the celestial pearl of the night sky. "It's stunning," I say, unable to take my eyes from it.

He nods. "It's a good sign for us."

"Why do you think that?" I like how he tries to see encouraging things whenever he can. It doesn't matter where he looks, he focuses first on spotting any traces of beauty, or even decency. I noticed that wonderful quality about him right from the first day he arrived here. It's such a contrast to my usual way of perceiving my surroundings.

"Because when the moon smiles at us, it's a sign from God. The moon symbolizes pureness, beauty, calmness. That's what eternal love is: selfless and innocent."

"Your love for your mother," I say and squeeze his arm.

"That will always be true, but I had in mind the love between a woman and a man. The one that starts innocently and never ends, despite destruction and death, despite wars."

"It's like you talk from your own experience?"

"I do," he says bringing a rush of unwanted disappointment to my heart.

Once more, I'm baffled. Why do I even experience these feelings? I'm happy for him, to learn that he loves and is loved in such a powerful way. But my voice is subdued when I say, "I hope to experience it one day, too."

FIFTEEN

BEATA

March 1940, Gretz

Spring came early this year, mesmerizing with its freshness and natural harmony. As I walk from the castle to the town, I feel the explosion of new life in the air. It's heartwarming after the long months of winter. The sun feels warmer and brighter as trees experience the blooming process that is so colorful and magically green. I listen to birds singing, and I watch for the first butterflies of the year.

If only there was no war. According to intercepted messages, the Luftwaffe increased their air raids throughout the spring. We haven't heard any news from Poland for a while now, so the atmosphere in the castle is nervous. Everyone worries about their families and the future of our country. But we do have our part to play in this war, thanks to our work in codebreaking and decrypting.

The Eglise Saint Jean Baptiste church on rue de Paris in Gretz was built in the fourteenth century. Pointed-arch windows decorate the light gray stone walls. A cross adorns the roof of the bell tower to the northeast of the building.

I take a seat in the same pew as Mrs. Moreau, who I know from my previous visits to the church. Marian and the other men sit up in the rows that the priest reserved for us, but I decide to stay with this elderly lady; she seems to appreciate my company.

After the mass, Mrs. Moreau convinces me to have a coffee with her. This isn't the first time she's attempted to invite me, so I agree. It turns out that she lives in a large brick building, two blocks away from the church.

"I live here with my only son," she says as we enter the mansion. "My husband, bless his soul, departed from this world eleven years ago."

The house smells of floor wax and freshly cut flowers. I follow her through an old-fashioned family room with a large chimney and into a vast kitchen. She points to me an amber-clothed table with a vase of flowers in its center.

I take a seat and watch her putting a polka-dot apron over her dark brown dress. "Your house is beautiful, Mrs. Moreau," I say.

She pats her silvery hair gathered in a bun at the back of her head. "My late husband built it when he owned his own construction company." She sighs. "My son sold the family business and does nothing."

I ignore her remark about her son as it clearly causes her distress. "I'm so sorry to hear about your husband," I say and offer her a sympathetic look.

"Thank you, my sweet," she says, as she stands stock-still with a small kettle in her hands. "Enough time has passed now for me to accept it. I'm looking forward to joining him one day over there, in the heavenly kingdom."

"Stop talking nonsense, Mother." A robust voice interrupts her.

I move my gaze to the kitchen door where a blond man fills

almost the length of the whole frame, his twinkling eyes set on me.

I bite at my lip, wondering how it's possible that the blond Casanova from Bar de Margot is now standing right before me in Mrs. Moreau's kitchen.

"Beata, my dear," the elderly lady says, "this is my son." Then she addresses the man. "This is the friend from the church I told you about. I invited her over for coffee. Will you join us?"

"My pleasure," he says and extends his hand toward me. "My name is Alphonse." He looks so different in his immaculate suit, definitely unlike the gigolo from the bar with his shirt open to expose his hairy torso.

I take his hand and say, "Beata."

He nods and kisses my knuckles. "I like your accent. What's your nationality?"

"Polish," I say without elaborating. Whenever I go out, French people point out my accent as "cute", so he isn't the first one.

"That's what I thought when I saw you last Sunday." He gives me a meaningful look.

I allow my lips to quirk, but I don't know what to say.

Thankfully, Mrs. Moreau breaks the silence. "Here, my dear, have some coffee." She sets blue-rimmed porcelain cups on the table along with a plate of croissants.

The dark roast coffee tastes heavenly with its smoky and intense aroma. It helps me to relax despite the awkwardness of this Frenchman sitting right across from me.

The old lady talks about the town's news while we add a word here and there. I'm pleased that her son speaks to his mother in a respectful manner.

Before I leave, she makes me promise to visit her again next Sunday after church. She also insists that her son walks me back home, and he readily agrees.

I have no heart to deny her kindness, so I go along with it.

"My mother adores you," he says on our walk toward the castle. "She's been raving about you for a while."

"She is so nice. I enjoy spending time with her."

For the rest of the way we talk about French food and wine, but when we are only minutes from the castle, I say, "Please, you don't have to walk me all the way home. I'm sure you have more important things to do."

"It's my pleasure. Besides, my mother asked me to escort you home and I cannot let her down," he says, displaying his perfect teeth.

When we approach the guard station, my chest tightens at the sight of Harry chatting with a guard. The last thing I need is for people to see me with Alphonse. Harry will surely remember him from the tavern and come to the wrong conclusion.

I lift my chin as we near them and can sense their eyes on us, but I pay them no attention. Instead, I stop and extend my hand to Alphonse. "Thank you so much for accompanying me here."

He kisses my knuckles, and says, "Again, my pleasure. I'm looking forward to seeing you next Sunday."

I nod and walk away. The guard knows me, so he doesn't bother halting me.

"Hello, gentlemen," I say without looking at them.

"Well, well, I see the French Casanova got his way with you." I hear Harry's voice a few minutes later. It's still warm outside, so I decided to rest on one of the tree stumps that encircle a barbecue pit in the center of a small square.

"Cut it out, Harry," I say in a voice devoid of emotion. I feel so drained right now. "I visited an elderly lady after church, and it turns out he's her son. So please cease all speculations because I'm not going to deal with any gossip of yours."

"And you are planning to visit the lady next Sunday as well, from what I've heard." After he says it, his mouth is pinched, and his face covered by a sour expression.

If I didn't know any better, I would think he is jealous, but that's not possible. Why would he be? "She asked me to. She's lonely."

"Her son can't keep her company?"

I grind my teeth. "Where are you going with this? Please be assured, I'm not giving away any work secrets to him." I treat him to a knowing look. "I'm not interested in getting to know him. I don't want to be rude to his mother. That's all."

He lifts his hands up. "All right, I didn't mean to upset you. Just got worried, that's all."

"No need to worry," I say, a little bemused. "Anyway, how are things over there?" I point to the castle.

"Busy as always," he says, then takes my hand in his. "Are you okay? You seem on edge lately."

"I'm fine, just missing home."

"Who's at home?" he asks while tracing my skin with his finger.

My flesh vibrates with sparks of electricity. The feeling is so delicious that I want him to never stop touching me like this.

"Just my dear friend, Joanna." I tell him the truth, then look away and continue. "I've no family. As a baby I was left on the steps of a church. I grew up in an orphanage." I don't know why I'm telling him this, but maybe it's because deep within me I care about the way he sees me. If he doesn't know the fundamental facts of my past, he won't be able to put together an accurate picture of me.

He doesn't let my hand go but squeezes gently. "Now I know why you're so damn strong. You don't want anything from anyone, and if someone does something for you, you seem uneasy."

I can't be upset about his words because I know he is spot on, but I don't like the direction he's heading in, even though his attitude seems genuine. I have judged people in the wrong way so many times in the past, and later been disappointed by them.

"It doesn't seem you can say this of your own experience," I say and slip my hand out of his. I can't let him get too close. I need mental peace in my life; I can't hold onto another burden of uncertainty from this man who is already in love with someone else, or at least that's what he suggested during the moonlit night. After Gabriel, I have more than had my share of it.

"You're right, my life was easier than yours. I was well taken care of when it came to my material needs." He reaches out and takes my hand back in his like it belongs there, causing my heart to give a nervous jolt. I like his bold gesture, even if it somehow doesn't feel appropriate that he moves forward and touches me like this.

"When I was eleven, I lost my mother. We were extremely close. She understood me in a way no one else ever could, so my entire world crushed when she died." His finger brushes my skin like a teasing feather. "Every happiness is only ever halfway felt, because there is always an immediate thought of her not being here. That day when I lost my mother, my heart began this excruciating journey, one it will never heal from. So, I learned to live with it."

"I'm sorry," I whisper. "I never had to endure losing my parents because I never knew them. You're lucky you got to cherish your mother for the first eleven years of your life." I wipe my tears and smile. "You know that there is no other man with whom I shed even a single tear?"

"I believe you." A gentle squeeze on my hand reassures me. I never had this emotional deepness with Gabriel despite the five years we spent together. Harry, practically a stranger to me, makes me feel understood. He listens like I'm telling him the most crucial things in the entire universe, and, unlike Gabriel, he doesn't judge me.

"Did you get any emotional support from your family?"

"Not really. I had a good relationship with my grandmother from my mother's side, but my father cut any contact shortly after my mother died. The fact that that side of my family lived in Poland, didn't help."

At his last words, I jerk my head back. "Your mother was Polish?"

"Yes, indeed. She met my father during his trip to Poland."

"And they fell in love," I say unable to resist a sardonic smile. "Did you learn to speak Polish?"

"That's all she spoke to me. It was truly my mother tongue." There is this wound of deep pain in his eyes, which I understand so well. "My last words to her were in Polish, minutes before she passed to the other side."

I squeeze his hand. "Can you still speak it?" My voice is quiet.

"I don't know. It somehow doesn't feel right. Don't ask me why, it's just how I feel. But I understand it pretty well." He grins, showing a line of white teeth.

I give an exasperated laugh, thinking of all the times us Poles have said something not so nice, thinking that the Brits and French didn't understand us. "Well, good to know."

His laugh sounds so healthy and genuine. I can't help but like this man more and more. Perhaps I've found a good friend, after all.

I realize how much I want to talk about Felka with him, when all these months I've kept her all to myself. The loss of her was just too painful to discuss with other people. I sense he would understand me in a way no one else could.

"My Felka was a teenage girl who lived in the same

orphanage where I grew up. She had so much joy and happiness in her despite her tragic past and so many misfortunes," I say. "I grew to love her like I would my own daughter and I promised to always watch over her. We had made plans for her to move into my flat once she was of age." I wipe the tears that never fail to arrive whenever I think of my girl. "The day Hitler's Germany decided to attack Poland will always be the worst in my life. Not only because of the war, but because it's the day I lost my Felka. The orphanage was bombed by the Luftwaffe. She didn't survive." My heart plummets to the pit of my stomach at the painful memories. "Nothing made sense once that precious girl died. Thankfully, I found enough strength in me to continue."

Harry pulls me into his arms and hugs me for a long time.

Minutes in his embrace seem like a peaceful eternity. If I was given a choice, I would stay like this forever. No words are needed, just the warmth of his touch. My belief in human decency is restored in the intimacy of this moment, restored because of this man who acts with his heart.

When I step to the side, we walk to the pond. I pick up a little stick at my feet and fidget with it, feeling uncomfortable after my confession. He probably thinks I'm a drama queen.

Harry throws a stone into the water, but then he says with a surge of panic in his voice, "Look, Beata, look!"

I jerk my head up and gaze into the pond. "What?" I insist, frightened.

"Look!" he says again. "There is a shark in the water."

SIXTEEN

HARRY

March 1940, Gretz

"Got you!" I say, and I can't resist the laughter that spills from me. She seemed so restless after telling me about her grief that I wanted to put a smile on her face.

When she looks at me confused, I say, "Have you forgotten that tomorrow it's April Fool's Day?"

"You're a sneaky one," she says but then bursts into genuine laughter. "For a second, I actually expected to see a shark in that pond. How silly of me."

I berate myself for not being able to take away the sorrow that she feels after losing her young friend more permanently. But this is the price, I think, for loving someone.

I pat her back. "I'm glad I was able to make you laugh. Listen, the truth is that more time is needed for you to learn how to live with this pain in your heart after losing your friend," I say while holding her hand. I like spending time with her when there is no one else around. In the castle, we're surrounded by crowds, everyone anxious to get the job done well.

"It's as if my heart is weighed down by a physically excruciating pain." She puts her other hand on her chest. "One night I thought I was having a heart attack."

"Losing your beloved friend caused shock not only to your mind, but also to your body. It will slowly get easier, I promise you that, but the wound will never heal completely. The only thing you can do is to accept that grief as a part of your being."

"Thank you for being honest with me," she says, her voice warm and sincere. "It makes me feel understood and truly helps me."

"Some people try to get it completely out of their system and make substantial changes in their lives, just like my father. I don't know if that sort of behavior is a sign of bravery, or cowardice."

"I want to remember Felka, so she's a part of my every day," she says, and her faint smile is so beautiful that I fight myself not to kiss her. We're talking about the sacred aspects of our lives, so such an act on my part would be stupid.

"It's how I feel about my mother too. Even though she isn't physically here, I keep reminding myself that she is more alive on the other side than we are here. It's just that our human brains are too limited to grasp at it."

"I appreciate your way of thinking and your beliefs. It's hard to cultivate such thoughts while dealing with our earthly problems."

"True. Think how much easier it would be to go on with our lives if we knew that our loved ones, who have departed from this world, are in the right place on the other side of the veil. If we could see their smiles at least once, or even to talk to them for a brief moment. Or be assured by them that they thrive and that one day we will be reunited with them."

"It would change everything." She sighs and wipes her tears away. "Life without them is a lonely adventure. I will never accept that Felka isn't here anymore."

"We have to believe our own voice deep inside us and trust in God."

"We humans like to touch and experience. To truly believe is an art on another level. Before I lost Felka, I didn't give much thought to anything beyond my everyday life. I prayed, went to Sunday church, but never really dug into a deeper understanding of our existence on this earth and after death."

"Like most people." I nod my agreement. "It's easy to concentrate on the material aspects of our lives and overlook the most important values that should shape us."

"Nazi Germany is a perfect example of this," she says. "Greedy with power, they forgot about the fundamental values and equality of all human beings. They represent the biggest tragedy of our times, and probably long beyond them too."

She nailed it pretty well, I think. "We must fight to win. It's the only thing we can do." I'm in awe of her. There aren't that many people with whom I feel so comfortable conversing about such various topics. Most people look at me awkwardly whenever I mention my belief in the afterlife. With Beata, it's natural to talk about it.

SEVENTEEN

BEATA

April 1940, Chateau de Vignolles near Gretz, France

I stretch and yawn. It's been a long day in this studio in the castle's attic furnished by a bar with a long table. Various landscape paintings bring cheerfulness to the place.

The air is crisp and fresh as we keep the windows open. I can't resist walking over to the table and reaching for a sandwich cookie filled with buttercream; I've learned that it's called a macaron. I enjoy its meringue-based sweetness, rich with fresh almonds.

Harry and the other men have been joking lately that my weakness for these exquisite sweets will one day make me betray them all.

French telegraph operators keep forwarding German messages using the teleprinter, and there are not enough hands to do all the work that we have here. Our cryptologists still break the Enigma codes using the perforated sheets. The Bomba machine had to be destroyed back in Poland, before the Germans had a chance to discover it. We have no equipment to build another one, unlike the British.

"Our specialists at Bletchley keep busy," Harry says, looking at Marian. "After getting the impulse from you, they've copied your replicas of the Enigma machines. Also, they're working on their own Bomba trying to take further what they were shown during the meeting in Pyry." His gaze moves to Henryk. "Though, as of now, the only way they are able to crack the Enigma codes is by using the perforated sheets Henryk invented."

"Our dearest cryptologists planted the seed," I say and smile with awe. "They're one of the most hard-working people I have ever met."

"Thank you, my friend," Marian says and smiles back at me.

I mean every word. They love their families in Poland and they'd give everything to be back where they belong. Still, they give their best while working here. It's a different story when it comes to how the results of our work are utilized.

We use the intercepted messages to prepare daily reports about Germany's plans and intentions, such as Hitler's planned attack on Norway and Denmark.

We also detect some signs of their vicious plans in regard to France, but some French dignitaries seem to think that Germans will not dare to cross their soil.

Bertrand's face betrays annoyance every time our resources are downplayed, or when they aren't taken seriously.

For my part, I don't think there is anyone in the world better informed of the enemy's plans than the French right now. We jot our findings on yellow paper cards marked as "Source Z", which are treated by the French command as "less important".

"Have I missed any news about our country from Bertrand?" Marian asks, taking his glasses off and leaning back in his chair. His face shows precisely the exhaustion we all feel right now, after twelve hours of constant labor.

"Not much besides the revelation that the Germans closed down the Polish libraries in Warsaw and opened up reading rooms for Germans," Henryk says, as a look of disgust flashes over his face.

"Yeah, supposedly their newspapers report how rich their library is," Jerzy adds, "while in reality, the rooms are empty because the drunken German murderers choose to rot in their godforsaken bars instead."

"I heard something else," Harry says in heavy accented Polish, surprising everyone, and making me so proud. For the last couple of weeks, I've spoken in my mother tongue to him whenever we're alone, but he hasn't said a word until now.

"Harry's mother is Polish," I say.

"Look at you," Marian says and grins. "And you hid it all from us until now?"

Harry simply grins back.

"So, what else about Poland did you hear, my friend?" Henryk says.

Harry continues in English. "It turns out that at the end of November, Governor General Hans Frank ordered that Jews must wear a white armband affixed with a blue six-sided star. If anyone who is Jewish doesn't wear it, they will face severe penalties."

"The damn Nazis think that everyone else was born to be their slaves," Jerzy utters.

Harry's words make a hole in my heart. Joanna's mother is Jewish. Does that mean she has to wear this terrible armband too? What about my witty friend who always wears the most fashionable clothes? Does this law apply to her as well? Is she going to be branded like an animal at the cattle market? I can't stand the cruelty of Hitler and his troops.

"I guess Hitler likes to mark people," I say. "I heard that the Poles who are deported for forced labor to Germany, are now marked with a letter 'P' on their clothing."

A heavy silence hangs in the air making me feel even more drained. I don't want to talk about it anymore. Any news from Poland is bad news, and I have the feeling there will only be worse and worse as this war continues its awful march.

Henryk must think the same because he says, "Beata, how's the Frenchman?" A cynical smile twists his lips. "He had his eyes on you even back then in the tavern."

"I don't know what you are talking about," I say, not stopping my process of decrypting another message. I know he's talking about Alphonse. Every Sunday, his mother, who is such a sweet lady, convinces me to stop by for coffee, and our meetings are always pleasant.

"Well, I'm talking about the handsome blond one who escorts you every Sunday right up to the gates of this castle," Henryk says.

I roll my eyes. "Oh, shut up, Henryk. Don't you have better things to do?" I scold him and go back to my task.

But it's too late. "Frenchmen have hot blood," Marian says, "and Polish women are wickedly beautiful, so the match is perfect." He winks at Henryk, and they burst out laughing.

I shrug. I know nothing is going to stop their teasing now. Doesn't matter what I say or if I explain to them once more that I'm only visiting Mrs. Moreau and that her son only walks with me because his mother insists on it.

So, I go along with their good-natured joking, as it's the most effective way to deal with them when they are clowns like this, having fun at my expense. "Well, how could I resist such a handsome, cultured *French* man like Alphonse," I say and bat my eyelashes.

Their laughter rings out and I know they appreciate my remark. But Harry stands up and leaves the room without a word.

"Someone doesn't approve of our sense of humor," Jerzy says. "Oh, those Polish women," he continues with exaltation, both hands on his chest. "They can break so many hearts."

"You comedians better go back to work," I say with a shake of my head.

I leave the attic to check on Harry. He surely didn't take our silly talk to heart? By now he should be used to our silliness, so what is it that's troubling him? He may not always understand the context, as he's not so fluent or familiar in Polish.

I knock on his door but when he opens it and stands shirtless in front of me, I want to jolt away. His face has this hard look, and his jaw seems to be tighter than usual.

I keep my eyes on his stern face, ignoring his torso and powerful shoulders. The citrusy tang of his cologne fills my nostrils and makes me feel even more dizzy in the face of his overpowering masculinity.

I swallow hard and smile, pretending not to be affected by my attraction for him. "I wanted to check on you."

"I'm fine, just need some rest," he says and folds his lips in a faint smile. But there is something else in his piercing eyes, and by now I know him well enough to detect it.

"I can clearly see something bothers you, but if you don't want to tell me, I understand. You don't have to."

I swirl around, intending to walk away, but he holds my arm. "Stay," he says in a tense voice. "I do need to talk to you."

I exhale with relief, as I do really care about this stubborn man. There is this special friendship between us that brings me so much comfort every single day. Thanks to him, it's so much easier to cope with all the pain I feel; he's always there to listen and console, or give advice. I want to offer the same to him.

The bedroom smells of him and feels so intimate. When he points out a chair to me, I take the hint.

"You seem upset," I say and meet his gaze properly for the first time since entering the room. His speculative eyes move to my lips and stay there.

"Are you involved with the Frenchman?" Not a muscle in his chiseled face moves.

I didn't know this way of him, and it scares me a little. "No," I say without shifting my eyes from his.

For a moment, his eyes show uncertainty, but he sighs and says, "Good. I don't want him to take advantage of you." His chin relaxes a little, and he looks more like himself again.

"Well, if I didn't know any better, I would think you're jealous," I say, trying to bring lightness between us again.

He doesn't answer but his gaze lands again on my lips.

His boldness unnerves me. He confessed his love for another woman, yet he plays his games with me. The need to retaliate grows in me. "I don't care about the Frenchman because I'm still in love with my ex-fiancé," I lie. I don't love Gabriel, it's as simple as that. Not after what he put me through.

His face shows no emotion. "Would you like something to drink?"

He only worries about the Frenchman hurting me, I tell myself.

I must control the physical attraction I feel for Harry. He is different from any other man I've ever known. He's gentler than most, but at the same time incredibly strong inside. The way he perceives the world is unique. He takes in every moment like it might be the last. His ability to talk about his feelings and his belief in the afterlife at first made me uncomfortable. Now, I enjoy it, and it brings me comfort.

Harry is eccentric in the best way possible. The woman he loves is lucky. Being adored by a man like him is a miracle in this gloomy world.

I wish I were her.

EIGHTEEN

HARRY

May 1940, France

Dearest Mother,

Her heart is not mine. She loves another man. But only you know what's in my heart... she never will.

April went by fast, marked by the start of the Norwegian campaign. Hitler wants more and more, and he will stop at nothing to get it.

I'm counting down the days until he begins his assaults on France, though not everyone agrees with me. I have the order to immediately return to England at the first sign of an attack on France.

We received wonderful news from Bletchley, though. They informed us that the 'Bombe', our advanced version of the Polish Bomba is finally up and running, thanks to Turing and his team.

Now the Enigma codes are being cracked much faster than with the perforated sheets. This is so important for the Norwe-

gian campaign, and it might be a game changer for Hitler's possible assault when it comes to France, or even England.

Knox wrote a "thank you" note to the Polish team. He also sent the first two messages that were decrypted thanks to the Bombe. He mentioned that these particular ciphers aren't important and just proof of their accomplishment, but when the Polish cryptologists saw them, they thought that there was something off.

Later, Marian explained that a while back they saw the Germans were sending some messages beginning with the "gelb", but those disappeared once the Norwegian campaign started. However, after long analysis, the Poles determined that Germans only use the "gelb" when they're referencing their plans in regard to France. Marian and the rest think that a future attack on France is the action called the "gelb". Time will tell.

I have a feeling I will be leaving for England soon. I dread the thought of separating from this beautiful girl who's stolen my heart. I can see she treasures our friendship, and I'm thankful at least for that. I wish I could change her heart though.

I miss you, Mother. Stay well over there, in Heaven.

Your Harry

NINETEEN

BEATA

May 1940, Chateau de Vignolles near Gretz

"What's the weirdest thing about you?" Harry asks. We're standing at the pond and he's teaching me how skim to stones on the water. It's a warm day for May, unlike in Poland. The air smells like mud mixed with geese poop.

"Why weirdest?" Since I told him the lie about Gabriel, his attitude toward me has changed, but we still meet for long walks and talks. He doesn't take my hand in his anymore, nor does he hug me. I miss that, but I shouldn't.

"Because it's something you wouldn't tell anyone." He grins.

I roll my eyes. "And what makes you think I'm going to tell you?"

"You owe me."

"What do you mean?"

"I saved a whole pack of macarons that were about to be eaten by your Polish peers."

I chuckle. "That's a strong argument. Well, let me think." I send another stone into the water and continue. "When I was five, I learned to read, and when I was six, I started learning German, of course in secret, from the orphanage's caregivers."

He squints his eyebrows together and a bubble of laughter escapes his throat. "That's the weirdest thing you ever did?" He playfully nudges my arm. "You're boring."

"You should ask me why I did it instead of insulting me," I say, pretending to be offended.

"Okay, princess. Why did you do it?"

"When I was six, a couple from Germany visited our orphanage. I heard them speaking this language that I didn't know, but I kept praying that they would pick me. They didn't, and I blamed it on the fact that I couldn't communicate with them. Something similar happened again when an English lady picked my friend Agata, instead of me." I look away into the water, trying to find the right words. "I thought that if I could speak other languages, people would think that I'm special and someone would want me."

"You're special," he says softly, but he doesn't take my hand like he'd done so many times before I told him that lie.

"It's your turn now."

"When my mother died, I started writing letters to her," he says in a matter-of-fact voice, a hard look in his face like he's ready for someone to laugh at him.

My heart melts. "That's not weird at all," I say in a quiet voice. "She's alive on the other side and I'm sure she can read your letters."

"Not everyone believes that. Most people would declare me crazy and send me straight to a mental institution."

"I don't care what people say. You can't please everyone. Why did you start writing the letters?"

"It helped me to cope with her not being there. Sometimes I wondered if she was around to watch over me, knowing I needed her."

"That is beautiful, Harry," I say. "Do you still write to her?"

"I do whenever something important happens that I wanted to share with her. I know that sounds weird."

"It shows your love for her, that after all these years, she is still so important in your life."

After we return to the castle, Bertrand orders everyone to pack. We are about to travel to Paris. The "gelb" operation has begun.

Germany has officially attacked France.

TWENTY

BEATA

Our departure from the castle was so hectic that I didn't get a chance to say "goodbye" to Mrs. Moreau. It breaks my heart to think that she will be looking for me at the church. This elderly lady made me feel like I had a family for the first time, someone who genuinely cares for me, like a mother. But it is what it is, and right now the war is the thing that rules the world.

Harry has already left for England, and now I feel so lonely without our talks. If not for Marian, Jerzy and Henryk keeping up a positive attitude, things would be so much harder. They always find a way to make me laugh or they do some of their ridiculous pranks, even though, now that France is fighting Germany's attack, we are much busier than before. We work constantly.

The fact that I'm back in Paris mesmerizes me. I yearn to go sightseeing this time and see all the famous places, experience the culture of the city. But there is no chance to even step out of this building. The war rages across the nations of Europe, and we need to give everything we can to contribute to the defeat of the aggressors. Perhaps I will visit after the war, when I can appreciate the richness and beauty of France's heritage.

I like to think positively; I like to believe there are good times ahead of us. It's way too easy to succumb to despair and misery, so we are doing everything we can to keep our spirits up, despite it all.

As before, once our cryptologists crack the daily keys for the Enigma machine, we continue our work on decrypting intercepted messages. We write them on yellow paper marked as "Source Z." As much as our results were ignored before, now they are highly sought after. Often even the French generals, or other high-ranking officers, wait at our door for them. The atmosphere is nervous, as we don't know how much longer France will be able to defend herself against Hitler's forces.

One day we read a message about an action called *Unternehmen Paula*. The following days, there are more and more radiographs mentioning it.

"Listen to this," I say as I point at one of the messages I've just decrypted. "*Paula* means Paris." I fail to leave out the tremor from my voice.

Marian and Jerzy stop their tasks and look at me, frowning.

"They are planning an air attack," I continue, "on the car factories in Paris."

Marian's face turns as white as the wall behind him. "Do they say when?"

"On the third day of June. I re-read the message to make sure I didn't make any mistakes while decrypting.

"I'm going to Bertrand now," he says and marches out the room.

"Hopefully they will be able to use this information wisely," I say to Jerzy, unable to shake off my dread.

≈

But, on the third day of June, many thousands of tons of bombs are dropped down on the Citroën and Renault factories. So many people die.

The decrypted messages keep warning of more air bombardments of Paris, so Bertrand decides that we must leave as soon as possible, before the German troops enter the city and it's too late to flee. The rapid German advance scares us all and brings on a miserable atmosphere.

We board a bus heading south. Our short interaction with Paris ended more quickly than it started. The Germans are about to take over this beautiful city, just like our beloved Warsaw.

We, on the other hand, need to continue our codebreaking and decrypting mission.

And so we are running away again.

TWENTY-ONE

HARRY

September 1940, London

Dearest Mother,

I'm relieved to say that we won the biggest fight for England. The Luftwaffe commander-in-chief, Hermann Göring, led his air force in its plan to fulfill Hitler's order to destroy London and occupy our country. But we won this murderous battle, and no German foot touched our soil.

I could write a book about it, Mother, but that's not my intention here. I just wanted to share this beautiful news with you.

We were able to defend our homeland in huge part thanks to Turing's Bombe. Göring and his peers used the Enigma machine to send orders, and thanks to our Bombe, the daughter of the Polish Bomba, we were able to decrypt their messages with the greatest speed.

I've another piece of news, too, but I don't think you'll like this one. I decided to cease working at Bletchley to become a secret agent. I was officially accepted and am about to begin my training. I will be a spy, Mother, helping to infiltrate German networks in France and Italy. The very thought of it fills me with adrenaline.

I made this change because I can't breathe in Bletchley. There are so many specialists here, and we're so lucky to have Turing. They will get the job done, especially now that the biggest problem of the Enigma has already been solved.

I need air, even if in the end I will pay the highest price for that air. If something was to happen to me, there wouldn't be too many tears shed. Father has his own family, and the only woman I love gave her heart to someone else.

I know you understand. Please continue watching over me. I feel your presence in every second of my life.

Yours,

Harry

TWENTY-TWO

BEATA

December 1940, Chateau les Fouzes, Uzès, the south of France

When I wake up in the early morning, I enjoy resting in the soft bedsheets for another hour. It feels like home, until I remember that I'm in France.

After leaving Paris, we had a short stay in Algiers in North Africa. Now we're settled in a small castle in Uzès, in the south of France, where Bertrand organized a station to listen to and decrypt radiographs from the German police, and the Gestapo, Wehrmacht and Luftwaffe. Thanks to that, we often warn the French Resistance about danger. This part of France is still in the *Zone Libre*, free from German occupation, unlike Paris.

I reach to the nightstand and tune the radio set, hungry for any news. The familiar male voice of the French broadcaster fills the castle's chamber.

"We would like to remind our listeners that on the twenty-seventh day of September, Germany, Italy and Japan signed the Tripartite Pact. They agreed to assist one another with all political, economic and military means should they get attacked by

any countries not involved in the European War. In November,
the pact was also joined by Hungary, Slovakia, and Romania."

Why am I not surprised at such a manipulative and disgusting act? As the broadcast continues, the speaker states that such an act is intended to prevent the United States of America from taking part in this awful war.

But I hope that America will finally get involved in this war, so that it ends sooner. Right now, the Germans are doing whatever they want. The terrifying news we received from Poland via Bertrand still sends shivers down my spine. I know these are only scraps of what is really happening there, but they paint a terrible picture that breaks my heart.

It turns out that Germany has a plan to knock down most of Warsaw and create a modern city where only Germans can live, and where any remaining Poles will be slaves. So far, they've been arresting the intellectual elite of our country, and executing them. They build ghettos and labor camps and terrorize the entire nation. And there is so much more of this awful news that it's hard to even think of it.

The fact that the Germans destroyed the Chopin monument in my beloved Łazienki Park in Warsaw pains me to no end. At the same time, if they stopped only at ruining monuments, we would be lucky. But no. They murder innocent people for nothing.

Lately, I dwell constantly on the tragedies of this world. I just can't get them out of my mind.

Still, the hardest thing for me is to remember that my Felka isn't here anymore. It hits me day after day, always with the same intense physical pain, an ache in my soul. Then, I convince myself that she is alive on the other side, that the line between the two worlds is thinner than we think. But every morning brings the same dull exhaustion and powerlessness.

Christmas is bittersweet this year, even more so than the last one because our hopes for the war ending any time soon are gone by now. I haven't heard from Harry since our parting in Paris. Missing him is like anticipating rain on a scorching day. I sense he can appear at any time, yet often it feels like I won't see him ever again. He left a huge imprint on my heart, and I miss him in a way that can't be described with words. But this feeling gives me the necessary strength to move forward despite it all. It helps me to keep my worries and my loneliness at bay, simply because I hope to one day see him again.

TWENTY-THREE

BEATA

March 1941, Chateau les Fouzes, Uzès, the south of France

Four brand-new, shiny replicas of the German Enigma are lined up in the castle's chamber, and we struggle to control our explosion of happiness. Bertrand brought the parts from one of the factories, and our engineer Palluth along with mechanic Fokczyński assembled the machines.

"This calls for celebration," Bertrand says, just as his wife, Mary, calls us into the dining room for dinner. She lives in the nearby city of Nîmes, but visits often to help organize food and the kitchen.

While codebreaking and decrypting, we focus mainly on German and Russian ciphers. In addition to us Poles, there are also French and Spanish teams, but the number of people is much smaller than before.

According to Bertrand, we are officially housed and financed by the Vichy government, but only officially. Bertrand plays his sneaky games; he makes them believe that he works for them.

At first, our team hesitated to continue working under

Bertrand because of the Vichy, but when we received orders from the Polish government-in-exile, we relaxed.

We're still to communicate with Bletchley. Of course, it would make more sense to work over there in England, but that's not possible in the present situation. So, we make the best of it, and Bertrand's savvy approach is helpful.

Here, we have much more time on our hands than in Gretz or Paris, but we can't leave the grounds too often for security reasons. When we do, we must stay away from the locals. Even though this is officially a free zone, German spies are everywhere, so we must be extremely careful and trust no one.

"Let's drink to better days," Langer says and lifts his wine glass, "in our beloved Poland." His last words bring a wave of sorrow to my heart. Will we ever be back home?

I often doubt it. First, we had to run to Paris, then to Africa, and now we are stuck here. I don't voice my worries; instead, I smile and salute with the others.

"The New Year didn't begin too well for Warsaw," I say in a quiet voice, referring to the new regulations about much smaller food rations. Bertrand keeps supplying us with such information from Poland. No one knows how he gets it, but we are thankful for it.

"I'm glad we can at least send packages and money to our families," Marian says. "But I wish they were here, safe with us."

I feel such sympathy for them. They often talk of how it would be better to bring their loved ones to France, but we all know that it's too dangerous.

Before Christmas, I sent a letter to Mrs. Moreau. She responded a month later that she is doing fine when it comes to her health. She laments in her letter that her son has been missing since October of last year. My heart goes out to this sweet lady. If only I could help her in some small way, but the distance is too great to even consider visiting her. I hope that Alphonse shows up soon, so her mind is put at ease.

After dinner, I help the cook to clean the kitchen. He is a sweet man and lives here with his wife. I like keeping busy when there are no work duties, so before bedtime, I walk outside to witness my friends taking turns in a competition to climb a snow-laden palm tree.

"What are you doing, you bunch of crazy Polish men?" I say and laugh, shaking my head. "Wait till Major Bertrand sees this." There is always something happening here.

TWENTY-FOUR

BEATA

June 1941, Castle les Fouzes, Uzès, the south of France

"Well, Beata, you cracked your first cipher," Marian says and leans back in his seat, a huge smile reaching his eyes.

I tilt my head slightly to the side. "It's just a hand cipher, nothing compared to what you gentlemen do." Despite my words I feel proud of my little accomplishment. This cipher gave me a hard time, but I did it. It's not like I will break many more as my time should be used decrypting vital messages.

"Don't underestimate your powers," he says with a wink. "Do you remember how our own engineer Palluth cracked the cipher used by the Abwehr?"

I nod. "My dream was to do only one, and I did it," I say, feeling warmth in my cheeks. "Besides, I have brilliant teachers." I truly mean it; all three cryptologists, Marian, Jerzy and Henryk, never hesitate to answer any of my questions and never get upset when I stop by to watch their work. They are the ones who took me under their wings from the moment we left Poland and who always make sure I feel safe and respected while surrounded by so many men.

According to the recent radiographs that we intercept, Germany's spying activity keeps increasing. For example, some senders of messages are agents posing as tourists. They watch the movement of ships in French and Algerian ports.

We also detect a lot of activity on German radio communication, where they relay ciphers and directions related to espionage. There is a lot of correspondence between the Kripo, Orpo and Gestapo.

Last month, we started reading radiographs from Russia. They are mainly reports against communists, partisans and Jews.

All in all, we extract a lot of important information for the war effort.

"I need to get some fresh air," I say to Marian. "I will be back soon."

"Go ahead. I'm about to finish for today as well," he says without lifting his head from his desk. He's probably in the middle of another huge breakthrough. That's how brilliant this man is.

I pass the palm trees in front of the castle and a huge fig tree, then after getting on my bike, I cycle along the avenue surrounded by trees on both sides.

Enjoying the fresh breeze on my skin, I decide to take a cycling trip to Remonlin. On the way there, I admire olive trees, blackberry bushes, and fields of herbs with thousands of butterflies hovering above. Sweet fragrances mingle with aromas of chamomile, rosemary and other herbs.

The whole time, I have this weird feeling that someone is following me, but when I turn to look, the road behind me is empty. I've been extra sensitive lately thanks to the intensified activities of German spies in the Nîmes area.

I pedal my way through the famous Roman bridge and three-tier aqueduct over the Gardon River. I leave my bike under a tree and walk to my favorite spot at the shore of the river where I lie down and enjoy the warmth of the sand on my skin.

I smell the familiar and mind-soothing scents of algae and fish mingling in the sizzling air. The monotonous sounds of water splashing over rocks and birds chirping feel blissfully relaxing after a long day of intense work. What a sweet highlight to my little codebreaking victory.

I stare into a blue sky with groups of clouds moving forward, just like we human beings do every day. Despite everything, we keep going, we keep hoping for better times. That's what my life in France is anyway—living, and at the same time waiting for something else.

"You should be more careful." A voice from nowhere. It comes without warning, so I jump to my feet.

A tall man in the shabby clothes of a laborer grins at me.

Forgetting the fright he gave me, I yearn to run into his embrace, but I stop myself in the last second. Instead, we smile at one another.

"It's you," I whisper, unable to take that silly smile from my lips. "Harry." Pure happiness overtakes me, a kind I haven't felt for a very long time. Warmth sips into my blood, my heart, my lungs. This man will never know how he makes me feel.

"Good to see you, princess," he says, his face serious now as our eyes meet and stay still for a longer moment, making up for all the emotions that aren't said aloud.

For a while, we sit next to each other on the sand and stare into clear waters of the river.

"Will you be staying at the castle?" I ask. I'm wondering why he's wearing those dirty clothes instead of his usual suit, but don't ask him that.

"Not this time," he says. "And you must promise not to tell anyone that you saw me." He takes my hand in his, just like he did before I lied to him about Gabriel. "Do you trust me?"

I gaze into his silvery eyes that are now probing mine, as if trying to figure out if he can actually trust me. But what I see in there is softness and hope. It eases my nerves and makes me remember again how it feels to be safe with someone. He always made me feel that way, so when he was gone, I missed him so much.

"I do," I whisper and squeeze his hand. "And I won't tell anyone."

His face muscles visibly relax. "Thank you. One day I will explain it all to you, but now I can't. For your safety and mine, no one can know that I'm here."

"I understand." I really don't but I genuinely trust him, so that's enough for me. "You know, throughout my entire life, I've never trusted anyone. Growing up in the orphanage made me wary of people. I've been on constant guard as if waiting for someone to decide to attack or hurt or abandon me." I press the side of my face to his arm. "But my heart tells me to trust you."

"I'm honored," he says. "Though I'm sure you trust your fiancé too." If I didn't know any better, I would think that a hint of annoyance aches through his voice.

I decide to tell him the truth. How else to build a friendship if not on honesty and truthfulness? "He's my ex-fiancé and he cheated on me. So no, I don't trust him."

"I'm sorry to hear it." For a moment we watch ducks gliding across the surface, bobbing their heads to fish. "But you still love him, despite everything." His voice seems somehow final and devoid of emotion, as if he's unable to grasp control. Or are these just my own feelings mixing into his words?

"I don't love him," I insist, "and I never did."

"It's not what you told me before," he says arching his brow.

"I'm sorry that I lied to you." My cheeks feel hot now but not to show my embarrassment, I continue, "When he showed his affection for me, I was very young and lost in the world after leaving the orphanage. He was independent and sophisticated. I didn't care about his wealth or his upbringing, but I was overtaken by his infatuation with me, a simple girl from the orphanage."

If he's still upset with me, he doesn't show it. Instead, he brushes a strand of hair back from my forehead. "You're more than that. "His voice is calm now, filled with a note of happiness. "You're smart and strong."

His words make my heart leap with joy, which is, I think, something that should not happen. He loves another woman, and he's only showing compassion for me.

He teases my lower lip with his thumb. "You're beautiful, my Polish princess."

I swallow hard, sensing he intends to kiss me, while conflicting emotions overtake me. I want to feel his lips touching mine, but at the same time, I don't understand his behavior. Has he suddenly forgotten about the other woman, the woman he loves?

His gaze is now steady on mine as if he's trying to read me. He must sense my confusion because he drops his hand.

"I must get going," he says, bringing a wave of pain to my heart.

"Already?" My voice cuts across my thoughts.

"I shouldn't be meeting with you at all, it's against the plan. But when I saw you riding your bike, I couldn't resist." He playfully nudges my arm. "Just to tell you that you must be more careful and not roam across the country freely like this. The Abwehr agents are everywhere. Trust me on that. Promise me that you'll stay alert all the time, and don't trust anyone, not even people in the castle. I mean, you can trust your Polish friends, but do not tell them about me."

I nod, unable to let him go, to tell him that it's okay if he leaves now.

"I will make sure to keep checking on you. I won't be far, as my duties now are in France, but you must be wary at all times."

He sighs and takes my hand. "I shouldn't be doing this, but can you meet with me in two weeks?"

I exhale with relief. "Yes."

After we part, I go back to the castle grounds, unable to blink my tears away. It was so wonderful to see him again after all this time. I intend to take as much strength from it as I can. Sometimes I wonder how it is that, even though I grew up in the orphanage and got used to relying on myself, I still look for someone to provide me with a wall of security. I failed for so long to find it, but then Harry brought it in the moment I least expected it.

He consoled my hurting heart and satisfied my need to talk with someone on the deepest level of emotions. And now, after not seeing him for so long, my heart leaped at the mere sight of him. I wasn't sure about deepening our relationship with that anticipated kiss today and he read me well. I'm so lost when it comes to my feelings.

What does he feel? Why did he want to kiss me when he loves someone else? Maybe I was wrong about him and he's one of those men who don't care about fidelity?

I arrive back at base just in time to witness my Polish friends hunting for frogs. They have spread a red blanket on the grass near some ditches. Their experiment turns out to be successful: lines of frogs jump onto it. Then, they pick up the blanket and dump all the poor creatures into a wicker basket.

The French team in our castle will be thrilled once the cook serves these amphibian delicacies. But when it comes to us Poles, we won't even touch them. We find it hard to even comprehend how someone can eat frogs' legs. But every culture has its own rules and traditions. There are plenty of dishes that are celebrated in our Polish cuisine that the French would probably find repulsive to try, like *flaki*, a beef tripe stew, whose name literally means "guts".

TWENTY-FIVE

HARRY

June 1941, France

Dearest Mother,

I wanted to kiss her today so badly, but I sensed her restraint. She isn't sure of her feelings, and I didn't want to complicate things for her, not now when her mind must stay sharp to survive.

I trust Bertrand that he will do everything to protect his Polish friends, but they all must be extremely alert to dangers. Lately, the German agents grow like mushrooms in the rain.

I have a sleeve of hope, Mother. Her heart is free, and I can only dream that one day it will be mine. That's all I can do for now.

Yours always,

Harry

TWENTY-SIX

BEATA

July 1941, Uzès, the south of France

I put on my dark gray pantsuit and comb my hair. It's not my place to try to look pretty for him. We are only friends. Good friends, but only friends.

I take my bike and head toward the large fig tree outside of the castle's property where we agreed to meet. He's already there, leaning against his bike, deep in thought.

This time he has on his regular suit and looks like the old Harry, unlike in those shabby clothes the other day. For a moment, his gleaming eyes take me in, but he doesn't smile or say anything.

"Hello," I say to break the uncomfortable silence. "I think it's going to rain soon." I motion to the dark clouds above.

He smiles at last. "Hello. Let's leave now, so we don't get drenched."

"Where are we going?" I ask before getting on my bike.

"With you, I'll go anywhere." He winks and a thin smile edges onto his lips.

His words give my heart a nervous jolt, but I keep my face

neutral. We are friends, only friends. I must remember that. "I do appreciate your humor," I say and smirk at him.

He grows serious. "I have good friends in Nîmes with whom I'm temporarily staying. Currently, they are out visiting relatives, so I made dinner for you. Are you okay with that?"

I'm taken aback that he went out of his way to do something so special for me. "You made dinner for me?"

"Does that mean yes?"

"Of course, I just didn't expect it, and as long as your friends are happy for you to bring a stranger to their home."

"They've assured me that it's perfectly fine with them. Let's get going as those clouds don't like us at all."

The ride is smoother than I anticipated and soon we arrive at a one-story house overtaken by ivy vines. It has an enchanted look.

Inside, the antique furniture is simple but chosen with taste. The entire home feels cozy and friendly, and the moment I enter it, I detect positive vibes. I've always had this ability to sense the house and the people who live in it. Here, nothing warns me; everything has an aura of peace and hope. But these are just my feelings, maybe others wouldn't agree with me, or I would change my mind if I got to know the owners.

Harry serves tuna fish with salad, and we enjoy white wine.

"I had no idea you're such an excellent chef," I say with admiration.

"It's just a simple dish, so I don't deserve your praise."

"You definitely do. I don't remember the last time I ate something so delicious, and I truly mean it."

"Well, I'm glad I guessed your taste correctly then," he says as he raises his glass. "Cheers to our time together."

After dinner, we settle on a sofa and talk about the war. "I can't believe it's almost two years since we arrived in France. It feels like only weeks went by."

He sighs. "Unfortunately, the war isn't going to end any day soon."

"When I left Warsaw, I was sure we would be back within months. How naïve of me."

"Don't judge yourself too harshly. No one knew how things would play out."

"Do you think that if the United States gets involved, that will speed up the end of the war?"

"It definitely would." He nods, turning his face to mine. "Let's hope it will happen one day soon, as we need all the help we can get in fighting those fanatics."

"I can't understand how human beings can murder in cold blood like the Nazis do," I say, and I feel my voice tremble. "They believe in this evil idea of them being superior, above others."

"Their nation was gradually being prepared for this since the last war. It's why Hitler wrote *Mein Kampf*, why it's present in German schools. The brainwashing was so consistent that they had enough time to implement it as a 'natural' way of thinking. They also made sure to expand their armed forces to ensure successful assaults, while the world stayed blind to it."

"Yes," I say, "but after the Great War it was hard to imagine that it would happen so quickly."

"True. Hitler took advantage of how angry and ashamed Germans felt in the aftermath of the Great War. They wanted to change their circumstances, and he promised to lead the nation to a better, stronger place."

"But at such cost," I say, thinking of home. We are both silent for a moment, then I ask, "How much news have you heard about the situation in Poland?"

"Enough to know how horrible things are there. There are no limits to those monsters' taste for torturing and murdering. They've lost their humanity."

His words tell me that he knows as much as I do, or even

more. "It's so hard to talk about it. I don't know how much more my poor broken heart can stand listening to such dreadful news."

He takes my hand in his; his touch is so calming and assuring. "Let's enjoy this moment. I don't know when I will see you again."

"You're right. You know, I'm sure not all Germans are like the Nazis, though. There are good people in that country too, but they are powerless and scared of those fanatics, and probably live in dread for their lives. Or that's how I imagine it."

"Definitely. The ones who have the courage to speak up meet even worse fates. But keeping silent is a crime too."

He is right, but who knows how we would behave in such extraordinary circumstances? "Not everyone was born to be a hero," I murmur.

He kisses my hand. "True. It's so sad that our generation has to live in the worst of times."

"It's not like we have had a choice."

He gets to his feet, breaking the desolate mood we have spun around ourselves. "Would you like some coffee? I have your favorite treats."

I laugh. "You have macarons?"

He nudges my arm. "You doubt me?"

True to his word, I get to enjoy my favorite thing in the world. "The last time I had them was in that attic in the Vignolles castle. Thank you, my friend."

He takes my hand in his again. His eyes meet mine and it feels like our souls connect. "I'd love to be more than that."

I don't understand his intentions. He has someone in London. Has he forgotten? Or am I interpreting his words in the wrong way? It must be that, so I ignore his comment and say, "Being here with you is like a breath of fresh air."

His finger traces my skin, this time sending currents of anticipation of something very foreign to me.

I clear my throat. "You know, every day is filled with work, and we can't even go out that much because of the threat of German spies." My voice is weak even to my own ears—he just shook me to the core with his sensual touch. I don't want things to be that tender between us, but it's like I have no say. He has no say. We can't stop staring at each other in wonder and excitement.

His hand travels to my ear and his thumb rubs it gently, making my heart skip a beat.

I leap to my feet and say, "I'd better get going or the boys will worry. It's unusual for me to be gone this long."

"Of course, let me ride along with you." His voice betrays a hint of disappointment and brings even more confusion to my already whirling mind. I know Harry isn't the type of man who would cheat on his woman, so why is his behavior so unsettling.

Just before we exit the house, he says, "Beata."

His voice is so quiet, I turn to him. That is when he pulls me into his embrace and kisses me.

I want to get away from him; his hold on me isn't firm and I could easily push him away. But after the initial rush, everything slows down as his lips press gently against mine. I know then that I will stay.

The blissful feeling sends me into an angelic state. I yearn for more and more of his sensual kisses, his flattering touch.

When we're done, I bury my face into his chest, basking in this intimate moment between us.

TWENTY-SEVEN

BEATA

January–September 1942, Chateau les Fouzes, Uzès, the south of France

After the news in December about the attack on Pearl Harbor, any hope of the war ending soon abandoned us. Now Japan is at war with the United States and England, and Germany has declared war on the United States. This conflict is going to last a long time and I often wonder if I will be able to ever return home. I don't have anyone close there besides Joanna, but I miss my old life and my beloved Warsaw.

I'm at the point when I do everything to focus on my duties without letting the outside news disturb me. Though the saddest days often come after a longer stillness. This time is no different. When Bertrand breaks the awful news, an instant numbness catches at my heart, as if trying to protect me. Jerzy, one of our cryptologists, is dead.

"Jerzy Różycki, Jan Graliński, Piotr Smoleński and Captain Francois Lane," Bertrand says in a voice laden with emotion, "you made the greatest sacrifice for France. We will never forget."

I cling to the wall beside me as a spell of dizziness washes over me. Just like that? We won't see them ever again? I will not be able to talk to my friend Jerzy who's the sweetest and most compassionate man in this world. And what about his wife and son in Poland? How will they go on without him?

I clutch a hand to my heart as Bertrand tells us what he's learned. "They perished in the Mediterranean Sea on the way here from our branch office in Algiers. Their ship, the *Lamoricière*, sank due to a mine explosion."

This terrible news affects us all, but especially our two cryptologists Marian and Henryk. Jerzy was a vital part of their team and they've been together on this Enigma journey since 1932. They'd known each other even longer, from Poznan University where they'd studied mathematics.

Jerzy was the inventor of the famous "clock" method, which made it possible to figure out the position of Enigma's rotors, or at least that's how I understood it when it happened. He was only thirty-two, still so young, but one day he will be remembered and celebrated in Polish history, I'm sure of that. People like him, of such trailblazing intelligence and dedication, cannot be forgotten. I remember the humanity in his dark eyes, and struggle not to weep. I promise myself that I will write to his wife, telling her of the deep admiration her husband inspired.

The following months drag on as we do everything we can to focus on our duties while facing the sad reality of Jerzy's and other men's absences. Life goes on, but it won't ever be the same. I know this sensation so well. Since losing Felka, it's as if I live with an open wound in my heart, one that won't heal. It's the price we all pay for truly loving someone—this draining pain inside you. You pretend that it's all fine, so the world outside leaves you alone. But only you know the truth.

It's why I got so close to Harry. He always knew what to say and do to make me feel understood. It's like our sorrow at losing the closest people to us mingled into one when we were together. We could talk without words.

In April, we discover an entire network of German agents in the area; they are observing the movement of our allies. Then we receive signals that the *Zone Libre* will be soon occupied just like Paris.

There are more meetings now between Bertrand and Langer, and the first goes on frequent trips to Vichy and the area near the castle. He even warns us to watch out for certain vans and cars. We might be escaping again soon—if we are able to.

The Abwehr agents drive around the area trying to track down secret radio stations, just like ours. We know what they are doing thanks to the intercepted messages we're able to decrypt. Some of the radiographs suggest they've taken an interest in our radio station and are trying to hunt us down, but they don't know our location. Not yet anyway.

One Sunday in September, I leave the castle at five o'clock in the morning, anxious for fresh air. After another sleepless night, there's no better cure for a troubled mind than spending time in nature. It seems that doing it so early is safe, but lately nothing seems safe.

The crisp autumn air calms my thoughts and soothes my skin.

"Beata," someone whispers to my left.

I freeze while alarm tingles my brain, but when the same voice urges me to step behind a nearby olive tree, I recognize Harry.

I exhale with relief and leap to him. Having been so terrified by his prolonged silence after our dinner together at his friends' house in Nîmes, I'm unable to control my elation at seeing him again.

He scoops me into his arms and before I realize what's happening, he kisses me with such untamed passion that my entire world fades.

The kiss is long and passionate and an electrifying warmth settles in my veins.

A moment later, he whispers in my ear, "I'm sorry. I just missed you so much."

I take a step back and ask, "What are you doing here?" It's my fault too for not controlling my emotions and forgetting about the woman waiting for him in England. But why does he keep disregarding her existence and provoking such intimate moments between us? I should simply ask him and end this. But I'm afraid of losing him.

"I need to show you something. Come with me."

Soon we are climbing into a small black Renault. "Where are you taking me?"

"There is one German spy that is particularly interested in your castle. I was able to locate where she stays and I need your help to eliminate her." His soft gaze takes me in. "If it's too much for you, please tell me and I will let you go back to what you were doing."

What he's said does scare me, but I tell him, "I want to help you."

"Good. This spy keeps sniffing around your castle and other houses in the neighborhood, and it won't be long before she takes a further step. After watching her for a while, I'm convinced she works for the Abwehr. I was going to handle it on my own but yesterday I received orders to relocate to another part of France." He gives me a meaningful look. "I need your help taking care of this before my departure, otherwise I wouldn't even consider putting you at risk."

It warms my heart knowing that he has been keeping an eye on our castle. "Just tell me what to do," I say, doing everything in my power not to betray my fear.

"It's going to be simple, but you must use your acting skills," he says as he starts the car.

I smile and speak loudly to beat the high-pitched drone of the engine. "I don't think I'd make a good actress."

He turns the wheel and we hit the dirt road. "Trust me, you will. Adrenaline does it to all of us. Anyway, princess, thank you for being such a good sport. I know I can count on you."

I find it hard to believe that he's including me in this action. Before he changes his mind, I say, "I will do my best."

He nods without taking his eyes from the road. "I don't need to tell you how important it is to keep this top secret."

"Of course, I'm used to keeping secrets." Since 1932, that's all I've been doing with the Enigma mission. And what Harry is doing here is incredibly important; that one particular spy could turn out to be fatal to us all.

Soon we enter Nîmes, called *the French Rome* because of its rich history going back to the Roman Empire, like the Arena of Nîmes.

Harry parks on a side street, under the umbrella of an enormous sweet chestnut tree. "She stays in this motel," he says, pointing out a long yellowish building, "and poses as a tourist with her little camera and straw hat."

"This doesn't surprise me," I say. "Given that Nmes is one of the warmest cities in France."

He smirks. "Her intentions are much more sinister than enjoying the sun."

A surge of heat rushes to my cheeks. "I didn't mean it to sound like that."

"I know. I was just teasing you. Relax, my princess."

His use of the word "my" makes me glow inside, but I don't

show it. "Sometimes I wonder if it's even possible to relax, after all."

He grows serious. "Well, you will after we make sure that spy doesn't bring the Gestapo to your castle." He gazes at his wristwatch. "If she follows her usual routine, she will be out in about half an hour, riding her bike and watching like a hawk for anything suspicious. Lately, her focus is set on your area, and more and more on your precious castle. Something must have attracted her attention."

"I'm guessing she's looking for signs of the Resistance, correct?"

"Yes, but not only that. Finding your team would bring her a huge promotion, that's for sure. Abwehr has a special section called Funkabwehr which detects radio activities, like the one you run. She might be sniffing around to alert them to the most vulnerable areas."

"And now she's suspicious of our castle."

"Seems like it. Now listen to me carefully, as I have a plan. Remember that this area is still free of German occupation, so there is a low chance that anyone will spot us this early in the morning, especially on a Sunday when people like to sleep longer. Please, don't lack confidence."

"I guess only people with a special agenda like us are out right now."

"Right, hopefully she will be out too, and soon."

He goes on filling me in with his plan.

"When she sees another woman in need, one who speaks to her as fluently in German as you, she's most likely to stop."

At the mere thought of what I have to do, my mouth goes dry. "Hopefully it will work."

Soon Harry hides in the back seat of the car, and I stand beside the open hood, pretending to be looking at something.

When I spot a woman on a bike in the far distance, I start

complaining loudly in German to myself. I act as if I don't even realize she's riding my way.

Only when she's about to pass me, do I jump to my feet and block her way, quickly spreading my hands in a gesture of defeat.

She stops with a screech of her bike's brakes and frowns, then her tan face shows confusion. Dressed in a white tunic and wide-leg linen trousers, she seems very sophisticated.

"I'm so sorry to stop you," I say in my flawless German. "But do you happen to speak German or maybe you know someone who does?"

For a moment her blue eyes assess me as if she's trying to decide if I'm even worth her time. "I'm in a rush," she says in German.

I exhale loudly. "What a relief to finally meet someone who speaks German. I can't understand a word of French, and I was just on my way to my hotel when smoke started coming out of the engine. It seems it's gone now, but my car won't start," I recite, while keeping the expression on my face suitably somber.

"It sounds like you need a mechanic. I don't know anything about cars," she says and makes a move to get back on her bike.

Adrenaline shoots through me as I realize she's about to leave. I touch her arm and implore in a pleading voice, "Please help me. My husband is a high-ranking officer in Paris and he will reward you for your trouble." I sob, truly pathetic now. "I should have listened to him and not come here, but I'm so bored over there while here the air is so fresh, so I decided to visit for a couple of days. I'm so close to my hotel too."

Her eyes betray that she's still not sure what to do. "What is it you want me to do? I told you I know nothing about fixing cars," she says, her voice softer now.

"My husband showed me what to do in a situation like this, but I need someone at the steering wheel who can turn the ignition while I spark the engine. An easy trick, even for me. It will literally take no longer than a minute." I smile with innocence. "Then I'll get out of your way. And please, I can repay you for this."

My last words seem to ignite her interest.

"Fine. Let's do this now because I need to be on my way. Also, you should ask the clerk at the hotel to call a mechanic for you," she says with authority, like she's speaking to a schoolgirl. "It's surprising that your husband allowed you to travel all the way here without a chauffeur."

"Yes," I agree, obediently. "I made a mistake and left without his knowledge. I needed a short break. But the first thing I'll do is call him to come and take me back to Paris. I'm lost without him."

She rolls her eyes but walks with her bike toward the car, then props it against the chestnut tree. She climbs behind the wheel and looks up.

I walk up to the front hood and say, "When I lift my hand, you must turn the ignition."

She nods her agreement right before Harry strikes the back of her head with his pistol. From that point on, everything speeds up. In no time, he drags her to the back of the car and ties her limbs. Then we drive away, glancing around to make sure no one saw our little piece of theatre.

My heart is still drumming wildly in my chest. "What are you going to do with her?" I ask, hoping he isn't going to kill her.

"I will deliver her into the hands of the local Resistance group."

"What if you made a mistake and she's innocent? She didn't seem malicious at all."

His lips quirk. "And that's what makes her an excellent spy. Besides, I have proof of her guilt. I've been watching her for a while now. I'm correct."

"I never thought I would be helping you catch a German spy," I say and shake my head. "Thank God this is still a free zone, or most likely we would have German soldiers chasing us by now."

"It's about to change." He nods with a somber expression. "Very soon, this will be an occupied zone too." Then I catch the glimpse of a smile as he says, "By the way, your performance was outstanding."

TWENTY-EIGHT

BEATA

October 1942, Uzès, the south of France

It's late at night and I can't fall asleep as droplets of rain knock on the castle's windows and roof. I struggle between nostalgia for my country and longing for Harry's presence.

Lately, I have been enjoying the Polish section of the radio station that I discovered not too long ago, so I turn the radio set on to a female broadcaster who is in the middle of announcing General Władysław Sikorski's speech, which he gave yesterday at a meeting at the Albert Hall in London. As he speaks, I picture his gimlet-eyed face. He's the prime minister of our Polish government in exile and commander-in-chief of our armed forces.

"I speak in the name of the Government of the Republic of Poland in the presence of this mass gathering to give witness to the tragic truth. This truth consists of persecutions of Jews in Poland which are mass, ruthless and exterminatory..."

Cold shivers run down my spine. Every time I hear a heart-breaking news bulletin from Poland, I'm unable to eat or sleep. It drains all my energy and turns me into a ball of flaming pain. But I brace myself and pay attention to the radio broadcast.

"Among these Jews are Jewish citizens of Poland as well as all other nations occupied by Germany, who have been rounded up into ghettos in: Warsaw, Łódź and Kraków, Lublin, Lwów and Wilno. Afterwards, driven further east, in the most dreadful conditions, treated much worse than herded cattle, they are slaughtered in the tens of thousands, down to the last soul..."

As the speech goes on, I listen with my heart in my throat. So, all these horrible things we've been hearing about the murders in the German camps in Poland are the truth? It's so painful to hear this dreadful tragedy confirmed. I can't even imagine what people in my own country are going through. This is so unjust. I refocus and tune into Sikorski's words.

"Even science has become a vassal for German executioners, as they discover and use ever-improved methods for the mass murder of people. Aside from the methodical destruction of the unyielding Polish nation during the past three years, these are the most blatant persecutions and atrocities, which Germany has engaged in..."

We had heard terrifying things about the camps, particularly in Oświęcim and Brzezinka, in the far south of the country, near Joanna's village. I hope that she and her mother are somewhere in hiding until this madness ends. I worry about my dearest friend daily. I miss her silliness, her freedom of spirit and love for life. The Joanna I know grabs every moment with her hands, like it could be her last. I could never fully understand her approach, but now I know to catch every minute. The war has taught me that there might not be a tomorrow.

If I could go back in time, I would change so much. I wouldn't be afraid to make friendships and to be open-minded toward new possibilities. I would enjoy life more, instead of exercising my fears and insecurities. But I'm an orphan child, so maybe I could never be like this? Living with the huge void of not having parents or any family at all is what created every particle of my being. Yet, I'm here—strong and ready to face the worst.

One afternoon in November, we notice that a German radio van has parked not far from our castle. The German agents begin searching the houses in our neighborhood. We all spring into action and switch off our radios, take down antennas, hide our equipment and anything else suspicious. Meanwhile, one of our men, dressed in gardening clothes pretends to be taking care of weeds near the road. He keeps an eye out and will signal in case of danger.

By sheer luck, the Abwehr doesn't come to search our castle. But that incident is enough of a signal for us that it's time to leave. And so, that's what we do the following day.

For the next couple of months, we hide in the French and Italian occupied zones, waiting for instructions. Every day we are extremely careful to stay away from German agents and policemen.

The plan is to find a way to cross the border into Spain and get to Gibraltar, and then England. This would be the best possible scenario, and I pray daily for this to happen, otherwise we will find ourselves in more and more danger.

TWENTY-NINE

BEATA

February 1943, Perpignan, the south of France

I've been stuck in this dusty, moldy attic for a week now. The French woman who was supposed to help me cross into Spain never came back.

At the end of January, we received orders to travel to the city of Perpignan in the south of France, where we were split into small groups and told that the crossing into Spain would take place soon.

Marian and Henryk stayed together, but I was introduced to a young woman with blonde hair named Charlotte. I was told to trust her. She brought me to this house and promised to come back the next day. Something either happened to her or she lost interest in helping me, because I haven't seen her since.

Two days ago, I walked back to the train station where we were split up, but I couldn't find any familiar faces there. When we arrived at Perpignan, it was dark, and everything happened so fast. They're probably gone by now, not realizing that I was left behind.

At this point I don't know what to do. The house is abandoned, so there is no one to talk to, and I don't know where to look for the rest of the team. I've never felt more scared than now. Still, I hope that Charlotte will somehow show up and tell me that she had to stay in hiding, but now it's all good and I will be able to leave here.

I have no more food, but I do have the money I made while working in France, though I need ration cards to get food.

A squeaking mouse scuttles across the floorboards, stirring up cobwebs drifting off the old rocking chair. I must go out and try to find some food. I haven't eaten since yesterday, and before then, I only had tiny pieces of a dry baguette that Charlotte left me. I measured a portion out every day and it lasted me for the first days.

I swallow hard, tasting only damp air and dust. I can smell the familiar scent of old books. The only good thing about this place is that it's filled with so many books. But how long can one person read without any food?

There is no trace of a crumb downstairs either, but this old house still has running water and electricity. This strikes me as weird. I do not turn any lights on at all as it's too risky. It's better to keep a low profile in case someone is watching the house.

I run my hand through my hair, and it feels rigid like wire wool. It's late at night, so I climb down the creaking stairs to the main house. In the bathroom I wash in ice-cold water and then I go back to the attic. It feels safest there, as I have the constant sense that someone is about to walk into this house.

I dry my damp hair with a stiff towel I found downstairs and put on the black suit I bought in a cute boutique in Gretz, the one Mrs. Moreau recommended. At the thought of the elderly lady, warmth squeezes my heart. I wonder how she is doing and if her son Alphonse ever showed up.

I spend the rest of the night lying on a floor of the attic and listen to the wind beating against the house. Sleep doesn't come, so I plan my outing in the morning. I've to find a black market and try buying food on the side, under the counter, away from the eyes of Germans and gendarmes.

At noon, without allowing myself to procrastinate any further, I put on my coat and hat, and I sneak out the side of the building, so neighbors can't see me. If they notice any activity in the house, there is a chance they will call the authorities.

Once out on the streets, I straighten and lift my head up. The crisp, cold air is bracing like an anticipated refreshment. If I act sure of myself, there is less chance of anyone stopping me. So, I do it. I walk like I'm too good to even talk to anyone.

Perpignan is only a few kilometers from the Mediterranean Sea, at the foot of the Pyrenees. When I learned that we would be coming here, I tried asking my French peers some questions about this city, but I didn't learn much. Someone said something about the gothic Palace of the Kings of Mallorca. Maybe I will see it at some point. Right now, the gurgling noises from my stomach remind me that I need food, not palaces.

Blood freezes in my veins just at the thought of approaching food smugglers, but I don't want to starve, so I cruise the narrow alleyways that feel like they're from medieval times, with their brownish brick buildings set close to one another.

I spot shops, bakeries and cafés along the Canal Vauban which runs through the center of the city. Then I enter a large square with the gothic-style Cathedral Basilica of Saint John the Baptist, and after walking further I realize there is an old, cloistered cemetery. Still, no sign of anyone looking like a food smuggler.

The Nazi swastikas are everywhere, making my empty stomach coil with disgust. Then, I spot an open-air market on one side of the square.

My mouth waters at the sight of stalls with food. Voices of smugglers lure patrons with their promises of regional wines or fresh fish from the Mediterranean Sea.

Is this all real, or is it a product of my imagination? I pinch my cheek and smile, realizing that there's a bunch of young boys running near the market, as if ready to warn of French gendarmes or Gestapo.

In no time, I buy some food with the money I brought with me, making sure not to have too much, so I don't look suspicious on the way home. After I pay, a lady in a beat-up coat leans toward me and whispers, "Take it and walk away immediately. The roundups are constant these days."

Once back in my attic, I devour a whole baguette and some Cantal cheese. Heaven. Pure heaven.

At night, I wake up to voices filtering up through the attic floor and the sound of steady footsteps. The first person I think of is Charlotte, but the voices belong to men.

Adrenaline shoots through my system while I try to grasp at my tumbling thoughts. What if it's the Gestapo searching the house? What if they decide to climb up here too?

THIRTY

BEATA

February 1943, Perpignan, the south of France

After catching hushed words in French, I know I'm safe, or at least I think so. The Gestapo would be swift and make a lot of commotion. These men seem to talk in low voices, which is why I only hear some of their words.

It must be the Resistance. We helped them a lot during our stay in the Castle les Fouzes, by warning them of the German spying activities we read in the intercepted messages. I'm sure our work there helped to save many lives.

For a moment, I wonder if it would be wise to appear before them. But what if they shoot me thinking I'm a German spy, before I even have a chance to explain anything? Would they believe my story? I resolve on staying undercover for now.

They leave a couple of hours later and then I beat myself up for not trying to do something. Maybe they could connect me to Bertrand or even Langer? Still, my gut is telling me I did the right thing by staying in my hiding place.

The next day, feeling braver after my last outing, I decide to go to the train station again. It will surely be crowded with gendarmes, but something is telling me to go there. Though, by now I'm sure my friends have crossed the Spanish border.

Charlotte promised to deliver new papers for me, even though I already have one set in the name of Juliette Toussaint. I guess the new ones were going to be of a better quality.

I can sit here like a scared bunny, or I can go out in hope of finding help.

When I look at it, not much has really changed in my life. I'm still an orphan, still alone and still in search of better days. True, my situation has worsened because now I'm by myself in this godforsaken city. Since our stay in Uzès, I've been perfecting my southern French accent with the help of the French staff there.

In the late afternoon, I leave the house, but after a brief walk, my very bones freeze at the sight of two German soldiers in gray-greenish uniforms, ruffles at their shoulders. They are coming from the opposite direction, heading right for me.

I straighten up, lift my head and crinkle a flirtatious smile while batting my lashes at them. My stomach is in my throat, but I do exactly as I observed Joanna do so many times when she liked a man and wanted him to take notice of her.

One of them smiles back and pulls the other one along to pass me.

I exhale with relief. I do have forged papers with me but one never knows how soldiers might choose to react.

After buying a newspaper from a young boy, I head toward the station with my faux confidence. Looks like pretending is my biggest weapon in this city. For once, I'm thankful to Joanna for her sophisticated speeches about how to appear independent and proud while getting what you need from men. Thankfully, the last part doesn't apply here.

Just when I near my destination, I overhear a small crowd of people whispering about a terrible roundup at the train station. I quickly turn and walk away.

Not knowing what else to do, and dreading going back to the attic, I take a walk along the canal. I summon my courage and enter a small café where I'm given a table. A savory aroma makes my mouth water while my stomach twists in excitement.

I order a cup of coffee and a crème brûlée, which turns out to be a rich, creamy dessert with a delicious sweet and tangy flavor. For a moment, I close my eyes and enjoy it, forgetting where I am and what I've been going through.

Felka's face comes to my mind, and I can't swallow anything anymore. She'll never enjoy the sweet and lovely things she deserves. I struggle not to let tears run down my cheeks, not in this place where wolves reside.

When I realize that a German officer to my left keeps watching me, I open up *Pariser Zeitung*, some Nazi-driven propaganda that I picked up from the little boy. I chose this one so that in moments like now, I can display it in front of the German officer. Normally, I wouldn't touch such garbage.

I open it to the second page and pretend to read it while sipping on my coffee and trying to form a plan. I have to cross the Spanish border, but how am I to manage such thing without any help?

"There must be something very intriguing in this newspaper," the blond German officer at the nearby table asks, a sliver of mockery in his voice.

I press my mouth into a smile. "Yes, indeed," I say in German, then I move my gaze back to the paper, realizing the entire article along with pictures is about German farmers raising Nazi bulls to impregnate Nazi cows.

But before I've chance to switch to another page, the officer leans above me checking the content of the article I'm apparently so engrossed in.

A surge of heat rushes to my face and I know my cheeks must be blazing crimson red.

Then the German bursts out a long, ringing laugh. When

he's done, his piercing blue eyes stay on my face, and I can't avoid the clear hint of a question in them.

Any other time before the war, I would be laughing with him at such a ludicrous situation, but not now. "I take a special interest in all farming subjects," I say, hoping he'll nod and leave me alone. The last thing I need is him bothering me or asking me for my papers.

He nods and says, "Do you mind if I join you to hear more about these farming matters?" His tone and appearance show no disrespect, or insult.

I'd better agree, or I might end up in a much worse situation than I'm already in. "Of course, officer." He is a handsome man and looks no more than forty. I curse myself for thinking of him as handsome. And that's all I need to think how much I hate him. The insignia on his uniform probably indicates that he holds high office in Hitler's forces.

"Call me Georg," he says and extends his hand.

"Juliette." When I take his hand, he kisses mine and once more his piercing eyes watch me.

"I'm curious to hear what's so exciting when it comes to farming."

I don't know what to tell him. The only time I ever stayed on a farm was at Joanna's parents. I try to remember what I liked the most. "I think every job is important and it's thanks to farmers we have milk to drink, bread to eat—and so much more," I say, sounding like a schoolgirl. But maybe that's a good thing.

"I agree," he says. "While growing up, I spent every summer at my uncle's farm near Bavaria. There were times when I worked really hard at harvesting, especially in my teenage years. It did me good, because now I know the value of hard work and determination."

I'm surprised by how personal his answer is, and by how easy it is to converse with him.

His eyes flash and then he smiles. "What else do you take an interest in beside farming?"

"I like problem solving and math." As soon as I say it, I realize my mistake. He does not need to know this. "But most of all, I enjoy playing piano," I add.

For a moment, he watches me like he's trying to assess what to think of my answer. "Math?"

"I liked it at school. It's not like I need it anymore."

"Too bad you didn't pursue it then," he says. "My sister studied medicine and now works as a doctor."

His attitude stuns me. Isn't Hitler always raving about a woman's place being at home as wife and mother? "Good for your sister."

"What music is most relaxing to you?" he asks.

The whole time he strikes me as cultured and respectful. But that's how they are—they play, then at the least expected moment they strike with brutality. I must find a way to end this conversation as his charming, fake attitude disgusts me. His uniform clearly shows who he really is and what he believes in.

"I enjoy Strauss," I say, which is a half-truth as there were moments in my life when I did like to listen to his music. I can't tell him that I adore Paderewski's compositions.

"I've some fondness for it too, as I appreciate how dynamic and modern it is." He seems to want to add something else but he stays silent.

"You describe it well," I say. "I'm so sorry but I need to get going."

He stands up and helps me put my coat on. "Let me walk out with you. I was about to leave as well."

My heart sinks. I feel so drained and not in the mood for any more conversation with this man. Besides, the last thing I need is to walk the streets with a Nazi officer.

Once outside, he offers me a ride, but I politely reject, stating that I enjoy walking.

"Before I let you go," he says as he drills his intense gaze into mine, "I would like to invite you for dinner tomorrow night."

In normal times, I would be taken aback by his good looks, and most of all, by his genuine approach. But I know this is just a game.

I gape at him, unsure how to reject him. Will he get angry when I do so? I shouldn't test my luck—I'm aware this man can arrest me for nothing—so I say, "I would love to accept."

He grins while a wave of relief moves across his face. "I will pick you up promptly at seven. What's the location?"

"My mother doesn't like strangers at our home," I lie easily. "It would be better if we meet here."

I can't believe that man asked me to dinner. I can't believe that I agreed. But it was just to get him off my back; I will not show up. I would rather die than date one of them. It would be a betrayal of everything I believe; more than that, it would be a betrayal of my nation.

The next day, I don't go. Instead, I read another book on the French Revolution. It's definitely more fascinating than going through the emotional hell of interacting with that man. I hope I don't bump into him ever again. I'll have to avoid the café where we met, and the surrounding area.

By not showing up for this date, I feel so proud of myself. It's my personal victory and it brings the kind of feeling that I need lately. I'm so useless here, not knowing what to do next. How has it got to this point, where I'm abandoned in a foreign country? Should I try finding a job and go on living here? How long would I be able to sustain that before being caught?

I resolve on talking to the French Resistance members when they have their next meeting here, which will hopefully be soon. I will ask them to connect me with someone who can help me cross the border.

I turn and twist at night while my heart feels like it's being squashed and squeezed by an elephant's foot. I truly don't know what to do or where to go. All I know is that I cannot go on rotting in this attic.

I stay inside for the next two days, afraid of Georg tracking me down. I don't want to even imagine the hatred in his blue eyes when he sees me. But my empty stomach forces me to go out the following day. I tell myself it's just a quick run to the black market. An officer like him surely doesn't frequent places like that, and I reassure myself that the French boys are there to warn of the first sign of danger.

I enjoy the touch of the sun's rays on my skin despite the cool air of February. Winters are so mild here, compared to the months of deep snow and Arctic temperatures at home.

I'm about to take the first corner into the square when I stop dead in my tracks.

THIRTY-ONE

BEATA

February 1943, Perpignan, the south of France

A tall man in a fedora hat and heavy coat is trotting my way. It is Harry. A wonderful feeling of weightlessness overtakes me and tears spring to my eyes. After weeks of terrible abandonment, I finally see a familiar face. In this very moment, I realize that I truly love this man.

His face stays emotionless while he looks both ways before pulling me into a narrow passage between two tenements. He hugs me with such strength that I lose my breath.

"I'm so glad to see you." His voice, whispering in my ear, is laden with emotion. "I looked for you the moment I learned you didn't cross the border into Spain." He takes my face between his hands, and I could swear I see a tear glistening. "Do you need to go back to grab your things?"

I swallow the lump in my throat and whisper, "I do."

An hour later, we are in a small flat in one of the tenements on Rue des Farines. Harry makes a pot of tea and I devour some of his bread and cheese. The apartment is sparse, with only a battered sofa in the main room, and a small table in the kitchen.

The empty walls and absence of furniture gives the feeling that someone just departed from here, taking everything with them.

As if sensing my thoughts, Harry says, "It's not much, but there is another room too, and it's safer here than many other places."

"It doesn't matter," I say, wondering if he has connections with the French Resistance. "I need to get to England. After we arrived here, they split us into small groups, so crossing to Spain would be easier. I was paired with a woman named Charlotte, but I only saw her on the first day. She never came back, and I didn't know how to get in touch with the rest. They're probably in England by now."

He gives me an understanding nod. "How did you manage to get food?"

"I bought it in the black market near the cathedral."

He tilts his head slightly. "That's extremely dangerous. If you were caught with the smugglers, you would end up in the Gestapo's hands."

Our gazes meet and I detect a trace of admiration in his eyes. "I had no choice," I say and shrug.

He sighs. "I know." For a moment he looks like he's trying to make sense of something. "I wonder why that woman Charlotte never came back."

For a second, I hear the sound of my heartbeat thrashing in my ears. "How did you find me?"

He stares down at his hands. "I've some contacts in Spain and when there was no sign of you there, I was worried. I couldn't get hold of Bertrand or any of the Poles, so I started checking 'the safe points' in Perpignan. When I met you, I was on the way to the house where you were staying. I finally got lucky after going through so many other locations. I can't tell you anything else for your own safety."

I nod. "One night, the Resistance members had a meeting downstairs, but I was too afraid to reveal myself." How little I know about him, I think. He once worked at Bletchley, and now he seems to be a secret agent. But which side he is on? The easy answer would be that he's on our side, but there is of course another, less pleasing option.

He touches his finger to his lips. "I do have information about your Polish peers."

Immediately, I grab hold of his arm. "How are they? I've been so worried about them."

"I don't have good news at all." His voice is apologetic now. "Marian and Henryk are held in jail in Spain. Most likely, they will be there for a couple of months and then get released. Hopefully by then Bertrand will be able to organize their safe transport to England."

"Oh no, I feel so bad for them," I say and clutch my fist into my chest. "But I hope you're right."

He nods. "Spain is free from German occupation, so they should be fine. I worry more for Langer, Ciężki, Fokczyński and Palluth. As far as I know, they are in German hands."

My heart sinks. "That's terrible. You know this for sure?"

"There is always the chance that my sources have given me wrong information, but unfortunately that's not the case."

"So, no one went to England?"

"Correct. The patrols at borders have intensified lately and to cross safely through the Pyrenees would be a miracle. At the same time, there is no other way available. Since Germans took over this unoccupied zone of France, sea escapes ceased, leaving the route through the Pyrenees as the only one available. Before the end of 1942, British navy vessels were coming in close to shore, so refugees could journey directly to Gibraltar by sea. But this isn't the case anymore."

My throat closes up and my stomach hardens in a knot of iron. "Then I'm stuck here."

He leans forward and takes my hand in his. His touch brings assurance even in this dire situation. "You must wait it out for a couple of months, until things get better. Meanwhile, I will find the right contacts and we will plan your crossing."

I make an effort to fold my lips in an appreciative smile. "I guess there is no other choice."

He nods. "I will make sure to visit you often and bring you food, but you have to stay low for the time being. People in this building are trusted and support the French Resistance."

An instant feeling of relief runs through me. "Thank you. I don't know what I would do without you."

"My pleasure," he says in French with a grin that exposes his white teeth.

"I thought you didn't speak French?"

"I knew I would need it one day, so I started learning when I was back in London."

"Look at you," I say and roll my eyes.

He brushes my skin with his finger sending a jolt to my heart. I love when he does that. "I will get you to safety. I promise, my princess."

THIRTY-TWO

BEATA

March 1943, Perpignan, the south of France

My first month in this flat goes by fast. Harry usually visits about once a week and stays for the night. He sleeps on the sofa while I enjoy the luxury of the large bed in the separate room. I offer to switch with him more than once, but he won't hear of it.

One evening, he convinces me to go out with him. We enter a bakery and take our place in a line.

The moment we do so, a teenage boy locks the door behind us and shouts to the people outside, "The bakery is closed for the day." Then he turns our way. "I will let out the patrons who are still in the store."

When our turn comes, a middle-aged woman in a white headscarf, whose face is covered with freckles, grabs a food ration card from Harry's hand. She inspects it quickly, then she gives him a long, somehow knowing look.

I pull on Harry's coat sleeve and take a step back, adrenaline surging through my veins. The card he gave her is forged, so we'd better run before she summons the authorities.

She drops the card into a container on the counter and says,

"For this I can only give you one loaf." Her lips form a thin line while she gazes to the door where the woman, who was in the line before us, argues with the teenage boy about what time the bakery should in fact close for the day, but soon she walks out into the street, and the teenager locks the door.

"That will do, Camille. Thank you," Harry says and smiles.

She packs the bread and, while handing it to him, she glances at me before saying, "Leon is working on one special loaf of bread."

"It's all okay, Camille, this is my good friend Beata. You can trust her."

Two conflicting emotions run through me. While I'm proud of him calling me his good friend, his words make me feel like my heart is shrinking. I hate myself for even feeling this. That kiss back then meant nothing. We drank a little too much that evening and everyone knows that wine has this effect on people when not stopped at precisely the right moment.

Camille nods at me, and her smile is friendly. "Well, as I just mentioned, Leon has some questions for you."

"Tell him that I will stop by tomorrow," Harry says and puts his hand on my waist. "We have to get going now."

She shakes her head. "I suggest you talk to him. We received an important piece of information today and I imagine you would want to know it right away." She winks at me. "I will keep Beata company."

He rubs the back of his neck, and his apologetic gaze settles on mine. "Would that be all right, princess?"

"Of course, go ahead," I say, as a reassuring smile clings to my lips. I'm not sure about staying alone with this woman but it seems that that man Leon has something important for Harry, maybe regarding his mission. Though it's hard to imagine that this little bakery could be part of any sort of resistance.

"Your French is flawless," Camille says, like it's obvious that I'm a foreigner. "What's your nationality?"

Damn! I thought I was doing well mimicking the southern accent. "I'm Polish," I say reminding myself that Harry trusts her, and it seems like they know each other well.

Her laughter rings out, filling the air around her with lightness. "Don't look so crestfallen. If Harry hadn't uttered those few words in English to you, I would have never known." She looks around. "I worry about him because he seems to lack some of the essential qualities of a good spy. Though he's a wonderful man and friend."

I don't know how open I can be with her, so I don't comment. Some people are good actors, mastering the ability of hiding their true intentions.

"Are you romantically involved?" she asks; her green eyes assess me, as if trying to figure out my truthfulness.

My cheeks must be turning scarlet now with the heat in my face. This woman doesn't dance around the bushes. "If you're as good a friend of Harry's as you say, you must know there is someone in England waiting for him."

"He never told me that." Laughter comes into her eyes. "I like you." Such a short statement but the air in the room shifts and I immediately sense that I'm finding a new, worthy friend.

"Let me help you with cleaning," I say, watching as she wipes down the empty bread shelves.

"Nah, I'm almost done. The real work is behind that door." She motions toward the back. "I'm hoping to find some assistance soon, or I will drive myself into the ground. Not much help from my dearest husband."

Her words remind me of my thoughts of trying to get a job. "I'm looking for employment. I don't have any experience working at a bakery, but I learn fast."

She looks up at me but says, "The position I can offer is more for a teenage girl. You know, doing dishes and cleaning after me in the kitchen. I'm afraid the salary is meager too."

"That's fine with me. Please, do consider me, as I can't stand sitting alone between the empty walls while Harry is out of town."

She nods and slowly smiles. "Are you able to start tomorrow morning? If you don't like it, you can always resign."

I jump up and down, unable to contain my elation. Even being a kitchen help seems attractive to me now, after all this time in hiding since I left Uzès.

"All right, all right. Let's see if it's something you can tolerate. You strike me as an intellectual." She sighs. "But the war has turned the world upside down."

At that moment, the back door screeches and Harry appears along with a short but stout man with a large mole above his right eye.

"I see you ladies are having a grand time here," the man says and extends his hand to me. "I'm Leon, Camille's husband. I'm sure you already caught a glimpse of our son Marcel. Those teenagers don't stay long in one place."

"I'm Beata." The culture emanating from this man makes me like him right away.

"Harry has told me a lot about you. Of course, only good things." He winks.

"I just hired Beata to help out in the kitchen," Camille says and places her careful gaze upon Harry, as if wondering what he'll have to say about it.

Harry fails to cover his surprise while glancing at me. "Are you sure?"

"Definitely. I'm looking forward to it. It will give me an outlet for the coming months. And Camille's already explained that it's a part-time position."

After saying our goodbyes and assuring Camille I will see her tomorrow, we head to our flat. We eat some cheese and bread and sip on dark, fragrant tea that Harry bought the other day.

"Camille and Leon seem nice," I say, hoping he will offer more information about them. "I assume I can trust them?"

"No less than you trust me. They're good people. I knew them before the war as Leon is a good friend of my father's. He was a professor at the University of Paris teaching art history and fine art techniques. Camille is an elementary school teacher. They used to visit London often, and that's how I got to know them.

"When the war started, they left Paris and came here to run her grandfather's bakery, as the old man passed in 1937." For a moment he seems to think hard, his forehead wrinkled. "They love children, and they devoted their pre-war lives to educating the new generation, and that's what they do now too." He lowers his voice. "Leon is one of the most skilled forgers in the French Resistance."

I forget to blink for a moment. "He forges documents?"

"Yes. Mostly for Jews, so they don't get deported by the Germans. But you will learn all this from them."

"I don't know if I could be so brave," I say.

"You are already. Look, you've been in this foreign country fulfilling the Enigma mission, facing so many obstacles."

I grimace. "Too bad I can't help any further with that."

"You Poles did all the groundwork for the Enigma. Trust me, we Brits are now able to use it in the most effective ways. It contributed greatly during the Battle of Britain. It was a game changer."

"Bertrand told us all about it. Still, I wish Poland and France could benefit more from our discovery."

"In the end, we all will," he says, holding my gaze. "In my personal opinion, it's thanks to the Enigma breakthrough and advancement that this war will end much quicker than it would without it."

I sigh. "I hope you're right. It seems like it will never end. And I'm so homesick."

He takes my hand in his. "I know, princess. The best we can do for now is stay hopeful. We will get you to London. I'm working on that."

"Thank you, my friend," I say uttering the last words with difficulty. How I would like to call him *my love*, but it's simply not my place.

He flinches, making me wonder if I just hurt his feelings. I only thanked him, after all, so why is his reaction so unsettling? "As I already told you, I want to be so much more than that." His stormy-gray eyes blaze into mine, making me question everything.

"Why are you confusing me so much?" I say, resolving to be honest with him and end this strangeness between us once and for all, so our interactions for the next couple of months can be decent.

"It's not my intention, princess," he says and presses his lips to my hand. "I'm just being honest with you. I can't hide my feelings."

"But—" A loud bang on the door cuts my words short. I freeze while our gazes meet. "Who that could be?" Gestapo comes to my mind; there have been so many arrests lately. I shiver at the thought.

He clears his throat and pulls me up by my arm. "Quick, we must hide you under the false floor."

"But I want to stay with you," I protest.

His grip is strong on me as he picks me up and runs to the bedroom. "There is no time to waste. The Gestapo has been on a rampage lately, breaking into flats and arresting all suspects without explanation."

"Let go of me, I will not leave you." I try to free myself from his hold. I would never forgive myself if he got arrested.

The banging intensifies. "Damn it, Beata, please listen to me." His eyes fill with pleading. "Please, darling," he rubs my ear with his thumb, "don't make this harder than it already is."

I swallow the lump in my throat and suppress my tears. "I want to stay by your side." I make sure to accent the finality in my voice.

He sighs. "Then at least stay here until I tell you it's all clear."

"Fine," I say and cross my arms over my chest. I have no intention of abandoning him. If this is an arrest, I will stay by his side.

I listen to Harry opening the door and to a woman's high-pitched voice yelling something about a man named Jean Paul. I exhale with relief when Harry tells the woman that she's got the wrong address—that person doesn't live here. Then there is the sound of the door closing and Harry's footsteps on the wooden floor. But he doesn't come back to me.

I lean against the wall and close my eyes. I know he's angry with me. My behavior was idiotic. I should have gone into hiding when he asked me to, so why did I do what I did? I can't explain it even to myself. It was as if I acted under this impossible, adrenaline-fueled fear of never seeing Harry again or, worse, finding him dead on the floor.

I spot him on the sofa with his face in his hands, so I perch beside him and touch his arm. "I'm sorry," I say, "this will not happen again."

He puts his hands down and folds them into fists, then he settles his blazing gaze on me. "You put us in an impossible position. I'm here to protect you and you acted like a school girl."

His words sting. I don't want to escalate his rage any further, so I repeat, "I'm sorry." I didn't know this side of him, but I'm not upset with his harshness. I deserve it for acting so foolishly.

Without another word, he pulls me into his embrace and draws his hand down my hair. "It's okay," he murmurs. "We are safe."

THIRTY-THREE

BEATA

April 1943, Perpignan, the south of France

I go every morning to the bakery where I tackle the dishes and all sorts of cleaning duties in the kitchen. These tasks aren't new to me. While living in the orphanage, I helped with cleaning chores from a young age.

Hard work was never something that I dreaded. I actually found solace in it and beamed every time Gloria, the orphanage cook, praised me. She was the person I felt closest to there, so when she suddenly left when I was twelve, I felt crestfallen. I'd lost the one person with whom I felt safe and comfortable.

I also help Camille with baking, but I make sure to listen carefully when she gives me instructions on how to place dough into forms, or how to cut out cookies.

She likes to chat a lot, but I don't mind since she doesn't expect me to participate actively in the conversation. Her husband, on the other hand, keeps quiet and can be seen only rarely. But I notice that even after many years of marriage they still show affection toward each other. It's so heartwarming.

It turns out that their son Marcel is a delivery boy, or he

assists Camille whenever she needs help while working behind the counter. We decided that it's safer for me to stay in the back, so I don't bring unwanted attention to my presence. Camille keeps telling me that in today's world no one can be trusted.

One day at noon when I'm about to head out home through the back of the bakery, Leon stops me. "Beata, let me show you something." He fixes his glasses. "Unless you're in a rush to leave?"

I shake my head. "Not at all."

"Follow me then," he says and disappears behind his laboratory, or at least that's what Camille calls it.

I close the door behind me in anticipation of finding out what Leon wants to show me. The scent of ink and paper hangs in the air, evoking wonderful memories of my school years.

"You see, before the war I taught my students the beauty of art and now I practice the art of deception." He chuckles. "Welcome to my little kingdom. I forge all sorts of papers here from identity and ration cards to passports, birth or marriage certificates. I basically modify old documents and create new ones."

"I can only imagine the demand for your work right now," I say and look at him with open admiration.

"You're correct. My work allows many Jews to avoid deportations to concentration camps in the east. To accomplish this successfully, I must produce documents of extremely high quality with gentile names. Every piece I create is a matter of life or death for those people in dire circumstances, so I put all my focus into it. I can't allow any errors."

"This is remarkable," I say, remembering Harry's words.

"I don't know how many people we've saved so far, but if I can spare only one life thanks to my work, it's enough to keep me going."

"We'll win this war thanks to people like you," I say quietly.

"I thought this would spark your interest. Harry told me about your background in decrypting. Very impressive."

"Thank you," I say, wondering if Harry broke the rules by sharing this with Leon. He must trust him unconditionally. I don't elaborate any further, not knowing what exactly he knows. I'm unable to trust people completely; the only exception to this is Harry.

"Don't worry, he only told me the basics," Leon says, catching my anxiety. "Besides, it will stay with me. Anyway, I wanted to see if you would be interested in assisting me here after your morning shift with Camille?"

"I would love to, but I know nothing about forging." Just the thought of helping him sends thrills down my spine. Finally, I could be doing something notable again.

"I'll teach you. You can start by watching me."

I nod my immediate agreement and so the next day I watch Leon forging signatures, reproducing watermarks, and creating perforations in stamps by using a sewing machine. The entire time he's exceptionally focused and his skilled hands move at a moderate, measured pace.

This is a whole new world for me. By observing Leon, I realize how hard this task is. I was always good at art at school, but this job is so important that the mere thought of doing it triggers palpitations in my heart.

This man cares for what he's doing like no one else I've ever met. Even codebreaking or decrypting doesn't rely on this type of precision.

"The most important and difficult task is to remove blue ink from paper. I use the lactic acid from cream, a technique developed by another forger in the Resistance network, Adolfo Kaminsky." He shows me the technique and I hold my breath for a long moment.

"Incredible," I whisper. "I don't think I could do it."

"Don't be discouraged. Come and watch me for as many days as you want, and when you're ready, I will give you a try."

"Thank you for your patience. These are such high-quality documents that you make. I'm sure they save lives."

"I hope so, I truly do. I'm doing my best. The next technique to master is duplicating typefaces. You must also learn to understand photoengraving to be able to produce watermarks, letterheads and rubber stamps."

As he goes on, my anxiety grows, but with the coming days, then weeks, I make progress, to the point he trusts me with the smallest tasks.

"Your hand doesn't lack precision," he says one day. "Not many people possess this ability. You would make a good forger, my friend." He beams and I relax just a little for the first time since I began doing this.

THIRTY-FOUR

BEATA

May 1943, Perpignan, the south of France

I can't stop considering Perpignan as a stepping stone to freedom. The hardest part is getting to Spain, from where Gibraltar and Britain would smile at us.

I've gotten a new set of forged papers from Leon, and Harry contacted a smuggler via the French Resistance who will help me get to Spain. The situation on the borders is a little better now, but we're to wait one more month before trying to cross through the Pyrenees. I feel nervous at the thought of it, but I can't stay here while my country is struggling. One more month and all of this will end.

I wish I had some news from Poland, but every time Harry stops by, he looks so exhausted that I don't want to overwhelm him even more. Whatever he's doing, it must be hard. Still, he always has a good word and a smile for me.

Today it's been two weeks since I saw him last, and that's so unusual. I can't help but worry. What if he was caught by the Gestapo? I tell myself over and over that he's fine and I shouldn't worry. He will return to me when he can.

After working at the bakery, and then at Leon's lab, I look forward to getting back home and resting.

May blooms with flowers and greenery, and the temperatures are high. I inhale sweet fragrances and set off in the direction of the black market.

When I get there, the usual spot is empty. Something must have happened, probably one of those terrible roundups. Well, I shrug, no shopping today.

On the way back, I make sure that no one is following me before I enter the tenement. The flat greets me with its savory aroma of cooked onion, potatoes and carrots that makes my poor stomach palpitate. Just the thought that Harry is back puts me in a blissful state.

He hovers at the kitchen stove, and as I wonder if he knows I'm there, he calls, "The soup is almost ready." He is making a potage, a heavy cream soup with boiled vegetables. He often makes it when he visits.

When he turns to me, layers of softness emanate from his gray eyes, and I wish I could run into his embrace and stay there for a very long time. I've missed him so much, but I've never betrayed how I feel about him. That other woman is waiting for him back there in England. Besides, there is no room for sentimental attachments during this war.

"Are you hungry?" he asks, still assessing me with his gaze.

"I'm starving," I say and take out a loaf and put it on the counter. "I got some bread from Camille."

He sighs. "I'm sorry that I wasn't able to return earlier."

I know that's all he's going to tell me, so I don't press for more but get busy setting the kitchen table.

We devour the soup and complement it with a bottle of red wine he's brought with him. The whole time, he keeps glancing at me whenever I don't look at him.

The wine brings relaxation, while his affectionate glances quicken my heart.

I stretch and say, "I'd better go to bed soon. The last days were exhausting, as I was worried about you."

"You worried about me?" He seems to be taken aback by my words. "Only because I cook potage for you?" He gives a mocking smile while placing his gaze on my lips.

I manage a shaky laugh. His eyes have this dark shade now, the same one that keep me awake every time I think of it at night.

After dinner, we clean up and I settle on the rocking chair he brought over a couple of weeks ago, saying someone had dumped it in the street. He walks over to the low table with its gramophone, another thing he managed to get for me, and puts on Edith Piaf.

"May I have this dance?" he asks with that earnest look on his face.

Dancing with him is as delicious as eating macarons. His wide shoulders and rugged strength make me feel safe while his piercing gray eyes send a tremor of excitement into my very soul.

The gramophone plays my current favorite by Edith, 'Tu es partout': *You are everywhere.*

"Well, this time I'm the one to tell you what this song is about." He grins. "Just pretend you don't know French and rely on my skills."

I laugh at the very idea but agree. "I'm intrigued to hear your interpretation."

"It's about a woman—"

"And how do you know it's about a woman?" I cut him short. "It doesn't say *she* anywhere."

He pretends to think for a moment. "But it doesn't say *he* either." A teasing smile crosses his face.

"Then it can be either."

"That's true. So, it's about a woman or a man left by a lover whom she or he can't forget. He or she is everywhere."

I can't suppress another laugh. "You make it sound like the story is funny while it is in fact tragic." I playfully nudge his arm. "You must stop this."

"Well, let's be serious then, because the last thing I need is you not liking me." After a moment of prolonged eye contact that tells me he isn't kidding at all, he continues. "The lover is everywhere, in the sky, sunshine, broken heart, dreams. She or he hopes he or she will come back one day."

"You're doing it again," I say and roll my eyes.

"But you said we don't know if it's a woman or a man."

I sigh. "Instead, maybe tell me what's the ultimate message here—in, of course, your subjective opinion."

"That loving someone without return is lonely and painful." The meaningful look in his eyes is making me blush. If he only knew.

"True, but I expected a more metaphorical approach from you, not so down to earth," I say, but then, without waiting for his response, I change the subject and tell him about my love for Padarewski's music. I would give a lot to hear it when I feel homesick.

He listens like nothing else matters, telling me that one day he'll find the perfect vinyl of my favorite music from home for me.

He moves his mouth closer to mine, sending jolts of nervousness through me, but also the anticipation of being kissed by him once more...

I gaze into his sensual eyes but turn my face away the moment his lips are about to meet mine. "We shouldn't," I whisper, so quietly I'm not sure he hears me, and close my eyes upset with myself for overreacting. I wanted that kiss, after all, so why am I so panicked? Because there is another woman waiting for him. It's not fair to her.

His lips touch my cheek and travel to my ear, then the back of my neck.

My entire insides melt as I want more and more of his sensual kisses. I've never felt like this—so shaken and at the same time so elated. But it's all wrong.

His arms pull me even closer, and he says, "Look at me." His voice is husky. "I can't live without you; I can't even breathe without you. You're on my mind every second of my life since that day I saw you in Poland."

I gasp in pleasure at his words, but my mind is racing. "You told me that you love another woman, remember?"

"I'm not sure what you're referring to," he takes my face between his hands, "but there is no other woman, and never was. Oh, Beata, you're the only one."

His words are like a breeze on a scorching day, bringing the sweetest relief to my heart. "We shouldn't complicate things, we are at war," I say knowing full well it's too late for my words.

"I was almost caught by the Gestapo, which is why I had to disappear for the last two weeks. It made me realize that tomorrow is not guaranteed. It's so important to catch every moment." His hand caresses my hair. "I love you, Beata. Please, let's give this feeling between us a chance."

I detect a trace of pleading in his eyes, like he's ready for my rejection. This man just made himself so vulnerable in front of me that my heart flutters wildly.

"I love you too," I say, meaning every word.

The moment I do, his lips touch mine, at first gently, sweetly tormenting. My nerves melt as our kiss deepens, our mouths seem to fit together in the most satisfying way. Sparkles of pleasure ignite my body, making it weak and entirely his. I put my hands to his neck and give myself wholly to the raw sensations pulsating in my veins.

After a long, long moment, he lifts his mouth from mine, his eyes flooded with passion. "If I don't stop now..." His voice is shaky.

"Don't stop," I whisper, lost in pleasure.

THIRTY-FIVE

HARRY

May 1943, Perpignan, the south of France

Dearest Mother,

There is one poem in your diary about the woman who loves without reciprocity. I wish I'd brought it with me, but at least I know it's safe in my apartment in London. Were you that woman, Mother? Did Father love you as deeply as you loved him? Sometimes I wonder and try to remember times the three of us spent doing things together. The more I think, the less I seem to know.

The other day I danced to Edith Piaf's song about the same fatal destiny, while enclosing Beata in my arms. She's my everything.

After you left, I felt lonely. Now I know it was the right price to pay for love.

I hated Father for starting his new family. It's why I built a wall, to make sure we kept a distance between us. I was sure you were angry at him too. Now I'm not so sure. Maybe you've been above it all, and you don't see it the way we do down here. I still don't know.

I bet you're as busy over there as you always were here. I wish there were visiting hours when I could hear your voice again and feel your loving touch. The day you left marked the beginning of my loneliness. It stops only with Beata's presence.

Be well, Mother. I love you to the moon and back.

Your Harry

THIRTY-SIX

BEATA

June 1943, Perpignan, the south of France

I'm only two days away from leaving Perpignan. José, the smuggler, will accompany me through this journey. Harry has promised to go back to England once his mission is over.

There is no certainty with anything anymore. I might get caught by Germans on this side, or Spanish police on the other. Harry was able to find out that Marian and Henryk were finally released from the jail in Spain. I pray every day that they find their way to England where they will continue working on breaking the Enigma ciphers.

Sometimes I wonder how different it would have been if we'd been able to go to England instead of France. Then our cryptologists would have worked on the Enigma ciphers without any breaks and obstacles. But it is what it is, and the French are the ones who offered us the hand of hospitality after we left Poland. We're thankful to Bertrand and his savviness.

When I enter the bakery, Camille's familiar freckled face greets me with a smile that reaches her eyes. The shelves are empty.

"I'm too late," I say and sigh, slumping my shoulders. "I was going to come earlier but I had a bad headache." Yesterday was my last day of duties at the bakery and lab because now I must focus on getting ready for the crossing.

I know that Camille has a particular fondness for Poles because when she was young, she dated a Polish boy named Franek. Even though things didn't last between them, they split in peace. Now, the thought of him brings happy memories to her. And now, as at other times, I am the beneficiary of such tenderness.

"Don't fret, my sweet. I put one away for you." She grins and takes out a loaf. She gazes around and leans forward. "When are you leaving?"

"The day after tomorrow," I whisper, as I put the bread in my duffel bag. "Thank you for this, my friend. I will never forget you and your kindness." I said my goodbyes to Leon and Marcel yesterday.

She nods. "Once all of this ends, make sure to write to us, and maybe one day even visit."

"I will." I take her hand in mine. "I promise."

She wipes a tear and says, "Take good care of yourself, child. You deserve happiness and I pray you find it with Harry."

"You too, Camille, take care. I will always remember your kindness."

Saying goodbye to Camille and her family isn't easy, despite the fact that I've known them for so short a time. In Poland I learned to be independent and careful, so I didn't get hurt. Here, having even one good person around changes so much. Sometimes it's worth taking a risk and letting others into our lives, even if in the end, we burn our own hands. How else to taste the real flavor of life?

I take a walk along the canal, admiring the beauty of this city. I try not to see the swastikas and the uniformed Germans, instead I concentrate on everything else and imagine this special place before the war. It's the type of city I would come back to in a heartbeat. Maybe the promise I made to Camille wasn't for nothing and I'll return here one day.

I cease my thoughts as I catch sight of Georg who is nearing me from the opposite direction. My blood pressure elevates as I long to make myself invisible. But before I get a chance to turn and walk away, he freezes, his eyes land on me, and an instant recognition registers on his face. He lifts his chin and glares at me, his hand traveling to his pistol in its holster.

My chest tightens as I clench and unclench my fists, but I'm trapped. There is nothing I can do; if I run, he will shoot me.

I feel numb. Joanna's voice in my mind tells me that I should smile and come up with some excuse for not making it to the date with him. But there is so much defensiveness and anger in his posture that the feeling of powerlessness wins. He will have his way regardless of my reaction.

His features suddenly relax as he drops his hand from the holster. When passing me, he stops and says in a chilling voice, "Be careful." Then, he marches away.

I can't stop my chin from trembling. What just happened? I manage to overcome the spell of dizziness that hits me, then walk back home on wobbly legs.

When I drop onto the sofa, I exhale with relief. This man, Georg, chose to be decent. But I also can't help but wonder if there is any other explanation for his walking away so suddenly. As conflicting emotions run through me, I know that I should be thankful that he didn't arrest me. On the other hand, if it weren't for him and his fellow Nazis, I wouldn't even be in this situation. Still, he could've behaved like his peers and changed my life into hell, or even ended it.

THIRTY-SEVEN

BEATA

June 1943, Perpignan, the south of France

The night before my scheduled escape, I can't get enough of Harry's warm touch; the citrusy scent of his cologne tantalizes my senses. While we lie in bed and talk, I yearn to cement every detail of him into my memory: the way he smells; the touch of his skin; his easy smile; the way his eyes sparkle the moment he sees me. If someone asked what it feels like to be happy, I would say it's being in the arms of someone dearest to you.

"I'm afraid of what tomorrow brings," I say and kiss his chest. "What if we are caught by the Germans or the French gendarmes?"

His fingertips travel down my arm to my hand causing flutters in my stomach. "It's the only possible route now; the only other choice would be staying here until the war ends. If you did that, you could get more involved helping Leon with his forgery work."

"We don't know how much longer the war will last. I need to reunite with the rest of our cryptology team and help them with our mission."

"I know, which is why I won't stop you, but believe me, if I only could…" He withdraws his hand from mine and pulls me closer. "You're well prepared for this. I'm sure that once you get to England, you will be assigned to continue your work on decrypting, but I do have an apartment in the center of London where you can stay as long as you wish. I hope to join you there soon, once my duties here end."

"I can't wait to be there with you," I say and kiss his lips, which feel so soft and electrifying. Excitement rushes through me and sets my heart on fire. For a heavenly moment, our lips dance in an exquisite symphony of exploring and touching.

He deepens the kiss by gently stroking my tongue with his, deliciously tormenting and teasing every nerve in my body.

I feel breathless but don't want this intimate moment to end. Our hearts beat as one while passion slips through my veins. I can't get enough of him, now or ever.

When he lifts his mouth, his eyes are a shade of the darkest blue, and his breathing is labored. "Every time I kiss you, the entire world stops. Why is that, darling?" His thumb caresses my cheek.

"I feel the same." I bury my face in his chest and close my eyes. "It's hard for me to talk about such deep feelings. I never had anyone to do it with while growing up, so I don't know how. Yet I cherish every time that you tell me how you feel, your deepest thoughts and the sensations you experience. Please, never stop."

"I won't. It will come to you with time. I talked with my mother about everything, but when she passed, it all changed. It was never the same with my father, even though I always knew he loved me."

"You have a good relationship with him?" I want to know everything about Harry, but there is never enough time to talk.

"Yes, we are on good terms, but we only ever talk about

things on the surface. He is very formal and doesn't like to show his emotions."

"But he remarried?"

"Yes, and I do admit that even though he had a new family, he never made me feel like I was less important. He always had time for me. The only thing I can blame him for is that he ceased any contact with my mother's side of the family in Poland."

I sigh my understanding; I can imagine how hard that was for him. "Well," I say, encouragingly, "it's never too late to meet them. I will help you find them after the war."

"I would love that, though I'm not sure if my grandparents are still alive. If so, they must be in their late eighties. I do have my aunt Kalina. I have wonderful memories of her from when I spent summers in Poland with my mother. I'd love to see her one day."

"You never tried looking for her?" I make sure my voice holds no trace of amusement.

"I thought they forgot all about me since they never called or visited." He sighs. "Besides, I didn't know how painful it would be going back to the places where I was so happy with my mother. I guess I'm a coward."

"It seems like you truly need to go and talk to them, hear their reasons for not reaching out through all those years. Maybe they were afraid for the same reasons you were. After all, you were raised by an Englishman with his new family, while they lived in another country and probably don't speak any English."

"True."

"Do you have siblings?" I ask, realizing how much I enjoy listening about his life, learning who he truly is.

"Only a half-brother, but we're as different as day and night." He gives a brief laugh. "He likes to attend parties and travel around the world. Well, not so much anymore when comes to travel, because of the war. We rarely see each other." He brushes away strands of hair from my face and kisses my forehead. "Tell me more about your childhood."

"There is not much to tell. As you already know, I was abandoned by my parents. Thankfully, a priest found me on the steps of the church before I froze to death. January's low temperatures can be harsh." I ignore the familiar surge of sorrow. "How heartless a person must be to do something like that."

"Maybe they waited in hiding to make sure someone saw you very soon."

"I would like to think that. It wasn't good, growing up convinced that my own mother didn't want me. If she'd brought me to the orphanage, they would have taken her name, and I would have a file like every other child in there. But I always felt like an alien with no past. She didn't even give me a name."

He wipes my tears. "You have no power over it, so it makes no sense to make yourself miserable."

"You're right." I sniff and wipe my eyes. "When I think of my childhood, sadness is the emotion that I always felt. While growing up, I wanted so badly to belong to someone. But that never happened."

"You're the strongest woman I've ever known," he tells me, and the sincerity in his voice is unmistakable. "You took your life in your own hands by learning all those languages. That's when you began your journey to become independent, but at the same time, compassionate. You have a heart of gold and I'm the luckiest man alive to call you mine."

I don't tell him that I often wonder what he sees in me. After all, I'm not insanely beautiful or anything like that. My personality isn't that charming either, I can be stubborn and difficult when it comes to showing my emotions.

I decide to change the subject, as I don't like talking about my past. "You live alone in your apartment?"

"Yes, but I also have a little castle outside of London, which my paternal grandmother gifted to me. I guess I'm a lucky man and material things came to me easily, unlike what you had to go through." Now I detect a trace of apology in his voice.

"Yet you're here fighting Germans, instead of living in luxury in your 'little' castle." I tease his bottom lip with my thumb.

He laughs lazily. "I will enjoy it when I marry you. You'll love the castle, princess. It was my grandmother's favorite when she was still alive, and I've a feeling you will fall in love with it as well."

"Are you trying to bribe me?" I say in a light tone, but in reality I'm overwhelmed with what he's sharing with me.

"I'm sorry." He pulls me even closer. "I didn't mean to come across as an arrogant Englishman. Please, forgive me, my love." His hot kiss complements his words, making me forget about the entire world. He urges my lips to part, and when I obey, our hearts beat in unison.

I'm welcoming every touch of his probing tongue, his devouring lips. Bliss runs through my skin and body and settles in the deepest parts of me. I don't understand why he makes me feel the way he does, as if I don't have any choice but to succumb.

Afterwards, I need to talk to him about how I feel, despite my hesitations. "I don't like being vulnerable," I say, "but that's how you make me feel."

His eyes soften. "You're safe with me because you make me feel the same. It's new to me too, something I never even thought I could experience."

"What if one day you change just like that man in Edith Piaf's song?" Once more, I strive to sound lighthearted, but the worries never leave me. This is something that's stayed with me from my orphanage years—this constant feeling of abandonment and disappointment at something good ending rapidly.

Harry already knows that side of me. "My heart is yours, darling," he says, his voice cracking with emotion.

I don't need any more words because his yearning eyes tell me all. This man loves me as much as I love him.

I lay my hand over his heart. "And mine is yours."

THIRTY-EIGHT

BEATA

June 1943, Perpignan, the south of France

José, a Spaniard with olive skin, assured us a while back that the safest route would be via a southbound train, and then crossing the Pyrenees by foot. If we are stopped for an identity check, I'm to pretend to be his wife and say we came to Perpignan to visit my relatives, but are now returning to our home in Madrid.

After our goodbye kiss near the train station where we met with José, I can't leave Harry's arms. The thought that I might never see him again brings sorrow to my heart. But time is running on, and I have to go. It's safer that Harry doesn't go any further with us.

Right before our departure, I overhear Harry swearing at José that if he abandons me or lets anything happen to me, he will find him and kill him. I pray José takes these words to heart. From what we've learned, Marian and Henryk were robbed by their guide and left alone in the Pyrenees. Langer and others were betrayed by their smuggler too. José is being paid generously, and I can only pray he turns out to be a decent man.

After one last kiss, I leave without another glance at Harry, or I would have no strength to go. At the train station, I feel the eyes of the French police, but we don't get stopped. The whole time, I keep my chin high and smile, pretending to be relaxed and with nothing to worry about.

We board a train to Ax-les-Thermes, a mountain town ten kilometers from the border with Andorra in the Pyrenees. We pass every document check, and upon our arrival, we take a cab to an obscure motel where we are to spend the night.

After dinner, which consists of dried fish and beans, José drops into bed and is soon snoring. I guess the four beers he drank at dinner help him sleep now.

As a *married couple*, we're given a room with only one bed. I debate for a moment what to do. The last thing I want is to join him. Who knows what he might get into his head at night?

I take a blanket from the bed and spread it on a cheap, stained rug. It's so hot in this room that José won't need it anyway. Without taking off my clothes, I lie on top of it and after thinking of Harry, I drift off to sleep.

In the morning, every bone of my body hurts. I chase flies away and get up.

After a quick face wash in a tin bowl, I devour a slice of bread and an orange. Soon we're on our way to board a train to Latour-de-Carol, the last station on the very border. From there, we will have to cross the Pyrenees on foot.

We don't encounter any problems with our forged papers this time either, but when we take off from Latour-de-Carol, two gendarmes stop us and request our documents. They ask questions about our presence in the forbidden border zone. José tells them the story we agreed upon while I stay silent, smiling in a friendly way at the two uniformed men.

"You've a beautiful wife," the younger one with dark hair

and a mustache says to José, while his gaze lands on my chest. "Aren't French women beautiful?"

I smile appreciatively and bat my eyelashes at him, thankful that I am wearing a modest dress that could not give rise to provocative ideas.

Then, all of a sudden, after José tells them that I've been living with him in Spain the last eight years and how quickly I learned his language, the younger gendarme decides to speak to me in Spanish.

I understand not a single word while his face reflects a question. He just asked me something and I do not understand it. I speak four languages, but the one I need right now that might decide my survival, is not one of them.

Seeing my hesitation, his eyes narrow and his face hardens.

I'm experiencing the sensation of not being able to take enough oxygen into my body, but instinctively I say the word that I've heard José use so often, "Sí." Then I smile flirtatiously and pray.

To my relief, he bursts out laughing and claps poor José on the shoulder; he is by now red like a crab.

Later, I ask José what the man said. It turns out he asked me if French men are hotter than Spaniards. After all, it seems I gave him the correct answer.

We spend the rest of the day in a bar where José drinks beer "for courage," while I can't swallow a thing. The hot air is stagnant, simmering with smells of sulfur and yeast mixed with a whiff of sweat.

Knowing that the critical part of our trip will be tonight, I force myself to eat some dried fish and bread. The whole time José is so quiet, unlike in the presence of Harry with whom he talked nonstop. But it's not like I'm talkative either.

"I need the rest of the money," he suddenly says in a savage voice, leaning forward in his chair at the bar's wooden table.

I wrinkle my nose. "It's not how you agreed things with

Pierre." Harry made José believe that his real name is Pierre and mine Angelina.

His nostrils flare but I can see he strives for control. "Pierre is out of the picture now. You're relying on me, and you either hand me the second half, or manage it on your own."

I want to shake this treacherous man. Everything I worried about with Harry materializes right now. "You're being paid generously. It's perfectly fair that you get the rest once I'm safely in Spain," I say with finality in my voice. "Besides, if you do as you say, Pierre will find you and put you through the most miserable death one can imagine." I make sure to use the exact same words I heard Harry say.

There is an undecided expression on his face but soon the rebellious look disappears, and he says, "Fine." For the rest of the day, he utters not a word to me.

We begin crossing the Pyrenees at night. It's so dark that I don't see much but I follow José whose mood is as rotten as before. But what matters is that we keep moving, and the truth is, if he wanted, he could have taken the money from me using his strength. Something stopped him, either the fear of Harry's words or his conscience. I'd like to think it's the latter.

After an hour of walking, the noise of a motorcycle makes us pause; my racing heart causes pains in my chest.

"Over there," José yells, while gunshots ring out. Too late.

THIRTY-NINE

HARRY

July 1943, Perpignan, the south of France

"Something isn't right," I say to Leon, unable to keep the panic from my voice. We're sitting in his office in dim candlelight. "Beata never arrived at the safe house in Spain."

He takes his glasses off and focuses on my words. "Are you sure? Isn't it too early to be saying this?"

"It's been three days since she left and today my contact confirmed that she is still not there." I feel my pulse picking up again. "It's like she vanished."

"You must be patient and trust her. She will contact you when the right time comes. I noticed how clever she is. She doesn't even realize it herself."

"True, but she might not be able to contact me. What if she's in the hands of the Gestapo?"

"You can't jump to the worst scenario. Maybe they have to wait it out before crossing the Pyrenees. Please, my friend, be hopeful."

I get up and pace back and forth. "The feeling in my gut

tells me that things went terribly wrong. Don't ask me how I know. I just do."

He sighs. "I'm not going to argue. I know you too well. You're not dramatic. Is there anything we can do at this point?"

"My contact is checking prisons in Spain." I drop to the chair. "That's all we can do for now. I have no way of finding out if she's in the Gestapo's hands. If the Vichy police caught her, she'll be immediately given away to the Germans."

"Maybe they're holding her at the Gestapo headquarters in Le Boulou," Leon says, rubbing his chin. "There is no way of getting in there."

"I pray it's not where she is. When is the next meeting of the Resistance?"

"Tomorrow night. But I doubt they would be able to help you if in fact she's held by the Gestapo. She needs our prayers and plenty of luck."

I'm beside myself with worry. I know deep in my soul that something is wrong, but at the same time, I still have a sliver of hope. "Maybe I'm just overreacting, and she will turn up in that safe house soon. Or maybe that bastard José left her when he received his money, and she doesn't know how to get there."

"Exactly. As far as we know, she might be safely hiding in Spain. You must keep your spirits high, my friend."

"I'm trying to. I hope you're right and she is safe." My voice breaks. "I can't lose her."

FORTY

BEATA

July 1943, Gestapo Headquarters, Le Boulou, 12 kilometers from the Spanish border

Sweat mixed with urine fills my nostrils as I sit in the corner of a large cell, accompanied by at least a dozen women, from teenagers to the elderly.

When I arrived four days ago, they all encircled me and asked millions of questions in French and Spanish, and even English, but I only shrugged and acted as if I didn't understand a word. And that's when they left me alone.

It's better that way, as one never knows who is a spy. As far as I know, one of these women might be working for the Germans, so it's better to be cautious.

Since I got here, we've received almost no food or water. They keep us like sardines, as more and more women arrive. Plus, we're in the basement, so there are no windows, and the air is heavy. The pungent odor from the bucket where we have to relieve ourselves makes me gag.

The realization that I'm in German hands hits me like a hammer. Throughout my time in Perpignan, I believed that I would succeed in crossing the border, despite Harry's worries. He knew he couldn't stop me, so instead he helped me. But now the worst has happened.

After they arrested us, they took away our papers and brought us here. Since then, I haven't seen José, but how could I, kept in this dungeon? José will probably come up with something to secure his freedom, while they will kill me.

My forged papers show my name as Edith Abascal, a French woman who married this Spaniard José years ago.

The situation I've found myself in is so idiotic that for a moment a bubble of laughter rises in my throat, but only until the thought of being in German clutches strikes me anew. Ironically, I don't know a word in Spanish, well, besides *si*. I put my hands over my face, blocking out this awful reality.

The plan was that once I arrived in the safe house in Spain, I would secure a new set of papers, ones for an English woman. It's all in vain now.

I do have some money and my Polish papers sewn into my undershirt. I pray they don't find them. I've thought about it, but realize I don't even have a way of getting rid of them.

The next day, a bearded guard calls out my name. I don't move, until he bellows again, "Edith Abascal."

I swallow hard and rise without a word.

"Why didn't you answer when I called you?" he snaps and pushes me forward.

We climb dirty cement stairs and enter a long corridor with so many doors. He knocks at one, and at once someone says in a firm voice, "Come in." Then, he pushes me in.

A bold man with a mustache and in German uniform points out from a desk to a wooden chair.

I obey right away. My legs feel so soft and wobbly that I'm afraid I would collapse.

When the guard leaves, the man drops papers to the desk,

then leans back in his chair. "Name?" he commands. I've never heard such a screechy, menacing tone of voice.

I raise my chin, ready to play the part of the confident woman with a Spanish husband. "Edith Abascal."

His nostrils flare as he lifts a stick from the side of the desk. "Name?"

All of a sudden, I have a sour taste in my mouth, and I forget to breathe. Something is not right. But I tell myself to act confidently. "My name is Edith Abascal and—"

He leaps to his feet and jumps toward me. "Stop lying, bitch." He lifts my chin with his stick.

I shiver at the touch of it, unable to stomach his breath that stinks of rotten eggs.

"Your so-called husband told us everything, including your ploy to cross the border and how he was paid for helping you." *So that's how he bought his freedom*, I think. His cold, probing eyes meet mine. "You do the same, and you will be released in no time as well."

I have difficulty swallowing the lump that's built in my throat. At the same time, I'm so thankful that Harry never told José our real names or gave him any real information. He always met with him far away from our flat. He might have betrayed me, but José doesn't know anything about me or Harry, or my work for the Cipher Bureau. My resolve is as strong as ever. The Germans can't find out about the Enigma mission. If they do, all our efforts are for nothing.

This particular German walks back to his desk and takes out a cigarette. After lighting it, he inhales slowly, then exhales whirls of smoke; the whole time his arrogant eyes stay on me.

My initial feeling of dread transforms into disgust for this snaky man. I have this overwhelming desire to spit in his face, but I brace myself. My situation is already terrible, thanks to that traitor José. If Harry only knew.

"What's your real name?"

I glare at the faded portrait of Adolf Hitler on the wall. I must visualize something beautiful instead, to gain enough strength to survive this hell. Only music can help me, so I imagine listening to Paderewski's "Mazurek Op. 5 no. 2". Melancholic tones transform into dynamic and graceful ones, then to an even more energetic and majestic cascade of notes. It all culminates in a joyful moment, but it doesn't last long, and is followed by painful chords.

He walks back with the cigarette clamped in his mouth and strikes my head with the stick.

I see bright flashes of light. I'm in such shock from the blow that I don't feel any pain. A surge of nausea hits me.

"Who helped you organize the crossing?" He remains in front of me, the stick in his hand.

Strong and dramatic timbres from "Mazurek Op. 5 no. 2" continue in my head, expressing Paderewski's love for his land, echoing rhythms of Polish folk dances.

This time he smashes his fist into my face. I taste blood on my lip and stinging heat in my face, but I instinctively cover my head with my hands.

He repeats this act of violence two more times, and the right side of my face feels numb.

"I'm giving you one last chance to cooperate before I send you to the biggest son of a bitch in this building. Anyone who finds themselves in his hands, dies in agony. He will knock out your teeth, tear up your fingers, smash your head. You don't want to know what else he's capable of. So, if I was you, I'd talk. And fast."

Bouts of dizziness set in. I swallow hard but don't budge. I'm doomed because I will not tell them anything. The throbbing pain in my face and head makes me close my eyes. I run my tongue over my teeth to make sure they are still there. They are.

He smirks. "Fine. José will lead us to this man called

'Pierre', so we don't really need you." His inquiring scrutiny settles on me as I open my eyes.

If that was the case, he would not be trying to get information out of me. He thinks I'm stupid. José has no way of locating Harry; we made sure of that, because we simply didn't trust him or anyone else. If I only had a way of warning him about José, just in case. The plan was that once Harry found out from his contacts in Spain that I arrived in the safe house, he would know I was safe. But, unfortunately, that hasn't happened.

The next morning, they bring me to another room. After the beatings yesterday, I didn't get any water or food, so I feel even weaker. I wish they'd just finish me off fast, so I don't have to stand this misery any longer.

The room is similar to the one from yesterday with another ugly portrait of Hitler on the wall. I walk toward it and spit at it. That single act of defiance brings some relief.

I gaze through the barred window with its view of another red-brick building. No chance of escaping. The monster yesterday said that I will now be interrogated by *the biggest son of a bitch*. Exactly his words.

The door behind me closes with a bang and heavy footsteps follow.

I freeze, unable to look up, but the person walks around the desk and settles in the chair. Then, an eerie silence deafens my thinking. He is here. *The biggest son of a bitch* is here.

I remain staring into the dirty floor with dark stains. Blood stains. I want to run far away from here, I want to run to Harry.

"Hello." The familiar voice rings out, compelling me to lift my gaze.

FORTY-ONE
BEATA

July 1943, Gestapo Headquarters, Le Boulou, 12 kilometers from the Spanish border

Georg leans back in his chair, his mouth curling in a gentle smile. The same smile he charmed me with in the café. He let me go the other day, telling me to be careful, so why then is he *the biggest son of a bitch*? I don't understand.

"I didn't expect to see you here," he says in a low voice. "I told you to be careful. Well, I understand that life happens, especially now during the war."

Our eyes meet, and while I struggle to control the confusion in my expression, his shows resignation, like he's not pleased I'm here at all.

"You have no choice but to confess everything, so I can get you out of this... difficulty. Why don't you start by telling me your nationality? I did notice a slight accent in your French when you spoke to the waitress." He lowers his head. "But you also spoke impeccable German to me. You're a cultured, intelligent woman."

"I'm French," I say. "Different regions have different accents."

"I knew from the moment you spoke that you're Polish," he snaps, and it takes everything in me not to flinch at his change in tone. "What are you doing in France? Are you a spy?"

"I'm French." I avoid his gaze; it unnerves me. I don't know how to figure this man out. Why is he so calm with me when his reputation is of that of a brutal torturer and murderer? It was so much easier to deal with the other brute.

"You're not Juliette or Edith, and you're not even Angelina." He smirks. "You're a Polish girl, but fine, have it your way. Which name do you prefer? Where's your identity card for Angelina?"

So José told them that my name is Angelina. What a snake. Harry was right to give him false names. "I'm Juliette, but I lost my papers in a fire, so that's why José gave me the other set of documents." I tell the story I decided on last night. I have to give them something. "My flat in Paris was destroyed by a fire and I lost everything. I decided to travel to Perpignan as my friend used to live there. But when I arrived, I couldn't find her. I met that man José and he promised to bring me to Spain and marry me. I wanted to start a new life not having anyone here, and not being able to find a decent occupation."

He smirks. "Well done, that's a nicely thought-out story. But I have another one. Most likely, you are a Polish woman, and so beautiful at that"—he crinkles a smile—"here for unknown reasons, so the possibility of espionage can't be ruled out. You tried crossing the border most likely because your mission in France came to an end." He sighs. "That's all you need to do: tell us why exactly you are here and who you work for, then I will set you free."

"I don't know what you're talking about."

He smashes his fist into the desk. "Damn it. Stop being stubborn. I'm trying to save your life."

I eye a whip on his desk.

He follows my gaze and I wonder if his face winces, or if it's my eyes playing tricks on me. My gut tells me that he doesn't want to hurt me. The *biggest son of a bitch* doesn't want to hurt me because he's the same charming officer from the café that let me walk away. This makes no sense at all. His behavior makes no sense. What will he do when he realizes that I won't tell him anything? Will he change his calm approach and beat me unconscious?

I make sure not to show any emotion. I will keep telling my made-up story, because telling them that I don't know anything only provokes them to hurt me.

And so, the same thing happens for the next two days. The same composed Georg, and the same me telling my false story. Throughout, he doesn't touch me once. It's all eerie and unnerving but at least I'm still alive. By now, in our cell, there is a rumor of one Gestapo man being extremely brutal and killing someone every day, usually it's one of the women who never comes back from interrogation. I've heard his name, too, repeated over and over.

Monster Georg.

It sickens me. The calm way he looks at me and speaks to me brings on a feeling of insanity. It makes me wonder if it's simply the calm before the storm. It eats me from inside.

In the mornings, we get a piece of bread and a little water. Nothing else for the rest of the day.

One afternoon they tell us to strip naked. By the time they return our clothes, it's late at night. When they do, my heart sinks.

My Polish papers and money are no longer in my undershirt.

I can't get rid of the dreadful thought that now they may link me with the Cipher Bureau. Were all those documents in Poland really destroyed, or is there something still lingering that will make my circumstances even worse? I pray as hard as I have ever prayed that they have nothing on me at all, that my name means nothing to them.

"The game is over, Beata," Georg says the next morning. "Beata. What a pretty name." His jaw is rigid. For the first time, he stands beside me. He smells clean, of chamomile soap. His face nears mine, his jaw rigid.

"You must start talking or you'll receive your punishment, and it won't be pretty. I can't tolerate your behavior any longer. My bosses need information, especially now we've found your Polish identity card."

How can it be that his breath smells of something sweet, like caramel candy? This man's demeanor is pleasant, yet he is a killer. Ice runs down my spine.

"I already told you the truth so many times. Please let me go."

"I can't, unless you give me something."

I sigh in defeat. "I don't know what you are talking about."

He closes his eyes as if trying to keep calm. "You must talk." Now, his pale blue eyes sink through mine, probing and probing for answers.

I settle my gaze on Hitler's ugly portrait. It's obvious he knows nothing of my involvement with their precious Enigma secret.

"Fine."

The moment he says it, the man who interrogated me the first day comes in, bringing with him a whiff of sweat and cigarettes. "I can't believe you still have this whore here. You go through others like flies, yet you're stuck on this one. I will take over from here."

Georg shrugs and says with malice in his voice, "I've already figured this hopeless bitch out and she's useless to us. Send her out east to the camp. I'm not going to waste my whip on this flea-infested ferret."

PART 2

GERMAN DEATH CAMP IN BRZEZINKA,
AUSCHWITZ II-BIRKENAU, POLAND

FORTY-TWO

BEATA

July 1943, train from France to Poland

On one sun-drenched morning, German soldiers usher us into train wagons, the type normally used to transport animals. Most are Jewish people, men, women, children, but there are also non-Jewish political prisoners, like me.

These are the very people for whom Leon works tirelessly, so they can avoid this cruel fate. Obviously, the ones on this train weren't lucky enough to get access to Leon's forged papers, or something didn't go as planned. Not in a million years did I imagine I would end up here as well.

When I enter one of the carts filled with hot air and the smells of sweat and vomit, it's already packed to the point there is very little room for any sort of movement.

I can't find an empty space but soon a boy who looks no more than five, calls out to me, "Miss, there is room here."

I lurch his way, collapse to the floor and lean against wood panels, beside the boy. "Thank you, sweetheart," I say and smile at him.

He smiles back. "I'm Samuel and this is my mama." He

points out a dark-haired woman who weeps into her handkerchief without paying me any attention. "Mama is sad because bad soldiers killed Papa last week." His expression drops and now tears gleam in his eyes.

I put my hand on his arm. "I'm so sorry. You must be strong for your mama."

"She only has me now and I have to take care of her. I promised Papa I would."

His mother hears his speech, and she pats his back and places a kiss on his forehead. "You're my everything."

The chaos inside continues, but soon the train makes chugging sounds, and we are in motion. People chat loudly, wondering if they are taking us somewhere in France or Germany.

Any stops are rare and the tiny amounts of water and bread we receive aren't enough, even when we are finally given something. The only place where we can relieve ourselves is a hole someone has hacked in the wood of the wagon's floor. I can't even imagine doing it, but soon I have no choice.

I make friends with the boy's mother. Her name is Sara, and she looks to be around thirty with her pretty, dark-complexioned face. Her sobbing subsided the moment the train started moving, as if she realized there is nothing she can do. She has to face the future bravely for the sake of her little boy.

As days go on in the airless wagon with its sparseness of water and food, the weak and elderly drop to the floor and die.

By now we are far out of France, heading east. Everyone is lethargic and we don't talk much, to preserve what is left of our strength. Even little Samuel, who was chatting away before, now mostly keeps silent, his head resting on his mother's arm.

Whatever water or bread we get, we make sure that he has it first before we take care of our own needs.

"When we arrive at the camp, we must stay together, so I can help you with Samuel," I say to Sara.

"Thank you, my dear. You're so kind."

Her words touch me, but inside I am in such anguish. *Oh, Harry, where are you?* my heart cries. Look at all these poor children here. Why is this even happening? Imagining I am talking to my beloved helps me find the courage to face another day. To think he warned me I might not be safe crossing to Spain.

When one day we realize that we've already crossed onto Polish soil, my heart sinks. I dreamed of coming back to my land, but not in these circumstances, not as a prisoner sent to a camp. It terrifies me.

When the train stops again, this time it's at our final destination. Soldiers slide the door open and bark at us to jump out and stay on our knees. Sara and I keep Samuel between us, trying to protect him.

The ramp down from the train bristles with armed guards and huge barking dogs on chains. They shout at us in German and, even though I speak the language, now I struggle to understand a word. I feel like I'm both in a trance and deaf.

I summon all my strength and listen carefully, knowing that it's important I understand what they're screaming at us.

They order us to form rows of five while separating children from their mothers. I struggle to look at Sara, knowing she is about to face the same fate as others before us. She doesn't understand German, so she might still not realize it as she manages to stay calm, while fear covers her face.

I squeeze the little boy's hand as they smack us with sticks, urging us to move forward. One guard shouts at us to let go of Samuel.

I instinctively obey, sensing that complying with their demands is the only way we can even hope to save his and our lives.

But Sara refuses.

The guard kicks her in the abdomen, his boot making her

stumble backward, then he simply grabs Samuel's arm and pushes him away.

The child screams for his mama.

I shout out, "Be brave, Samuel, we will find you." I know he hears me because he turns his head and settles his terrified eyes on me, then he nods before the guard ushers him forward. What a brave boy.

Sara scrambles back to her feet and yells, "My child, give me back my child."

I hold her in place and whisper, "If you want him to stay alive, you must calm down. It's the only way." The world slows down as she sobs.

FORTY-THREE

BEATA

August 1943, German death camp, Brzezinka

I stand still while a woman-skeleton in a striped dress and head covering shaves my hair. Her large black eyes are sad, her skin is flaky and dry.

"Don't ask questions," she whispers gravely, "just do what they want, or they will kill you."

I suppress my tears and bite my lip, but I nod. I know she is right because a moment ago I witnessed a guard shooting a woman who refused to give away her baby. At least Sara and Samuel are still alive, as far as I know. We were separated right after they took Samuel.

I found myself along other women on our way to this barracks where right away we were ordered to strip naked. I wish this was all a bad dream, but I know better.

That monster Georg picked hell for me, just as he assured me he would. I thought there was nothing worse than being in that interrogation room with him, but how wrong I was. I wish he had tortured me to death, so I didn't have to be here.

After shaving our heads, they tattoo crude numbers on our left forearms; from now on, according to them, we are only numbers. I refuse to look at what was inked into my skin. I feel no pain, just hollowness and numbness, like I'm not a human being anymore.

My senses are brutally awakened under streams of ice-cold water in the crowded shower stall. Afterwards, we are brought into a large room where I put on a striped dress and wooden shoes. No underwear, no sign of our old clothes or belongings. I feel something crawling on my skin but before I get a chance to examine it, they bark at us to move.

It must be late because it's dark outside. We are taken to an ugly wooden barracks where the first whiff of its airless room nearly knocks me to my knees. The odor of unwashed bodies and urine, and something else I'm not able to describe, intensifies the stagnancy of hot air.

I suppress my breathing but then I feel dizzy, so I take in a gasp of the pungent stench. One, two, breathe, one, two, breathe, one two, breathe... Don't think, just do it. Numbness wraps itself around my soul again. How are people expected to live in here? The answer comes to me right away: they have no choice, just as I do not have one either.

Thanks to a dim light from candles held by women prisoners who help us settle, I can see that the barrack block is crowded by three-tier wooden beds. There must be hundreds of women in here.

I leave the lower bed to a middle-aged woman who seems fragile, while I manage to climb into the top one. I realize soon that I'm to share it with another woman who's already asleep. It feels like I've landed on a paper mattress stuffed with something uncomfortable.

The commotion of all these women in the barrack block eventually quietens down.

I'm glad the other woman isn't awake as streams of silent tears run down my cheeks. My mind is still spinning. I heard Georg telling the other German to send me east, but I didn't know it would be here. I thought he was talking about a camp in Germany.

While working in France, we heard terrible things about this place. Now, for the sake of my survival, I pray it's not as bad as they said. But it is. I knew that the moment we got to the platform and the train door opened; I knew it the moment that SS guard killed the Jewish woman. And her poor baby. My heart still shatters into a million pieces at the thought of it.

Who could be so cruel as to take children away from their mothers? There was this tall, dark-haired officer with his hands in white gloves that kept asking if there were any twins among us. I don't understand any of this. I'm unable to suppress a sob.

"Shhh," the woman next to me mumbles. "You must be strong, or you won't survive," she continues. "What's your name?"

I swallow the lump that constricts my throat. "Beata."

"I'm Halina." Her voice is softer now. "It's good you picked the top bed as down there they have to deal with rats. How did you end up here?"

"I don't know. My only *crime* is that I was caught crossing the border from France to Spain," I say, deciding to tell her the truth. I must be extremely careful to never say a word to anyone about the Enigma mission, though. If this piece of information ever reaches the Germans, they will torture me, and my friends will be in even more danger. I don't even want to think about how this could jeopardize the use of the Enigma secret in defeating Germany in this dreadful war.

"You're a political prisoner then," Halina observes. "Are you Jewish?"

"I don't think so, I mean, I'm an orphan, so I don't know. But I was raised Catholic."

"There is no indication anywhere that you have Jewish ancestors?"

"That's right."

"So, do yourself a favor and whenever someone asks you the question I just did, always answer that you are not Jewish. It will give you a higher chance of survival, though everyone's fate here is doomed." She sighs.

"There were a lot of Jewish people on the train with me," I say.

"Many transports of Jews," she murmurs, her voice even quieter now, and shaky, "they send straight to gas chambers. They strip them of their belongings and inform them that they are going to take showers. Instead of water, they release killing gas. Women, children, elderly, anyone unfit for work."

Nausea engulfs me. Do her words mean that Sara and her sweet Samuel were poisoned in this unimaginable way? I pray it's not the case. I must find them. I squeeze my eyes shut while not feeling coherent enough to talk more, but I manage to say, "I don't believe this. How can one human do this to another, to innocent children?"

She ignores my words. "So, my friend, as you see, you are the lucky one. Remember, it can always be worse, and you must do everything to stay alive. Don't think about how it's not fair here, because that can put you in your grave quicker than you think. Instead, focus on moving forward and finding a path through this hell."

She's right. I must accept I'm here. I must fight for survival. Maybe it's possible when one obeys the rules? I just have to bury my past, keep my codebreaking work secret.

Lying next to Halina with her jutting bones, I realize she is like all the women prisoners I glimpsed today: extremely gaunt and malnourished. Soon, I will be the same, but as Halina said, I'm lucky I wasn't sent to my death right away. Her words are like a bucket of cold water and make me realize once more how important is to focus on surviving the next hour, the next day. I must do it for Harry, for my homeland.

"Pray that you get assigned to work inside," Halina says after a longer moment. "The outside labor is brutal and kills even the strongest. Try to stay near me, and I will see what I can do. But sleep now."

FORTY-FOUR

BEATA

August 1943, German death camp, Brzezinka

The first gong sounds at half past four in the morning. I relieve myself in a ditch dug in the ground with a basket placed inside it. Then we receive a breakfast of watery tea that tastes like boiled hay. That's all. No food.

I feel weak. It's been two days since I last ate, and before that, all I had was a sliver of black bread here and there. But I don't have much time to think because at the sound of a second gong everyone rushes outside, so I follow.

We line up in rows of ten in a large square in front of the barracks where counting begins. I make sure to stay beside Halina. Just like me, she wears a striped dress over her gaunt body, the stubble of her black hair contrasting with her brown eyes. They must shave prisoners' hair constantly, I realize.

A stout female guard walks back and forth while the counting goes on. Her gimlet eyes travel from woman to woman and, if she doesn't like the way someone looks at her or stands, she exercises her whip on our heads with perverse delight clear on her round face. She glares at us while shouting commands to the prisoners who are supervising the counting. I learn that her name is Liesel. I'm determined to avoid looking at her at any cost.

At last, while the camp orchestra plays marches, everyone walks away to their designated working area. I wouldn't have expected to hear this music here, not in the place where innocent people are murdered. Is this a cruel joke?

I'm instructed to go with a group heading out of the camp. Halina said yesterday that those who work outside go through the hardest labor, which inevitably kills even the strongest. I swallow hard.

But as I watch in amazement, Halina leaps over to the officer who guards us and hands him a piece of paper. He scratches at his head while he reads it, but then he nods, so Halina hurries to me and pulls me by my hand.

We follow another group of women. "How did you convince him to let me go?" I ask quietly while we march.

"I showed him a written order stating that Kanada needs more workers. I found it the other day after Inga threw it away. And now it saved your life."

"Thank you," I whisper. Why is she telling me about *Kanada*? "But I don't—"

Halina cuts me off. "Let's stay silent now as they watch us like hawks. Whatever you do, do not look our guard Inga in the eyes. You will meet her soon. She is a pretty blonde on the outside, but her heart is a chunk of rotten meat. Be careful."

It turns out that Kanada is a complex of warehouses filled with the belongings of people arriving at the camp. I realize that its name is a dark joke; this Kanada is very far from the Canadian land of plenty of our Polish imaginations. Our job is to work on sorting things. Everything seems chaotic, but just the thought that Halina is here with me gives me courage.

I'm in the same group as her. We open the hems of dresses and shirts where we often find money or jewelry, or other belongings. The whole time we are closely supervised by Inga, whose blonde braids form a crown at the top of her head, and other SS guards who prowl around us. Just like Halina said, she's cruel. Whenever she doesn't like something, she hits our heads or backs with her stick. It seems like Halina is the only one not touched by her.

I do everything to work fast, so she doesn't have reason to hurt me. To my relief, at noon we get an hour break. As soon as I am given a chipped and dirty bowl and a spoon, Halina tells me to take good care of it because if I lose it, I will not get a new one.

We take our places in line to receive our share from a large pot of soup. My mouth is watering even though the aromas aren't too tempting. In this moment, I would eat anything. The emptiness in my stomach makes me feel on the verge of puking, except there is nothing to vomit with.

It turns out we are served a watery liquid with a very small amount of barley and a few tiny potato cubes. I gobble this slop right away, trying to suppress my disgust for it. At least, I tell myself, I'm able to put something in my stomach.

For the remainder of our break, we talk quietly, making sure no one can hear us.

"Since last year, they allow us to receive packages from outside and to send letters," Halina says, narrowing her eyes, "but only for non-Jews."

I do a double take before saying, "That's not fair." Then I remember how Halina warned me not to think of *fair* or *unfair* in this place. We talk in low, almost inaudible voices, and I'm afraid someone might be listening to our conversation, but it seems no one pays us attention.

She stares down at her hands. "They do much worse." She looks around and continues, "They don't allow Jewish mothers to keep their newborns." Her chin trembles. "When my cousin Teresa arrived here, she was pregnant. At the labor they took her baby boy by the legs and suffocated him in a bucket of water." A look of limitless sadness passes across her face. "Shortly after, they murdered Teresa in the gas chamber and burned her body in the crematorium."

"I'm so sorry," I whisper, and take her hand in mine.

She quickly pulls it away and looks around. "Act like we are talking about food or work."

I nod. She's right; we shouldn't bring attention to ourselves. People get punished or killed for nothing here, I learned that much on my first day.

"There is a separate block for children," she goes on. "Sometimes when I'm able to steal extra food or clothing, I take it to them."

My heart sinks. I feel speechless. That's where I need to look for Samuel. "Those poor children. I will try to help them too."

A thin smile edges her lips. "That's all we can do, keep trying. But most of all, take time to learn your whereabouts here. The weakest are treated the worst, and we women have it much harder than men."

For the rest of the day, we are busy with our dreadful work, which we finish just before the seven o'clock roll-call. This time, it is prolonged by an inaccuracy in the number of prisoners. But shortly afterwards, we receive a supper: a small piece of black bread that tastes like sawdust with a thin layer of margarine.

I look forward to washing myself, but it turns out we have to undress in the barracks and walk naked outside to the bathhouse. Just the thought of it makes my heart palpitate. What about my dignity? How can I comply with something so humiliating? The voice of reason whispers in my head that I have no choice. But, unable to even stomach the thought of it, I end up not washing tonight.

Halina tells me that I didn't miss out; there were way too many people for the available facilities, and most didn't get to do any washing before the first gong announced it was time to get back to barracks. That's it for my hygiene today. Now I understand why it smells the way it smells in this barrack block.

At nine o'clock, the final gong brings on the night silence. Once it seems like all the women are at sleep, I ask Halina more questions about Kanada.

"All the belongings stored in there were stolen from prisoners like us, but mostly they are from other Jews who were killed in the gas chambers on arrival," she whispers.

I have a heavy, cold feeling in my stomach. My hands have held clothes marked by the blood of innocent people. Touching these things is a disgrace, an act of disrespect for the memory of the murdered. But what choice do I have?

"Everything in good shape is sent to the families in Germany," she continues.

I have a bitter tang in my mouth. Do people suspect where all these things come from? Doesn't it make them wonder that for them to receive these items, they must be taken away from others? To be more precise—they are taken from the innocent, dead victims of Hitler's sick ideology. Nausea grips my body.

"What has happened to this world?" I whisper.

On Sunday, I go to the secret market, as it's our only day free from work. The market gathers in the far back of the camp, and it's where people trade things. For one set of cashmere gloves that I smuggled out from the Kanada warehouses, I get a nice-sized chunk of bread.

I hide it under my shirt and head toward the children's barrack block in the hope of spotting Samuel. Two days ago, I saw Sara in the walking cordon of women led by SS guards. She must be living in one of the barracks assigned to Jews. I hope to be able to talk to her one day.

My entire life, I thought that fate had dealt me the worst possible hand the moment my mother abandoned me. But now, I understand how wrong and selfish my thinking was. I always had food, clothes, and most of all, enough dignity to survive. I even found a way to learn different languages, and at the age of eighteen, I went out, with complete freedom, into the world.

As I watch the children in this miserable, filthy, lice-infested barracks, I feel like someone is ripping my heart out of my chest. Who gave humans the right to put these precious children through this? The reality of them having only the slightest chance of survival hits me like a sledgehammer. They don't even have the basics necessities for life. They are neglected, malnourished and forced to exist under the cruel eyes of monsters.

To my relief, I spot Samuel who sits in a corner, his eyes glassy. He looks so lonely.

"Samuel," I say, a lump in my throat.

When he lifts his head and our eyes meet, an instant smile comes to his face.

I jump to him and pull him into my embrace. "Oh, Samuel, my dearest, I'm so glad to see you here." After Halina's words the other day, I knew that if I didn't find him here, he'd most likely been sent to the gas chamber.

"I'm happy to see you too."

"How are you?" I look around. So many children lie on beds, staring into thin air. Their faces are skinny and fatigued.

"It's not that bad," he says and folds his lips into a faint smile.

"You must carry on being brave and do what they tell you. Try not to catch the guards' eyes, always mix with other children. Can you promise me you'll do this?"

He nods. "I promise."

"I know it's hard to understand and I know how unfair it is

that you're here without your mama but try to think of this as a special challenge."

His large eyes brighten. "Yes, Mama told me that. She promised to visit as often she can. She said it's just a game and that when I'm hungry, I need to think of home and remember my toys, and when Papa took me to the zoo."

So, Sara was able to come here and reassure her little boy. This news is such a light in the darkness. It brings me hope that if we support each other, we can survive the worst.

I take the chunk of bread I've brought with me and put it in his hand. "Your mama is right. You can do this, sweetheart. I believe in you. I will come every Sunday too, I promise."

FORTY-FIVE

HARRY

December 1943, Spain

I follow him as he walks home from the local bar, and when I'm sure that no one can see us, I grab his arm and push him inside a narrow passage between two stone tenements. I sense his initial shock, but he quickly recovers and tries to wriggle himself out from my grasp. I give him no chance. Fury fuels my strength.

Once I have him pressed against the wall, I touch the blade of my knife to his neck. I quieten my heavy breathing and say, "You thought I would never find you, huh?" I make sure my voice carries enough violence to scare the hell out of him. "Big mistake, José."

"What do you want from me?" He looks me in the eye, as if he's genuinely confused about what I could in fact need from him.

"I told you I would kill you if you betrayed me." I press the knife harder to his skin, causing its blade to release the first droplets of his blood. He needs to realize that I'm not joking around here. "Where is my friend? Tell me now or soon you will bleed to death."

His bulging eyes tell me I've convinced him about my intentions here. "I will tell you everything, but please don't kill me," he begs. "I have little children at home."

"I'm listening," I say without flinching. "You have two minutes."

When I move the knife away from him, he swallows and says, "I don't know where she is."

I press the blade to his neck again.

"All right, all right."

Tears show in his eyes. What an actor.

"The Germans arrested us in the Pyrenees, not far from the border. They took us to the prison in Le Boulou. And I never saw your friend again. I swear on my mother's life."

"Then why are you here while there is no sign of her?"

"I have no idea. All I know is that I got released days later. I told them some lies, that's all I did. I thought the same thing happened to her. I had no way of finding you."

I look at the sheen of sweat covering his face. "You aren't telling me something. What is it?" I intensify the blade's pressure, allowing it to pierce his skin. "My patience is running out."

"I don't know." His entire body trembles. "But I heard that they're sending people on cattle trains to labor camps in the east. Maybe your friend was put on one."

FORTY-SIX

BEATA

December 1943, German death camp, Brzezinka

Winter this year is so brutal that people would give everything for extra layers of clothing. I know that a lot of women who work at Kanada, trade stolen goods for bread, just like Halina and I do. Whenever there is an opportunity, they also hide pieces of fabric under their dresses. Some manage to smuggle out bigger things like shoes or sweaters, but one needs real bravery and luck to do that.

A few weeks ago, Inga caught one woman trying just that and she subjected her to the most terrible beatings. We had to watch Inga battering her entire body—until she lost consciousness. Then, the same day during the evening roll-call, the poor woman was flogged over a stool. She died a few days later in the camp's primitive hospital.

Afterwards, no one attempted any more stealing for a while, but slowly things went back to our previous routine. People have to survive, and that requires taking risks. Still, we're much more careful now.

And I don't risk trying to smuggle bigger things anymore. I

hide only underwear, slips or thin scarves. These fabrics are in high demand because they aren't given to us at all. We want to keep our dignity, so we wash whenever possible, and we try to have the basic things. Often, they come at the cost of food, which is already in such short supply.

I think often of my beloved Harry. Will I ever see him again? Does he know I'm stuck in this hell? He's always on my mind when I fall asleep and when I wake up in the morning. Always. I wish I had a way to write to him, but I don't even know his address in England. And I guess he's probably still on his mission in France.

Plus, a letter to him could lead the Germans to realize that I was involved with the Cipher Bureau. After all, my work there started in 1932 and continued for so many years. And now with Germans ruling our country, they might know more than we think. And so, I adhere to the same advice I gave Samuel and make sure to sink into the crowds of humanity that fill this place. I give all my strength to my allocated labor, so Inga doesn't ever have reason to seek me out.

Even Halina doesn't know about my past. It's safer for her that she doesn't. I told her about my love for Harry but mentioned nothing about Bletchley Park or his spying activities.

The only thing that stops me from losing my mind, or throwing myself at the electrified barbed wire fence, is the thought of seeing him again. This gives me the strength I need to go on.

One morning we are given an unusual instruction. We are to undress and go naked to the field outside of the camp.

It's only four o'clock, so it's still dark when we line up on the field. A mixture of rain and snow is falling down on our shivering bodies while Liesel informs us that we are here because they are sanitizing our clothes to rid them of lice.

I want to yell in her face that there are less drastic ways of doing it, that we don't have to stand in the cold like this. But I bite my tongue, remembering what's happened to others who speak out. I don't want to share their fate, so I must comply.

After hours of shivering, I realize that it's their way of getting rid of the weaker ones among us. More and more women are collapsing, and we can't do anything. The SS guards, dressed in their warm coats, make mocking faces at us while sharing obscene jokes.

They treat us worse than animals. So many times, I've spotted Liesel stroking her dog with affection, straight after beating someone to death. Nausea churns in my stomach at the thought of her ferocity.

Exhausted, I don't care about the German soldiers ogling my naked body. I fight to keep myself up on my feet, so I can stay alive. The temperatures must be close to zero, but I know that today's weather is mild compared to yesterday's. Still, I struggle to stop shivering as I slowly sway to one side. But someone's hand grabs mine. It's Halina. Her raw gesture renews my strength. She is trying to survive this misery. I should too, for Harry.

The moment Liesel turns our way, our hands drop. That woman would beat us to death with her whip if she saw that connection between us.

I don't know what time it is, but it must be hours since we first came here. My vision is blurry while every muscle in my body is numb. It costs me my entire strength not to sway. Whenever Liesel notices someone losing strength, she leaps up and smacks them in the face. Usually, that act of violence drops the poor woman to her feet, and then to death.

Concentrating on keeping my body still, I forget to be angry at that sadistic German woman. It's as if what she does to us is normal and we are simply performing our regular duties. It's like all of this is normal. As I absorb that, I refuse to let my mind waver. Not even a bit—my body's strength relies on my mind.

Only when it's turning dark do they order our return to barracks.

I'm afraid that my wooden legs will fail me, but I'm somehow able to walk slowly. Someone from above must be watching over me. I think of my Felka. She is here with me; I believe it with my whole heart. How else would I be able to endure such cruelty?

As we set on the walk back in our rows of four, my heart weeps for all the women left behind. They didn't have enough strength to survive this brutality. Their suffering came to an end out in that frozen field of death.

When we get our clothes back, they are still infested with lice. Whatever they did to them didn't work. I doubt they performed anything today besides killing so many of us and plummeting the rest into even deeper misery.

The night after that, Halina whispers to me about the resistance movement in the camp. I'm stunned to learn that one exists in such a place. She talks about her boyfriend being involved in it and how a man named Witold started it. He was able to escape in April, but during the time he was here, he gave hope to so many.

"One day, we will run away from here too," she whispers with a yawn.

I want to hear more, but soon she drifts to sleep, and I don't blame her. After the inhuman labor we carry out here, it's hard to function on any level, and the few hours of sleep we can seize are our only restoration.

FORTY-SEVEN

HARRY

December 1943, London

Dearest Mother,

Leon was able to find out that Beata was sent to the German labor camp in southern Poland. I can't contain the pain in my heart, Mother. Why my Beata? It's all my fault. I will not stop until she's free. Please watch over her.

The things I've been hearing about the camp are not good. There's a report by a Polish officer, Witold Pilecki, who intentionally let the Germans arrest him, and he ended up in the camp where Beata is now. He remained there until April this year, when he successfully escaped.

In his report, Pilecki writes about people being murdered by poisoning in gas chambers, their bodies burned in crematoriums; German medics performing inhuman experiments; people dead of starvation, typhus... There are so many more details that I find them hard to put down on paper.

He also describes the hunger as the hardest battle of his life.

He shared the report with the world, but many refuse to believe it.

I believe him, Mother, which is why my heart bleeds every day. If only there was a way of getting my Beata out from that hell. I tried convincing my chiefs to send me on a mission to Poland, but to no avail. They say it might be possible after the war ends, to assess the situation there, but not before.

If only I could speak Polish without an accent or speak German at all, then I'd find a way of going there and posing as a prisoner or guard. Instead, my hands are tied, so all I can do is pray every day for her strength. She must survive this.

I hope she remembers how much I love her. I hope she knows I can't go on without her. Mother, I need her.

The war situation changes every day. I just hope it's not too late when it all ends.

I'm back in London, so I've sent her a letter. I asked my Polish friend to translate it for me. It will be delivered to his relatives in Poland, and they're going to send it to Beata.

I realize that every letter is surely being censored by the Germans, so I was very neutral in it. I just want her to know that I think of her and that I'm waiting. I asked her to write back to me at the address in Poland, and from there it will eventually reach me.

I made sure that I stay incognito as if they somehow connected her with me, she would be in an even grimmer situation because of her involvement with the Polish Cipher Bureau. I know it's a far stretch, but one never knows, and it's wise to be extremely cautious.

I also gave my friend money and asked if his family can send her packages. He said he will see what they can do.

Oh, Mother, I need to find a way of going there. I'm thinking of her every day and doing what I can to reunite with her. There is not a second when she is not on my mind. I would *give everything to hold her in my arms, to hear her beautiful voice.*

Yours,

Harry

FORTY-EIGHT

BEATA

December 1943, German death camp, Brzezinka

Christmas Eve is as busy as any other day, with more belongings being added to Kanada storage each day. With every transport that arrives, I feel like another piece of my heart dies. Still, I perform my duties in hope of survival.

By now, I've lost so much weight due to the meagre food rations we receive, and I don't have anyone outside to send me food packages.

The women living in our barracks are mostly Polish, but only a few are Jewish. The blocks across from us are occupied by Jewish women and, from what Halina tells me, their conditions are ten times worse than ours. They sleep five on one bed. I can't even imagine it. My heart goes out to Sara. We're able to exchange a few words here and there. I continue to visit Samuel every Sunday and I know that Sara goes to her beloved child whenever she can.

I try to bring some food to the other children too, but my offerings are like trying to stem a flood with your thumb. I'm not able to get much from what I sell at the camp's black market.

I'm glad, though, that Halina has it a little easier than most of the other Jews in the camp. I suspect it's because of our guard Inga. A while back, Inga used Halina to steal some diamond rings that Halina found in the hem of a wool coat, and because of that, the guard has a lighter hand when it comes to her.

In the evening, we receive a small ration of black bread, thinly layered with beet marmalade. After the first gong that prompts us to stay inside, almost all the Polish women decide to celebrate Christmas. At home, we would have a traditional Christmas Eve supper that consists of twelve meat-free dishes, like mushroom soup, stuffed carp, pierogi, piernik gingerbread... my mouth waters at the memories. We would share an unleavened wafer with our families and friends, while giving our best wishes to each other.

Here we have no beautifully prepared dishes or wafers, but to feel at least a hint of normalcy, we share our bread rations and gift each other with uplifting words.

We wish one another health and happiness, even though in this situation our words seem cruel. But we want to feel the same way we did every year on Christmas Eve when we were at home. These brief minutes of pretending aren't going to hurt, despite the tears in our eyes.

Someone begins to sing "Silent Night," in a low, shy voice. I clear my constricted throat and join in, and the tears run freely down my cheeks.

"Silent night, holy night
All is calm, all is bright."

As we continue, our voices grow stronger and stronger, so the guards outside must definitely hear us. They could shoot all of us, if they chose. I tremble at the thought of it, but then I chime in again.

"Silence," a voice barks out in German. "Unless you want to sing in German." Then the same male voice belts out, *"Stille Nacht, heilige Nacht,"* followed by a shaggy, drunken laugh.

A bitter tang settles in my mouth. I don't want to contemplate how much I hate them.

I look for stars through the gaps between the barracks' wooden boards. According to Polish tradition, we only begin our Christmas Eve dinner after spotting the first star in the night sky. I didn't get a chance to do it before we shared our bread.

To my astonishment, instead of a star, I see someone crawling on the ground from the Jewish women's barracks toward the electric barbed wire fence. Lately, there have been more and more episodes in which the desperate attempt suicide by throwing themselves on the fence. It's an immediate death. Whenever the guards notice in time, they shoot at those people, because they think that dying like this is too easy.

Does this person intend to do the same? My gut is telling me that I'm right and my heart is telling me that I must do something, while my mind orders me to stay inside. It's a huge risk because right now we are forbidden to leave our barracks. I could be shot on the spot.

I make my decision in the way I usually do when I'm under overwhelming stress—I cease thinking and let my heart do its job. I quietly slip out. I make sure no one notices me, especially Halina because she would attempt to stop me.

Guards are talking nearby, but thankfully they are behind the other barrack block, although I can smell the smoke from their cigarettes. I edge in the shadows of the wooden buildings in the direction of the crawling woman. When I get to her, she is already crossing a gate.

I touch her arm, making her flinch, but she is wise enough to keep quiet, her dark eyes peering at me in the pale moonlight reflecting the snow on the ground. Her hand is icy.

"Don't do it," I whisper, my voice gentle. "Go back to the barracks and try to survive. One day, this misery must end, I promise."

"I can't do it," she whispers back hoarsely, "I can't go on." She chokes. "I want to die."

"You won't make it to that fence before they shoot you. Guards watch from the tower; their eyes are everywhere."

"Let them shoot me. I don't deserve to live."

We are hidden in the shade of a gate, so as long as the guards don't walk this way, we still have some time. "You do, we all do," I urge. "One day we will go back to our old lives. You must find strength in your heart to keep fighting. Don't let those monsters break you."

"You don't understand," she sobs, "I committed the worst sin possible." She wipes away tears with her trembling hand. "When we arrived, they took away my daughter. I let them do it, I didn't fight for her even though she cried and called for me." Her voice is empty. "I didn't fight to keep her with me. Yesterday, I found out that she died in the gas chamber." Her voice breaks. "My precious little girl trusted me. I was her entire world, and she was my... my only child... I have nothing now. I have no future to look forward to."

"I'm so sorry." I gently squeeze her hand. "Still, you must go on. You had no choice. If you'd said something to those SS men, they would have shot you both. I witnessed such a thing when I arrived here. The woman only asked not to be separated from her baby and she was murdered a moment later. You could not have known your daughter's fate when they took her away from you, because what they do is unthinkable."

She sobs. "Why did God do this to me?" she almost wails. "Why did he take the life of my precious baby, of so many precious babies?" Her sobs intensify, making me nervous that the guards will hear us. "Why?"

I don't have any answers for her. Every night I ask myself the same questions. I could tell her that God gave us humans free will, and whatever we create on this earth is our choice, not His. I could tell her that if all people had God and love in their hearts, then wars would not happen. I could, but I will not. Not now, anyway. Her heart is broken and right now there are no words that could heal her pain.

Instead, I hug and rock her. "Shhh... It will all be okay," I whisper in her ear. "Your little sweetheart is in God's arms now. She is happier than you think. All you need to do is be strong for her. One day you will notice some signs. She will come through for you because she knows how much you suffer. She knows your love for her."

I listen for any movement but there is only silence.

"For now, remember that the love between both of you isn't lost. There is more to it than what's here. Her earthly body died, but her spirit and soul live on. Take comfort in it. You need that comfort now more than ever, so you can survive this and keep the memories of your daughter alive."

My quiet words convince her to abandon her plan and so she carefully crawls back to her barrack block, and I slip to mine. I promise to visit her on Sunday, after our chores.

For the first half of the night, I can't sleep for thinking of her and this death-drenched place we find ourselves in. I don't blame her for almost giving up. Would I be able to go on if I couldn't save my child from such a brutal, lonely end to their short life?

FORTY-NINE

BEATA

March 1944, German death camp, Brzezinka

Late one evening, I receive a letter and a package. I can't believe my eyes and wonder if it's from Joanna.

Halina was very tired today, so she's already asleep on her side of the bed. I reach for the envelope from under the mattress with my trembling hands. It has already been opened, of course, for censorship.

I hope Joanna knew not to write anything sensitive here, especially when it comes to my work for the Cipher Bureau; though, as I tell myself, it's not like she knows much anyway. But sometimes one word is enough to activate a chain of suspicions that culminates in action. I must avoid this at all costs.

Well, the rational part of me says, if there was something in this letter to spark their attention, I would be arrested by now.

At last, after so much mental turmoil, I start to read.

Moja Ukochana,

There is not a day or night when I don't think or dream of you.
My work on the farm is hard but it brings a lot of satisfaction. It
starts in the morning and ends at night, but I will do everything
to continue, and to find a way to get it done.

I love you, my darling. Please take good care of yourself
because you're my everything. My sun, my moon, my heart.

Please write to let me know how well you're doing.

Yours forever,

H.

I can't believe this letter is from Harry and that he knows
I'm here. I touch the first words: *Moja Ukochana. My Darling.*
It's a very vague letter, but that's because of the censors. Harry
is smart. The work on the farm means his mission. He wanted
to let me know that he knows I'm here and that he loves me, and
most of all, that he's fine. He would do everything to get me out
of here, if he only could. I don't doubt that.

My Harry is alive. He still loves me. Now I know that all my
perseverance wasn't for nothing. One day I will see him again,
feel his touch, hear his warm voice.

There is an address on the envelope, an address in Poland.
Surely, Harry isn't here, I think. It must be that he found
someone to send it to me. But how did he manage to get the
letter to these people?

I wish I could write back to him, but I have neither paper
nor pencil.

The moment I open the package, a strong whiff of *kielbasa*
fills the air and makes my mouth water. I close my eyes and
inhale it even more.

I shake Halina's arm. "Look what I have." I bring it closer to
her face.

The smell awakens her in seconds. "Where have you got this from?" she whispers with disbelief in her eyes.

"I received a package from Harry. Shhh," I tell her as I break off pieces of the precious sausage, and we both chew the *kielbasa* with tears in our eyes. It tastes so wonderful despite its dryness, which indicates that this package was on its way here for a very long time. The delicious smell awakens some of the women around us, and I pass pieces to them, making sure to put away some for Samuel as well.

The rest of the package consists of biscuits, two oranges, sugar cubes, a bar of chamomile soap wrapped in a small towel, and other treasured items.

I hide the soap and towel under my mattress, planning to exchange it later for paper and pencil, and the rest I resolve to take to the children's barrack block.

That night I fall asleep knowing my Harry is waiting for me. One day, I will feel his lips on mine again and our tears will mingle in a dance of happiness. One day, I will be safe again in his arms.

Since my first day working at the Kanada warehouses, I've been keeping a low profile and working hard. So far it has kept me out of trouble and out of sight of the guards.

But then, one morning, our guard Inga arrives late for her shift, and she appears to be in an extremely bad mood.

"Why are you working on this pile when there are plenty of unfinished piles from yesterday?" Inga shouts at Halina. This is so unusual that everyone stops and watches the scene. This is the first time we have seen Inga confront Halina in such manner.

My friend only understands a few words of German, but

she tries to explain her reasons in Polish while pointing at the clothes.

Instead of calming Inga down, her behavior has the opposite effect. Next thing, Inga is shouting at poor Halina that if she doesn't find a way to explain this issue to her, she will be severely punished.

I detect a hint of amusement in the guard's face; it's as if she takes pleasure from the fact that Halina can't defend herself. She lifts her hand with her stick and Halina's face flinches.

I must help my friend, even at the risk of my own life. "She's saying that the morning guard ordered us to attend to this pile first, so we're only obeying orders," I say in German, expecting Inga to turn on me and beat me up. But I had to speak up for my friend.

As she swirls around and settles her pale blue eyes on me, her livid expression softens. "Tell her that I understand that now and to continue as ordered," she says, not taking her gaze from me.

As we resume our duties, Halina looks at me with gratitude while my hands still shake from the confrontation. We all know how this could have played out; much more trivial issues have taken people's lives.

After lunch, Inga nears me. "Your German is fluent."

With a dropping sensation in my stomach, I nod and continue my unstitching task, hoping she leaves me alone. This woman's inhuman behavior scares me to death.

"Why did you keep it a secret?" She curls her lip.

Without betraying any emotion, I say in a quiet voice, "I'm trying to do my duties here the best I can. I didn't think my German speaking skills would be useful."

"You Poles are so primitive." She sneers a hard smile. "But I shouldn't be surprised. We're here to teach your barbaric nation some civility." She pokes my arm with her stick. "Look at me when I talk to you."

I put down the elegant dress I'm working on and lift my gaze to her face. "Yes," I say, ignoring the tightness in my gut.

"People with your skills can be more useful than this general labor. Soon you will get a new work assignment."

True to her word, the next day I'm sent to a new workplace. It's in the canteen for the SS guards.

My duties start in the kitchen, where I help prepare meals by peeling potatoes or doing various other menial tasks. Then, I'm one of the twenty waitresses serving food to the SS men in their canteen. Afterwards, we clean up and do the dishes. This job is so much easier. It requires so much less labor, is less heart-wrenching, and there is no one here like Inga to watch my every move.

But serving them weighs heavy on my conscience. They kill; I know their brutality has no boundaries. These men and women belong on trial, they belong in prison awaiting the death sentence for their crimes.

If I had enough power in my hands, I would make them suffer the pain they inflict on innocent people. Instead, I crinkle a smile every time I serve them and act like I'm happy to be here.

Where is the outside world? Why don't the world's powerful leaders gather and send their troops to end this hell on earth? It's hard to believe that they don't know the extent of what is being committed here. Until the middle of 1942, this camp held mainly Poles like me, here because of their activities against the Nazi regime, but now it's a place of mass murder.

We don't eat the food we prepare for them, instead we receive the same awful watery broth as other prisoners. Some girls join the SS men during their meals when invited, but I'm in the group that stays away. I would never eat with any of them. I would rather gladly consume the tasteless liquid from that dirty pot. It sits better with me, even though every spoonful makes me feel truly nauseated.

One day, away from my serving duties, I sit outside eating my food ration. This time the broth consists of boiled nettles, and I am bemused by its punchy flavor.

"That doesn't look too appetizing," a sharp but familiar voice in German says.

I drop my spoon.

Freezing shivers run down my spine.

What is Georg doing here? There is no trace of anger in his voice nor is there a weapon in his hand. Why is he talking to me?

I clear my throat, trying to appear natural. "It's very good," I say, unsure how to react to his unexpected presence.

"I don't believe it," he says, his teeth glinting white as he gazes down on me, a hint of amusement in his eyes.

I can't believe he is talking with me openly like this, not showing any sign of recognition, like he's conversing with a stranger.

I follow suit and wonder if I should just get up and excuse myself, but then I would have to go back to the canteen while I still have another fifteen minutes of break. I decide to stay, "There is delicious food in the canteen today," I say, hoping he just leaves.

Instead of eagerly rushing to fill his stomach, he laughs lazily. "Are you trying to get rid of me?" His eyes probe into mine, as if assessing whether what he's just said is in fact true.

Now he sounds more like he did back in France. "I enjoy chatting with you," I say and crinkle a smile, while disgust coils up in my core for acting like I'm flirting with this monster.

He nods and says, "Well, I'm looking forward to seeing you inside the canteen, Beata." He narrows his eyebrows in satisfaction at knowing my real name.

Unable to stop myself, I recite the number that is inked into my skin. "We are only numbers here." I hope this will stop him from acting like we're both happily living our normal lives. Though, when comes to this man, I'm confused.

His behavior in the Gestapo headquarters was so weird. He didn't touch me, didn't lay so much as a finger on me, through those days of interrogation. And now he's here, right before me, conversing lightly and laughing as if he's been reunited with his dearest friend. I don't understand this at all.

He gives me a mocking smile, while his eyes twinkle, then he marches away.

I realize that I've forgotten to breathe.

Maybe there is more to it than I think and he's on some sort of mission. Maybe the Germans know I was involved with the Cipher Bureau and that's why he took the approach he took in France and now here.

But I soon disregard that possibility. If that was the case, they wouldn't send me to this camp. Instead, they'd have kept me in France and tried to make me talk and betray my friends and country. Still, I should be careful, especially with Georg. If he suspects something, he will use his sneaky ways to doom me.

If he only knew that I was involved in solving their precious Enigma secret, he wouldn't play his gentle games with me. There is no way, I reassure myself, that he knows about the Enigma mission. That secret has been kept very well, and I will not change this. I would rather die.

That evening, right after supper, two Polish men come over to repair some beds in our barracks. One of them is Antek, Halina's lover. They knew each other even before the war, then met again in this camp, in such terrible circumstances.

While the men work, Halina and others encircle them, but they restrict their talk to silly subjects. There are ears everywhere around us, and some people would earn a chunk of bread by ratting on others.

I already know from Halina that Antek belongs to the secret Resistance movement in the camp. They're planning an escape, but I don't know any details. Halina said that I will learn more when the right time comes.

I can't even imagine how dangerous it is to form any sort of Resistance here, where the most trivial thing can put you into the hands of death.

Back in France, I was always in awe of the French Resistance. Here, it's like being in the mouth of the lion. I don't know if I would have enough courage to be part of the escape Halina mentioned to me. She, though, is determined to accompany her lover. That's how she is—strong and unstoppable when she sets her mind to something.

I wonder if Harry would want me to take the risk and try to escape when the opportunity arises, or if he would rather I stay here and do everything to survive. I wish I knew. I miss him so much that every night I dream of meeting him in England. It's where we planned to reunite once his mission in France ended. Then cruel fate decided another path for us. Now I feel like we've been denied the chance for our love to ever bloom.

The next day, I am at work as always in the canteen when Georg stops on his way out the building, and hands me a sweet roll.

This gesture is so surprising that I give it back to him, worrying that it's a sort of test. I've seen it happen so many times—prisoners are wrongly accused of stealing food and punished later.

Instead of walking away, he leans in and whispers, "Don't worry, Beata. I expect nothing in return. You remind me of my sister. That's why I'm doing it." He places the sweet roll into my pocket and marches away.

From that moment on, never again do I reject his *gifts*. I take them all to little Samuel. Georg's acts of kindness bring a smile to the boy's trusting face.

FIFTY

BEATA

June 1944, German death camp, Brzezinka

One day, the cook designates me to stay longer to deliver a supper to one of the commanders. I can only imagine he is one of those in charge of the guards patrolling the camp's perimeter fences.

I comply, knowing that any questions would only lead to painful beatings with a stick or whip, or some other weapon.

I'm escorted from the canteen by two guards who lead me to a black car. I get inside while holding the food basket for the commander in my shaking hands. This is all so awkward that I hope that none of my fellow inmates notices me.

The car passes the camp gates and cruises along a dirt road for a few minutes. Then it halts in front of a two-story modern villa.

I can't stop my heart palpitating as one of the guards opens the car door and shouts, "*Raus,* you Polish slut."

I'm out in no time and edging my way toward the villa's stone steps. The whole time, I have this empty feeling in the pit of my stomach. Why me?

Before I get a chance to knock, the door swings wide open and a stout lady in a white apron appears. "You must be that girl the commander sent for," she says in German; her sour expression only makes her wrinkles sharper.

I clear my throat and reach out with the basket toward her. "I'm only bringing supper." I want to hand it to her and leave as soon as possible. This woman doesn't stir good feelings in me at all, nor does this forbidding house.

But instead, she steps aside and gestures for me to walk inside.

I swallow hard but obey. The house smells of vanilla and cinnamon. My mouth waters, but I suppress my stomach so as not to make any noise. Because of this escapade, I will surely miss out on my supper portion of black bread. Which isn't good, as lately, I've been feeling weaker and weaker.

The woman closes the door behind me and takes basket from my hands. "We don't want lice here, so you must immediately wash yourself. Follow me."

"I don't understand," I mumble as I wipe at my mouth.

"You're not here to ask questions, but to do as you are told." The arrogant tone of her voice is final. "Unless you don't care about your own life."

She leads me to a bathroom and orders me to take a quick shower. "You've fifteen minutes, and not a second longer," she says and points her finger at me. "Understood?"

I scrub the dirt of the camp from my body, then put on the light blue summer dress that she left.

I don't understand any of this, but I just want it to be over with. Nothing can be worse than the camp, where every minute might be my last one.

The woman is waiting outside the door. When I come out, she takes me in with her scrutinizing gaze. "I don't know what he sees in you but I'm not the one to make decisions here. Follow me."

She leads me to an elegant family room with high ceilings and burgundy furniture. The white-clothed table is set for two, but there is no one here.

"Take a seat," she says in a sharp tone. "On this side." She points to the left. "Commander should be back soon."

I yearn to shout at her that I don't understand what is happening here, but it would be pointless. This harsh woman doesn't want to hear anything from me.

"Don't think about running away either," she instructs. "There are guards everywhere."

When I'm alone, I still don't move. My eyes devour the schnitzel and mashed potatoes and green salad, but my mouth stays shut. Whatever this means, it's certainly nothing good.

I hear steps on the wooden floor and swallow hard. My heart stops for a split second.

FIFTY-ONE

BEATA

June 1944, German death camp, Brzezinka

"I'm glad to see you here, darling," Georg says, his lips folding in a sarcastic smile.

My mouth goes dry and my words stick in my throat.

He looks wickedly handsome in a tailor-made suit that complements his athletic physique. His blond locks are freshly combed and the smell of his cologne with its notes of sage is tantalizing. Without the Nazi uniform, he is an attractive man. Of course, that's only if I didn't know about him what I do.

His pale blue eyes take me in. "I know, I know, you're surprised to see me." He tilts a chair out and settles in, opposite me. "You avoided me in the canteen. I was invisible to you even when I kept gifting you with little treats." He lifts a bottle from the table. "Wine?"

I nod, not knowing what else to do. Does he want me to pay for the food he has given me? If not, why this circus?

He fills two glasses and lifts his. "Cheers to our meeting."

I take a sip and summon my courage to ask, "Why am I here?"

He motions to the table. "I bet you're starving. Please dig in."

I don't wait for another invite and devour a schnitzel and some potatoes. If he plans to kill me, at least I will die with a full stomach.

He examines me the whole time with his all-knowing eyes, like he is the ruler of life and death. "That day when I saw you in that little café, I knew you were special. How angry I was when you didn't show up for our date. I tried looking for you everywhere, until I saw you again in the street." He stares at my short, almost cut to the skin hair. "And you were so scared to see me that I let you go. My gut told me that it wasn't the last time I would see you."

"Why are you telling me this?" I ask. "And what am I doing here?"

He keeps ignoring my questions. "And then they brought you to the prison for interrogation. I wasn't going to hurt you. I found a way to convince them not to murder you but to send you here. That's all I could do for you."

"Thank you," I say quietly, despite the alarm tingling inside me. Is he going to hurt me?

He seems pleased by my response. "Then I saw you in the camp's canteen."

"What do you want?" My voice is shaky.

He leans back in his chair and takes an appreciative sip from his glass. "When I saw you again, I decided that we're destined for each other. How else you can explain fate putting us together in the same places? I went to the camp's commandant and called in a favor he owed me for saving his life."

I'm too afraid to ask what exactly he intends to do with me. If he has the commandant's blessing, he's free to do as he pleases. "Let me free then."

He shakes his head. "I have quite different plans. As I mentioned before, fate keeps putting you my way, so I'm going to take this as a good sign. You have a lot to offer." He watches me for a moment longer, before continuing. "You're a beautiful woman. With good nourishment, you will gain your weight back and your stunning hair will grow again. Your skin will turn healthy."

"What's your plan?" I ask, hoping for this farce to end soon. One part of me screams to run far away from this man, while the other part reasons that such an action would earn me a bullet in my back.

"I dream of nothing but coming home to a bed warmed by you. We're destined for each other, and we can both benefit from such arrangement," he says, drilling his sparkling gaze into me as if expecting to find delight.

My mouth goes dry. "Is this an offer?" My mind is foggy right now thanks to the merest sip of wine and the presence and words of this intimidating man.

"Yes, indeed. Though, please be assured, your body isn't all I want. I yearn for your soul too. I want you whole."

As I sit across from this man and listen to how he wants to possess every aspect of me, my clarity of thought slowly comes back. He wants the impossible, something that is not worth the sacrifice even if it costs me my life. The murders he committed of the innocent women in the prison in France and his function as a commander in the camp tell me all about his lack of humanity, yet he wants to mix me in this *dirt* too.

I say in a cold tone, "Everything about you disgusts me. I'd rather die than let you touch me in the way you want."

His eyebrows narrow and his lips form a thin line.

I ignore his hostile expression. "So you either hurt me," I say, "or let me go back to the camp."

His jawline tightens and it's clear he's fighting for control. "What makes you think you can reject me like this?" Gone is his composed voice from a moment ago. "Who do you think you are?"

"In this place, I'm just a number," I say quietly.

"The hell you are." He smashes his fist into the table causing plates to clatter while his wine glass hits the floor and shatters.

It feels like every sharp particle of that glass penetrates my heart. This man just exposed his true nature—that of a Nazi slaughterer.

His face is as red as his wine, but he says in a calm voice, "I'm only trying to help you. If you don't stay in this home of mine, you will rot to death in that camp. Look at yourself"—he takes in my figure from head to toe—"you are like a skeleton. How long do you think you can go on until typhus or some other sickness eats the life out of you?"

He gets up and paces back and forth.

"I'm offering you luxury, care, tenderness. I will nourish you back to health and to the way you were before you ended up here. Please, accept my kindness. One day you will grow to love me. The true and powerful feeling doesn't come right away, you must earn it, and most of all, deserve it."

As I listen to his pathetic speech, I can't help but wonder if he's insane or if he's playing some cruel game at my expense. "Why me, Georg?"

He returns to lean back in his chair. "I remember you from Perpignan as pretty and confident. But I also sensed right from the beginning that your true beauty is inside you. Your eyes told me this at our first encounter. Since then, you intrigue me to the point that I can't stop thinking of you."

He might be insane, but I must not make him angry with harsh words anymore. I've noticed that kind words drive him into a softer place, while harshness makes him lose his temper. Even so, I truly don't understand why he's so fixated on me.

I change my approach. "I apologize for my disrespectful words from before. I liked you right from the beginning too," I say, averting my gaze. I'm not such a good liar, so I'm afraid he will read me. "You're handsome and kind, and if only my heart didn't belong to another man, I would be thrilled with your offer, with your willingness to save me from the camp."

What I really want to tell him is that he is a blood-soaked murderer. I want to spit in his face.

My softness does its job; this time he stays composed. "What's the use of loving another man if you won't survive long enough to see him again?" His tense, low voice fills the room with an uncomfortable eeriness.

I decide to play it a little differently with him, since he seemingly cares to be viewed as *my kind protector*. "Is there anyone there waiting for you in Germany?" I ask gently.

"I have a wife and four children," he says without a wince.

What a skunk. "Do you love your wife? Do you adore your children?"

"Of course I do. What kind of question is that?" He seems genuinely upset by my inquiry.

"What would you feel if someone poisoned your children in a gas chamber?" I pause, but of course he doesn't reply. "Let me assure you that the pain would be unbearable."

He seems deep in thought, his face like an iron, watching me with his eyes reflecting disgust.

I go on, "How would you feel if your wife was forced into hard labor while men who believe they are the rulers of life and death used her body in exchange for the mere hope of survival?"

"Enough," he says with finality, as he gets up. "Go back to where you belong and don't ever dream of another chance. You're dead to me."

FIFTY-TWO

BEATA

August 1944, German death camp, Brzezinka

I use all my strength to pick up a large stone and place it in the wooden cart. I continue to wade through the field, grabbing smaller stones. I remain bent over, as for the whole time I'm not allowed to straighten up.

I don't wipe the sweat from my forehead as there is no point. My mouth is dry like the Sahara Desert, but I won't get anything to drink until noon. I focus on my task, ignoring paralyzing pains in my back. This has been my job for the last two months, since I rejected Georg.

My strength diminishes with each day that I work here. The fact that I am laboring so hard now hasn't meant an increase in my food rations. This is my punishment for not wanting that insane man.

Once my cart is filled all the way to the top, I push it along a wooden board placed above a ditch, in the direction of the main pile. But for a second, I lose balance and the wooden cart falls over the board and into the ditch, spilling stones all over.

It's not the first time it's happened, so I rapidly put the cart back on top of the wooden board and kneel down to gather stones from the ditch.

The SS guard with his familiar monstrous face leaps over to me and barks, "This stupid bitch did it again. Useless whore." He goes on hitting my back with his stick while I keep picking up the stones.

By the time I'm back at the barracks for the night, I have no strength to move. I chew my black bread ration and drink some water. I know my days are numbered; I won't be able to handle working in the fields much longer.

"You need to go with us," Halina whispers when we lie on top of our bed. She begged Inga to help me and bring me back to the Kanada storage, but the orders about my work came from the commandant himself, so there was nothing that could be done.

It's Georg's doing. He sometimes pops in during our evening roll-calls, every time drilling his eyes into me, as if checking if I'm still alive. I make sure not to look at him. It's easier this way. I can't afford to lose control and attract Liesel's attention to me.

Thankfully, he doesn't go any further when it comes to punishing me and doesn't involve Liesel in his ploy.

"Beata? Can you hear me?" Now Halina touches my arm and I detect concern in her voice.

"You know I'm in no shape to escape. I would slow you down and we would all get caught." I sigh. "And I can't leave Samuel. Sara is fighting typhus right now."

"Then I'm not going either. I can't leave you like this."

"Oh, Halina, you won't help me by staying. Besides, I will be fine." I take her hand in mine. "The work in the field is not that bad," I lie, glad she can't see my face in the darkness. "Are you sure you will be able to do it without being caught? Maybe you should stay here if it's a safer option?"

"The plan is watertight. The boys have worked on it for so

long, and there were others before us who escaped and were never caught." She sighs. "I want to do this, Beata. The only thing that could stop me is you asking me to stay."

"I will be fine," I say, trying to sound convincing. "I will pray it all succeeds and that you'll be free very soon." They are set to escape tomorrow night.

"And I will find ways to send you packages." Her voice is cheerful. She truly believes it all will be fine.

Like she said, Antek and his friend have worked on the escape plan for a long time. From what Halina explained to me the other day, the two men are laboring on building new barracks at the far end of the camp called Meksyk. There they dug a ditch, which they camouflaged with a turf, so the SS guards don't notice it.

Halina, Antek and their friend Grzegorz are going to hide for the night there, and when the right moment arrives, they will sneak out.

The next day goes by fast. In the evening, Halina doesn't come back to barracks; she is probably in that hiding place already, waiting.

Because of that, the count during the roll-call is off and that puts Liesel in rotten mood. She takes her aggravation out on the weakest of us.

At night, I twist and turn, unable to sleep worrying about Halina. Did they escape already, or are they still waiting? The good thing is that it's only the end of August, so the nights are still warm. I pray for the success of their mission.

The following day is uneventful at work, the same brutal labor weakening my health more and more. By the time night falls, I'm convinced their plan has ended up in success. I eavesdrop on other women whispering here and there about the escape last night, but other than that, there is no commotion.

Maybe the Germans want to keep quiet about it since they

weren't able to stop Halina and her two friends? I'm so happy for her—she is finally free.

Friday is a rainy day, but it doesn't stop us from working on the clayish fields. My wooden shoes keep slipping off my feet, causing so much more hassle on what is an already hard day.

I'm exhausted to the point that it takes everything I have to walk back along the dirt road to the camp. We enter a roll-call square and begin lining up, but Liesel and the guards shout at us to keep moving in the direction of the men's section of the camp.

When we are told to halt, my heart stutters at the scene before us. I bite on my chapped lips, feeling the salty taste of blood on my tongue as dizziness sweeps over me.

Hanging from the wooden gallows is a sign: *We're back again.*

And two human figures: Antek and Grzegorz.

No sign of Halina.

"Look at those men, Polish sluts, so you can see how traitors are treated. There is no escape from here." Liesel utters a long, demonic laugh. "We also caught one of yours." She glares into our faces. "We will extract the necessary information from her, then she will be hanged."

They have Halina.

FIFTY-THREE

BEATA

August 1944, German death camp, Brzezinka

There is no way. I don't know how to save my dearest friend from the hands of the murderers. I'm struggling myself to survive every hour. Halina will be executed in a few days.

Today is Sunday, so there is no work. Instead, we are expected to take care of chores like washing or sewing our clothes. But I can't even move; I'm paralyzed by Halina's impending execution. I don't care about the aches and pains shooting through my broken body.

I don't even take pleasure in another package from Harry. He arranges these frequently. In his last letter he told me, in a careful paraphrase, that for my safety he won't send letters anymore. He's waiting for me, and I'll do everything to survive this. For my Harry.

I realize that I must go to Georg and beg him for mercy. I've nothing to lose and I owe that much to Halina. Then, I remember his final words—I'm dead to him.

Hollowness and exhaustion overtake me again. He won't do anything for her. Now, whenever he sees me, his face is hard like a stone, and the only reason he shows up once in a while to the roll-calls is to check on the progress of my slow demise. It brings him a sick satisfaction.

If I had stayed in his cocoon, within his insanity, when he wanted me to, I would have a chance to save Halina. On the other hand, would I even know about her troubles? I did the right thing by rejecting him, and I will never regret it. But how much will this matter when Halina is hanged?

I think and think, and there are no ways I can even attempt to help her. I feel like I'm choking. There is nothing I can do, and in a few days, I will witness her execution. Liesel has already informed us that we all will be watching, so we learn our lesson from her death.

At noon, I devour a cup of broth, and decide to take a walk outside our barracks area, in hope of clearing my mind. The other option would be to try approaching Inga, the guard from Kanada. It's a huge risk, though, because she might beat me unconscious for daring to ask her. I never saw anyone as vicious as her—well, maybe Liesel can compete with her. I wonder what these women did in their normal lives in Germany. Do they have loving families there, parents waiting for them?

In the end, I decide to walk closer to the German canteen in case I can see Inga there, though my gut tells me it's dangerous. Inga will not move a finger to help Halina. She's happy that Halina is doomed, so she doesn't have to worry about anyone finding out about the stolen diamond rings.

I'm about to turn back to the barracks when a familiar voice approaches me from behind. "It's not wise to be here," Georg says, with no malice in his face, but no compassion either. It's like he's put on a mask, so people can't read him.

Encouraged by the fact that he isn't screaming to alert others to my presence, I say, "Hi, Georg."

He looks around as if making sure that no one can see us. "Well, it's good seeing you."

Just as he attempts to stroll away, I summon all the courage I have. "I need help." Saying those words out loud scares me to death.

Instead of shouting at me, he says in a voice devoid of emotion, "I shouldn't be talking to you. For your own safety, please keep on walking to your barracks."

Casting my good judgment aside, I move forward and touch his arm. "My friend Halina was arrested while escaping. She's in Block Eleven now. Please help her if you can; she is as innocent as your sister."

He thinks for a moment. "You know what I want in return if I help her?"

I nod with a sinking heart. "I will do everything you want. Please, help her," I say and then charge away, so I don't hear his refusal.

Stricken by the thought of being unable to help Halina, I spend the rest of my day fixing my clothes. It doesn't take my mind away from her, so it's pointless.

Every day upon my return from fields, I expect to see Halina hanging like a broken doll from the gallows. I know the sight of her will kill me; I already have no more strength to go on. I grow weaker and weaker with each day that passes. I will not be able to survive the labor in the fields. It is brutal enough to kill the strongest.

By Friday, there is still no news about my friend. Knowing her, she's refused to give them any information about how they were able to escape.

She's probably going through terrible interrogations. I don't want to think what they're doing to her. In the end, they will hang her anyway, regardless of whether she tells them something or not. How unjust this all is.

It feels morbid, and selfish, but I keep dwelling on the fact that if the Germans learned about my past and my Enigma involvement, I would share Halina's fate. Should I use my secret to free my friend? Would offering them information save Halina? It's possible, but I simply have no authority to do so. There are too many lives—and the safety of entire nations—at risk.

Then, it is Sunday again, and Georg enters our barracks right after the second gong announces our bedtime. He jumps toward me and pulls me outside by my arm. His grip is so strong that I feel no circulation in my hand.

As he keeps dragging me, all I hear is the sound of my own heartbeat thrashing in my ears.

He stops in the passage between the barracks. "I will kill you, Polish slut," he shouts.

I close my eyes, awaiting the first blow, but there is nothing.

Instead, he whispers in my ear, "Your friend is safe. I was able to send her away on the transport to the Third Reich for hard labor." He teases my bottom lip. "Now it's your time to pay." His eyes penetrate mine like he's trying to assess if he can trust me. He must be satisfied with what he sees because his voice softens. "I will have you in my villa in no time."

When he takes his hand from my mouth, I whisper, on the verge of crying, "Thank you for saving my friend."

He nods and then bellows, "I thought you were the bitch stealing food! Go back to your barracks now before I change my mind."

I do as he demands and slip into my barracks, knowing it's only his performance in front of the night guards. Thankfully, Liesel and the other monsters aren't here.

For the first time in this camp, I feel elated. Halina is safe and that's all that matters. A new sparkle of hope returns to my heart. *Thank you, God, thank you.* I don't care what I have to pay for her safety. The price is not important anymore.

FIFTY-FOUR

BEATA

October 1944, German death camp, Brzezinka

In October I'm moved from field labor to the canteen's kitchen where again I'm to do dishes, peel potatoes and everything else that the cook needs. This time, though, I strictly stay in the kitchen and do not serve food in the canteen. I think it's Georg's hand in this.

After all those months in the fields, I must look too sickly to be serving food to the SS men. The fact that I don't have to see those slaughterers brings me so much peace.

There are three of us helping the cook. He is a skinny man with a bristly mustache who moves quickly around his cooking duties. He often gets annoyed that we aren't fast enough, but other than that, this job is a breath of fresh air compared to the fields. I don't know how I survived all those months out there. The intensity of that labor is why I still feel dizzy and extremely tired.

Back in August, they started the first transports of prisoners to Germany. Halina left on one of them, or so Georg claims. I believe he's telling the truth.

Rumors say that the Soviets are getting closer, which is why the Germans began organizing the transports out of here. They have started destroying documentation within the camp. They are murdering the Jewish prisoners who were forced to service the gas chambers and crematoriums. As a result of that, on the seventh day of October, the prisoners attacked the SS guards. Unfortunately, the protest ended tragically for the prisoners. Hundreds of them died.

I often think of Halina and how she is managing. She loved Antek fiercely, so going on without him must be torture for her. I just hope that she is as strong as always and keeps her fearless spirit high.

One evening, Georg blocks my way out of the canteen's kitchen. My muscles tense. I haven't seen him since August, and his sudden appearance terrifies me. Deep in my soul, I was hoping that he's resigned himself from bringing me to his villa to collect his *payment* for saving Halina.

"I missed you." He smells of cigarettes and his eyes are red.

I swallow hard, but before I can answer, the cook's voice rings from the back.

"What's this commotion? Georg? What are you doing here? I had no idea that you work in this camp."

"Hello, Hans. I didn't know you were here either."

The cook utters sardonic laugh. "What a small world."

"Yes, indeed." It's clear that Georg isn't thrilled to see Hans.

Hans's mouth gapes open, exposing his missing upper tooth. "I see you're talking to my kitchen slave? At least she isn't a dirty Jew, and she works hard, so there is no harm in having her here."

"Why would I waste my time on this Polish pig?" Georg chuckles mirthlessly. "I must go back to my duties. It was a pleasure seeing you again."

The cook lights his cigarette and a moment later exhales clouds of smoke. "He used to be my neighbor back at home," he tells me, as if I am suddenly his confidante. "He had problems with his head from early childhood. Once I saw him walking naked on the roof of his parents' house." He looks at me, as if realizing I'm still standing here. "What you're waiting for. Get out of here, you stinking Pole."

I don't wait for him to say it again, I hurry away while trying to grasp what I've just heard about Georg. I knew he wasn't mentally stable because of the things he said when he summoned me. Or the fact that he comes to roll-calls and stares at me. Does he even have a wife and children, I wonder, or is that one of his delusions?

I'm not surprised that the Nazis give power to people like him. They pull the very worst criminals out from their prisons— and make them officers.

Thanks to my work in the kitchen, I'm able to steal a potato or a chunk of bread here and there. Whatever extra I smuggle under my clothes, I bring to Samuel and the children in the camp. By some miracle, Sara managed to get back to *health* after typhus and now visits her little boy again.

In the old times, I used to take chocolate to the children in the orphanage, as I wanted them to feel that others care for them. Now, I bring simple potatoes to these children, so they have a higher chance of survival.

The day after the cook tells me about Georg, we are summoned for an extra roll-call, where they force us to watch a man being hanged for killing one of the SS guards while attempting to escape from the camp. He is young, full of a vitality that is so rare here; no more than twenty-five, his rawboned, tanned face beams with strength and courage.

My heart bleeds for him. I pray for a miracle to save him, but no such thing happens. Someone from our crowd calls on everyone to turn their backs to the man, so he can die with dignity.

At first no one budges, but then slowly one after another we turn our faces away. I and the other women do the same, even though Liesel rushes toward us with her whip raised in a blaze of fury. But it has no power to it; she would have to assault all of us—there is not one person among us who didn't turn.

With our backs turned to him in a final gesture of respect, the man on the gallows calls out, "*Niech żyje Polska!*" over and over. "*Long live Poland!*"

Then his voice dies out.

FIFTY-FIVE

BEATA

November 1944, German death camp in Brzezinka

Georg stays away, but I have no doubt that I will be seeing him again soon. I detected it in his eyes, in that look of triumph that made me sick to my stomach. When one day he sends the car for me, I feel like I have a stone in place of my heart. I saved Halina and now I have no choice but to pay for it.

The same ill-tempered woman greets me at the door. I clean myself and put on an emerald dress that seems somehow familiar. Is it possible that it comes from the Kanada warehouses? Its soft fabric burns my skin. Who is the woman who wore it before me? Is she still alive? I shiver; it's all I can do not to wrench it from my body.

On the table is the same meal as last time, schnitzel and potatoes, but this time I don't have to wait long before Georg arrives.

He changed. Standing before me is the man in the same suit as before but now deep wrinkles are visible under his eyes. He's aged so much in these last months. I would like to think that his conscience has caught up with him and it's showing in his looks, but I'm sure that's not actually the case.

He smirks. "Are you ready to taste our paradise?" he asks, and I'm thrown sideways by the lust in his gaze. He motions to the table. "Help yourself."

Overpowered by disgust for him and by my gurgling stomach, I chew some meat, while struggling to swallow. I would rather die of starvation than go to bed with this brute, but this time I have no choice.

He raises his glass, which is filled with vodka, "Cheers to our upcoming night." What a dramatic switch in his attitude. Gone is any pretense of being a gentleman.

I take a sip and restrain myself from vomiting as a surge of warmth runs through me. I'm about to let this man use my body, like a doll without heart or soul. I know I did right by saving Halina and I would do it again if I had to, but it's pure misery to give this man what he demanded in return. Yet, I have no way out of it.

"How do you like my choice of music?" he asks and awaits my answer.

For the first time I realize that the gramophone is playing a composition by Strauss. "I like it," I say.

"You told me so in France." He gulps another shot of vodka, leaps to his feet and extends his hand my way. "Can I have the pleasure of this dance?"

I cringe inside. "Stop your games, Georg. Let's get this over with, so I can leave."

"I'm trying to be romantic, and you keep rejecting me." He chuckles. "Well, as I earned you, I now intend to enjoy myself. If not for the strings I pulled, you would already be dead in Perpignan and your Jewish friend would be hanged."

I know he's right, but still I give him a pleading look. "You can have any woman you want. Please let me go."

"Not this time. If you don't repay me for saving your

friend, you will leave this house dead. Enough with this nonsense." He grabs my hand and pulls me to the staircase. When I struggle to follow him, paralyzed by what's in store for me, he scoops me into his arms and climbs the stairs, the whole time singing in German some sentimental old love song.

I remain unmoving, knowing that to try to escape would be equal to death at the hands of one of the guards outside.

"I can't wait to drink your freshness but I will be gentle," he whispers, his breath reeking of vodka and cigarettes. What a far cry, I think, from his usual pleasant fragrance, belying his cruelty.

He throws me onto the soft sheets of a large bed; his hungry eyes watch me while he takes his shirt and pants off. Then, for a time that seems like forever, he makes use of my body.

I lie motionless while tears pour down my cheeks. All I feel is loathing for this man. His every touch causes pain, his gentleness causes nausea.

An eternity passes as he fulfills his needs, then as soon as he is done, he gets off me and sits on the edge of the bed smoking a cigarette.

I'm unable to move my body; he has poisoned it with his venom. I feel disgraced—dirty and disgusting. How will I go on after this?

"We're square now," he says and sighs. "I didn't expect you to be so exciting. If it makes you feel better, you're the only woman I've cheated on my wife with. There's something about you that makes my blood hot. I don't know how to explain it."

He goes on chatting like we just committed this act together, as if we were both willing participants. His words convince me even more that he lives in his own sick world.

"Of course, I would love more response from you, but I understand it's our first time. One day, I will drive you to an endless sea of passion."

My stomach clenches as I gasp. "We agreed to one time, nothing beyond it."

"Don't play the rigid prude," he snaps. "I know you enjoyed my lovemaking. I was tender and patient with you. I let you experience it in your own way without forcing you into anything. There are many women that would give everything to take your place."

"Let them then," I say, finding my voice. "I'm not one of them."

He goes on ignoring my words. "I know you would love more but I can't give it to you. My orders are to leave for Berlin in two days."

Relief spreads through me, and I seize the chance this news offers me. "My health is deteriorating," I plead. "Please have mercy and help secure my release from the camp."

"I can't, even if I wanted to," he responds. "You must pay for your treachery. You refused to give me your heart despite my many sacrifices. I had to take you like a soulless doll today. You deserve your fate."

He gets up, still naked, and stubs out his cigarette in the ashtray. "Get back into your rags." He's like a stone as he exits the room.

As December passes and the New Year arrives, I feel weaker with each day. It's as if every ounce of strength stored in me is now disappearing. I can't stop thinking of Harry and if I will ever see him again. Will he understand when I tell him about Georg? I can't hide that terrible truth from him; it would be unfair.

The first few days of the new year, I feel feverish and jittery. I wonder if it's due to my desperate longing for Harry. But I'm also full of dread at the thought that I may have typhus. Despite feeling so wretched and the unrepairable damage Georg inflicted on me, I still find enough will to get up each morning for work in the canteen's kitchen.

I now go more often to Samuel, with odds and ends I steal while the cook's back is turned, to make sure he has enough food. Like everyone, he's lost so much weight, but he's alive, so there is still hope we'll survive this. I will do everything I can to save him. I haven't seen Sara for a few weeks now, and Samuel tells me she's stopped visiting. I do my best to reassure him, but... is she still alive?

If not for Harry and little Samuel, I would have given up a long time ago.

FIFTY-SIX

BEATA

January 1945, German death camp, Brzezinka

I'm bedridden, waiting to die. It all started three days ago when I collapsed after getting up in the morning. For weeks I've been coughing, bringing up phlegm and suffering from this sharp pain in my chest. Now my fever is out of control, and my entire body hurts from my brain to even the tiniest muscle. I have no strength to move, and no one has bothered to take me to the camp hospital. At this point, I don't even know if there is one. Since being bedridden, I have eaten nothing, drunk nothing.

A week ago, on the seventeenth day of January, the SS men set most of the prisoners on an evacuation march out west. It is clear they are afraid that the Soviets may arrive any moment now. Only people who weren't in any way fit for the march stayed behind in the camp. I'm one of them. Even though I collapsed only days ago, I was in a terrible condition for weeks before that. So, I knew I would not survive that journey, wherever they are taking them to on their pitiful march.

Since then, they continue with their mass shootings; they drag Jews into the squares and murder them. They are on a mission to kill all of us who are left here. I pray that I die in this bed as quickly as possible, so I don't have to go through the horror of being forced into the square.

As more time passes, I don't know what's going on around me anymore. I can't open my mouth, that's how dry it is, and I have this constant hum in my head. Soon I will join Felka on the other side. I hope Harry forgives me for being unable to survive this.

Then, finally, I fully succumb to the darkness, so blissful and peaceful.

"Miss Beata, please get up." Samuel's tiny voice keeps playing in my mind, but I find no strength to open my eyes. I feel water on my lips and the voice continues, "Miss Beata, please get up. We are free. The Soviets are here."

The boy sobs and I wish I could hug him for the last time, but my awareness drifts away and I'm lost in darkness.

FIFTY-SEVEN

BEATA

February 1945, Kraków

I wake up in a white room filled with rays of light, as a nurse in white linen robe leans above me. The pleasant scent of clean sheets makes me dizzy; it's nothing like the pungent odor of the barracks. Am I in heaven?

"Miss," the nurse says, "are you okay?"

Am I okay? Why does her voice sound so real? Why do I feel her touch on my skin? I thought in heaven there was no sensation of physical touch. Pain shoots between my temples. The last thing I remember is falling asleep on my bunk in the barracks.

She looks at me with urgency in her eyes, "Can you tell me how you feel?"

I clear my scratchy throat. "Where am I?"

"You are in the hospital in Kraków."

"But I was dying in..." I don't have enough strength to continue.

"That's okay," she says and brings a glass filled with water to my mouth. I take a few sips. It tastes so good.

"That's enough for now. Stay calm, and I will tell you what happened. When, on 27 January, Soviet soldiers liberated the camp you were in, they found you unresponsive in one of those filthy barracks." Her expression becomes very somber. "You're lucky. They discovered the bodies of hundreds of others, shot by the SS troops as they desperately tried to evacuate the camp."

All of a sudden, my body feels cold with the heaviness settling in my chest and limbs. I remember how the women in my barrack block were praying that the SS men didn't kill them before the Soviets arrived, which we all knew was about to happen. I didn't have any hope for myself; I knew I was dying, yet I'm here now. "So many people were forced to leave and march out west," I whisper.

She nods. "I heard they were packed into trains and taken to Germany. I guess most of them survived." She busies herself smoothing out my sheets, then continues. "When the Soviets found you, there was a little boy who wouldn't leave your side, who kept insisting you were still alive. Thanks to him they brought you to a field hospital organized by the Red Cross, but your condition was so critical that they decided to transport you here. We've been supporting you intravenously with liquids, or you wouldn't have survived. You're severely dehydrated and malnourished, and still fighting pneumonia and typhus. It's a miracle you've pulled through, out of this."

"Samuel," I say and smile.

She smiles back. "Well, now we're going to make sure we slowly return you to your health."

"Do you know what happened to the boy?"

"Yes." She gently strokes a stray hair from my face. "He was reunited with his mother who he found in the field hospital, the same one where you were brought. I know all this because I was working there at the time."

"God bless you," I say, as warmth surrounds my heart.

She nods, squeezes my hand in recognition. "Is there anyone we should inform that you're here?"

I carefully give her Joanna's information, though I doubt they will be able to reach her. After all, the war is not over yet.

But next week, I can't quite believe my eyes when Joanna enters the hospital room. Her enormous, sunny smile fades the moment she sees me.

"Beata, is that you?" she says, seeking confirmation in my eyes. She hasn't changed at all, still the same pretty girl with shiny black hair, only her outfit is much simpler than the ones she used to wear. She, too, is much skinnier.

"Hello, Joanna," I say and smile with warmth.

She jumps to me and takes my hand. "My poor little thing. What have they done to you in that awful camp?" She lifts my hand and touches it to her soft cheek.

I'm not ready to talk about it, not even with Joanna. It looks like the war hasn't been so brutal on her, and I sense she will never understand what I went through.

In fact, the pitiful way she looks at me makes me feel like a leper. "Please, I don't want to talk about it. But thank you for coming here."

"The Red Cross found me as I still live with my parents. I never returned to Warsaw. But let me tell you, I heard the city is all in ruins now after the Uprising."

I only nod. It's too hard to even think of it.

"You heard about Gabriel, right?" She wrinkles her nose.

I shake my head. I've no idea what she's talking about. Probably she's got some torrid gossip about Gabriel's love affairs. Before the war, I learned more than I needed to know about that from her.

"He was killed back in September 1939, fighting the Germans," she says in a softer voice.

Soreness settles in my throat and lungs. "I had no idea." It never even crossed my mind that Gabriel might be dead.

"How ironic," she continues. "The son died protecting our country while the father did business with the Nazis through the war."

Sudden tiredness overtakes me. "It's so nice seeing you after all these years," I say. "Thank you for coming to visit."

She takes the hint. "Of course, you need to rest, so I will get going." She touches my hand. "You will always be my dearest friend." Her gaze is pained, full of sorrow.

"And you'll be mine," I say.

I spend two months in the hospital as a patient and then, when I am well enough, I work helping the nurses. I am assigned a tiny room in one of the hospital's outbuildings, where the staff live. Because of my fragile health, my duties are light; mostly, I read to children or talk with the adult patients.

The Soviets liberated Kraków even before the camp, so it seems safer to stay here for now. Who knows what the situation in Warsaw and the rest of the country might be like? I'm far too weak to travel, and the last thing I need right now is to face more Germans. But it seems like we're now under Stalin's regime here. I don't want to even think about what that might mean.

Slowly, I gain some weight and my hair grows back. There were moments when I didn't believe I would ever get to this point. I was sure that my life was over when I ended up in that horrible camp.

I think of Halina a lot. She had such a strong will to live and there was so much happiness in her despite the harsh conditions in the camp. She loved a man with whom she wanted to start family, instead he was hanged like so many others. I hope she's able to go on living with such unbearable pain inside her.

Every night I dream of still being in the camp. The SS

guards are dragging me and the women from my barracks out into the square. There, they shoot at us. In the distance, I hear Georg's obnoxious laugh. I always wake up drenched in sweat, unable to go back to sleep.

How can I start my life over after enduring all of this? Is it even possible? But I fight my everyday battles, determined to move on.

There must be a reason God kept me alive, though I don't see it myself. I have no hope for any dream of a happy future, even if Harry is still alive. If he saw me now, he would probably not recognize me. The mirror tells me that I'm not the same woman he knew once.

I could not handle seeing pity in his eyes, just like I did in Joanna's.

The change is not only in my physical appearance; the worst damage was done to my mind, my soul, my consciousness. I'm broken from the inside and that can't be repaired. Harry wouldn't want the woman that I have become.

FIFTY-EIGHT

BEATA

June 1945, Kraków

Our enemy Germany was officially defeated last month, and so Poland, after nearly six interminable years, is no longer at war. But our hospital is still overcrowded with patients.

After work, I mostly stay in my room, only sometimes I like to take a walk by the river to admire the red-roofed splendor of our royal Wawel Castle. It's a miracle it wasn't destroyed during the war. But there are rumors that the Germans looted its collections of valuable artefacts and jewels.

I don't know what this city looked like during the war, but I can only imagine swastikas everywhere and swarms of German military personnel. Now there is no sign of any of that; instead, uniformed Soviets crowd the streets.

At the hospital, the management keeps reminding us to be cautious and not to walk the streets alone in the dark. There are more and more cases of women or girls being raped by Soviet soldiers. I'm sure there are many women whom we don't see, those who don't come to the hospital after being hurt by those brutes.

Joanna never came to visit me again. Seeing shock and then pity in her eyes was not easy. It made me feel like an outcast. I should visit her, so we can talk some more. When she came over, I was still in the depths of a kind of post-camp shock, and I didn't even ask her how she managed to survive the war. Maybe she mistook my behavior and now thinks that I don't want to see her.

Though sometimes I feel like it's easier to stay away from my old life because nothing can be the same anymore. There is no point hurting myself further by being overly sentimental about the past and what has been lost forever.

I enjoy working at the hospital, I feel useful when I'm helping the nurses. It leaves me no time for overthinking, which I can't afford to do as there are too many black clouds hiding under the surface of my heart. I convince patients to smile again and to laugh, while I'm so sad inside. Yet, helping others brings some purpose to my life, it starts to heal this painful loneliness in me.

Felka, Jerzy, Gabriel... Will I ever see them on the other side?

One evening, the sun is still high in the sky as I'm about to leave the hospital at the end of my shift. A young nurse runs down the corridor after me. "Beata," she gasps, "Mrs. Tawoczek wants to see you in her office."

I have no idea what the head nurse might want, but I dutifully knock on the pale green office door and enter at her brisk, "Come in!"

"Take a seat, Beata. I have received an unusual phone call," she says. "A man from England is looking for you. He's on his way here as we speak. His name is Harry Smith. Does it sound familiar?"

I feel like I'm going to faint. Harry? Here? How did he find me?

"It does," I manage to say, "but I do not want to see him."

She takes off her glasses and scrutinizes me. "It seems like this man made a substantial effort to find you. Are you afraid of him? Does he intend you harm?"

"No, of course not," I stutter. "He's a good man."

"Then you should have the manners to inform him yourself that you do not wish for any further contact with him," she says with finality in her voice.

I like, and trust, Mrs. Tawoczek. She opened her heart for me right from the beginning, when she found out that I grew up in an orphanage and don't have any family. Thanks to her, I have a job, a room to live and food to eat from the hospital's kitchen. Sometimes, I wonder at my luck in meeting good women with huge hearts. Felka, Mrs. Moreau, Camille, Sara, Halina and now Mrs. Tawoczek.

I should be honest with this woman, so she doesn't judge me wrongly. "I don't want him to see me like this." I stare down at my hands, and continue, "I'm just a wreck of the woman he once knew, and I could not stand to see the pity in his eyes."

A look of understanding flashes over her face. "Is he your friend, or are there deeper feelings involved?"

I decide to be entirely truthful with her, so she fully understands the situation. "I love him."

"Trust him, then. If he's worthy of you, the way you look won't matter. Especially when, believe me, you look healthier and healthier every day. You've already gained some weight; your skin keeps improving and your hair grows beautifully. I like that shade of blonde, by the way." She pauses as if trying to find the right words before continuing. "There are so many who came from the same place who would give everything to be in your shoes."

"I know," I say in a broken voice. "I'm thankful every day

that I survived. I met an amazing woman on the very first day I arrived at the camp, and she helped so much. Thanks to her, I was given much easier work than the labor outside. First, in the warehouses, then in the canteen. I only did hard labor in the fields for a short time."

"I know it's hard to even imagine," she says, "but you are among the lucky ones. So many innocent people perished." She sighs. "Be positive, my dear, as that will help your healing journey. And most of all, don't run from your life before the war. Give this man a chance, he might prove to you that he's worth it. If not, you'll have the strength to move on."

"I guess I'm used to disappointments," I confess, as I think about the amount of pain inflicted on my heart... Can it take any more?

"This time there might be no disappointment," she says, one side of her mouth twisting into a kindly smile. "You're young, you deserve happiness."

I nod and leave it at that, without elaborating any more about my insecurities when it comes to meeting Harry.

A moment later, I walk through the hospital's gardens, enjoying the sweet scents of flowers and the melodious sounds of chirping birds. The entire garden blooms with green trees and bushes. The one thing about nature is that it always comes back to life, even after the longest winters.

It was so hard to reach acceptance after losing Felka. My entire world crumpled right before me, while everything else kept moving on. I still can't comprehend it. But what I saw day after day in the camp changed me forever. People poisoned with gas, babies murdered in cold blood... The list of horrors is endless. Every day, I try not to think of it, or I would not be able to get up in the morning.

I perch on a wooden bench and take in all the beautiful colors around me. In the camp everything was black and gray. It made me realize that before the war I took a lot for granted, that

I didn't appreciate the beauty of simple things. There are so many others who will never again feel the sun on their skin, or smell the blossoming fragrance of flowers.

I know my thoughts are chaotic, but it's been like that since my stay here. In the camp, I focused on surviving the next hour, the next day without thinking beyond those moments. Halina told me to do this on those first nights in our shared bunk. Maybe her wisdom is why I was able to cling to life.

I often wonder what happened to the children from the camp. Closer to the end, I was so sick that I couldn't see them. Were they liberated with Samuel, or it was too late for them? I didn't see any of them here, in this hospital. Yet, I know there are many other places, including the field hospitals created by the Red Cross.

Lost in contemplation, I forget all about Harry, until I hear a voice throbbing with layers of sorrow from behind me. "Is it really you, Beata?"

FIFTY-NINE

BEATA

June 1945, Kraków

He's here. My Harry is here. I'm too paralyzed to turn his way. Shock and pity, that's what I'll see in his eyes. And that will kill me.

Instead, I close my eyes, and stay completely still while fear clutches my heart.

I know he kneels before me because he takes my hands in his. The touch of his skin makes my heart beat fast from a combination of excitement and fear; it brings warmth and tears. But I keep my eyes shut.

"Look at me," he says gently. "Darling, please, look at me."

I summon my courage and at last look straight in his eyes, ready to confront nothing but pity, which has by now surely intensified.

But his beautiful grayish eyes emanate only softness. They tell me everything.

I forget about all my worries and insecurities. I let him embrace me in a tight hug. We both cry while he kisses tears from my face, and then our lips engage in untamed passion. He kisses me hungrily, with an urgency that takes my breath away. It's as if he's trying to make up for the time we have lost, for every moment we have spent apart.

I dreamed of this day for so long that I cherish every sensation of his touch, his gentleness, his presence. My Harry is here; despite it all, he's here with me.

I don't know how long we stay like this, but at some point, he says in a hoarse voice, "I'm taking you from here." There are still tears running down his cheeks.

With so much emotion in my body, I'm unable to speak, so I press the side of my face to his chest. I fought for so long to stay alive, but it's not until now that I truly feel alive. It's like Harry is the missing air that my lungs have now gained back.

"Say something, darling. I want to hear your voice." He breaks off and buries his face in my hair.

The moment he does so, I wish I still had my long, thick hair. I lift my nose and sniff. "You still want me?"

He takes my face between his hands, his eyes burning with admiration. "How could I not want you? You are my everything."

"And you are mine," I whisper. "It's just that I'm not the same I was before, and I thought..." I bury my face into his chest without finishing. How can I explain it to him in only a few words?

He pulls me closer. "You're the most beautiful woman I've ever known, inside and out." He runs his hand down my spine sending sparks of electricity through me. "Can I invite you to dinner tonight?"

"I have a better idea," I say and smile while our gazes meet and stay connected. "Why don't you join me for supper in my room?"

"Are you sure? I don't want to make you feel uncomfortable if hosting me will cause your neighbors to gossip."

"I don't care what others say. We deserve time alone, which we wouldn't have in a restaurant."

He grins. "In that case, my answer is yes."

Of course, we don't eat that night because we can't get enough of each other. When he takes my shirt off, I close my eyes to avoid seeing the pity in his eyes. I rapidly turn away as pain and shame surround my heart. What made me think that this handsome, beautiful man would want me the way I am now, with my ugly, camp-inflicted skinniness?

But without another word, he pulls me closer to him and holds me for a long moment.

"You're a warrior, Beata. When I look at you, I see pure beauty. What you went through made you stronger, made you unique." He turns me to face him again, and gently kisses every particle of my skin. His lips brush my nape, travel to my lower neck, down my breast.

Our lovemaking is urgent, but at the same time is sweet, filled with passion and tenderness.

Afterwards, we cuddle, and I wonder at this bliss in my heart. How can this man make me feel this way? With him, I realize, I forget it all; I feel like I'm the same Beata as I was from before the war.

"I was serious when I said that I'm going to take you with me to England," he says. "I'm sorry, darling, but you have no choice. If I have to, I will kidnap you."

I answer with a soft laugh. "You don't have to, because I dream of nothing else. But how am I going to leave Poland? I'm sure the borders are now patrolled by the Soviets."

"Leave it all to me," he says, "but we do need to depart immediately. The war has only just ended, so there is still a lot of chaos. Soon things will change." He gives a long, low sigh and shakes his head. "Especially now that the Yalta Conference in Crimea has put Poland in the hands of Soviets."

I flinch and a sour taste fills my mouth. "We went from one regime to another."

"Unfortunately, yes."

"I would only need one day to visit my friend Joanna who lives near Kraków," I tell him. "I wasn't too warm toward her when she visited me here, and I need to apologize to her. She means so much to me."

He thinks for a moment. "Why don't I drive you there tomorrow morning, so you can spend a day with her? Then I will go back to Kraków to take care of some things before coming to get you."

"Thank you," I say. "And now I really must ask if you know anything about our cryptology team."

"Marian Rejewski and Henryk Zygalski made their way safely to England back in 1943," he says, "where they enlisted in the Polish Armed Forces and continued their work on ciphers. I'm sorry, I know nothing about the others."

"Hopefully they didn't end up in German camps like me." I sigh. "I want to tell you about my..." Words fail me, but I know I should tell him what happened to me in the camp: I need to confess about Georg.

He pulls me closer and whispers, "Shush, sweetheart, we have our whole lives for that. You can tell me when you're ready."

I feel a sudden release of all tension. He's so gentle and understanding. "I will, darling. I will tell you everything one day."

SIXTY

BEATA

June 1945, Tyniec, a village near Kraków

The motorbike ride with Harry to Tyniec, the village where Joanna lives, was a quiet adventure. We got lost once or twice, but eventually Harry dropped me off where I told him to and promised to come back and get me at four o'clock.

One thing about my Harry is that he adapts quickly to new places and situations. First in France, and now here. I don't even know where he got that awfully loud, bone-shaking bike.

I have no trouble finding the right house thanks to my summer trips here with Joanna. My friend sits on a bench in front of a wooden shack with a straw roof, a bunch of chickens eating grains at her foot.

In her dark, simple clothes, she looks nothing like the sophisticated and elegant girl from Warsaw. The war has changed her too. I just didn't see it in the hospital; I was too busy with my own traumas.

"Would you care to take a walk with me?" I say and smile at her.

If she's surprised to see me, she doesn't show it. She was like that in Warsaw too, always sure of herself.

"I knew you'd visit me when you were ready," she says.

"I'm sorry for the way I treated you in the hospital," I say, wanting to be honest with my friend. "I was fighting my own demons."

"I understood," she assures me, "and I don't hold it against you. You went through hell, unlike me, who was hiding away like a rat."

I ignore the tightness in my chest, and say, "I can only imagine the hell you went through, too."

Her features soften. "Come inside. I baked an apple pie and will make some coffee. My parents aren't home; they've gone to the market."

The inside air is rich with the scent of lavender, but my nostrils detect a whiff of mold too. "It looks different here," I say when she prompts me to take a seat at a table covered by a lilac oilcloth.

She settles a kettle on a white-tiled wood-burning stove and turns my way. "First Germans lived here and later it was looted by the Soviets." She sighs heavily and drops to the chair across from me. "Our neighbors hid my mother and myself all through the war in their cellar. They're good people, so they shared their food with us. My dad was abroad with General Anders."

"I'm so sorry you had to go through this," I say.

She touches my arm. "Don't be sorry for me. It's a miracle that you survived the camp. I've heard about all the terrible things that happened there." Empathy flickers in her eyes. "You look so much healthier now. Your skin looks radiant. It was such a shock when I saw you in the hospital, you were so poorly."

"I'm still not ready to talk about the camp," I murmur. "I'm sorry."

She takes my hand in hers. "I understand, trust me, I do. The whole war we were hiding, constantly worrying about being caught and transported to a camp, if they didn't just shoot us on the spot. Every day was a struggle to stay sane while confined in the cellar. But we were going to do everything we could, so that we weren't found." She sighs again. "And I had no idea that you were in the very place of which I was scared to death. The irony."

"It's so hard to believe that you spent all those years in a cellar."

"We had no choice. It was the price we paid to stay alive, but there are so many countless Jews whose hiding places were discovered, and then they were killed or perished in those awful death camps."

She stands and picks up the whistling kettle, then pours hot water into two glasses with iron handles. A heavenly aroma of freshly ground coffee fills my nostrils.

"I was a political prisoner there as they arrested me while crossing the border from France to Spain." I close my eyes and try to suppress tears.

"Let's not talk about it," she says with compassion in her voice. "I only wanted you to know that I feel your pain. I thank God every day that he saved me from going through what you endured."

She grabs a plate with cut pieces of apple pie and places it in the middle of the table. For a moment we enjoy the hot coffee and homemade pie.

"So delicious," I say and smile. "I missed your cooking."

She smiles back and rolls her eyes. "Do I need to remind you how you complained every time I tried making something new?"

"I know, I know. I took so much for granted back then."

"We all did."

"So, what's your plan? Are you going to stay here or go back to Warsaw?"

Her green eyes gleam. She pulls off the scarf that's been

covering her head to reveal her lustrous curls and natural beauty. "I'm getting married next month and moving to Kraków."

"That's wonderful news." I leap to her, and we hug and hug and hug. "I'm so happy for you," I say, leaning back to look at her radiant face. "Who's the lucky man?"

"We knew each other from before the war and then, when I came here in September 1939, he bumped into me in Kraków. Waldek brought food and whatever supplies he could for us during the war."

"He sounds like a nice man. Do you truly love him?" I ask, but her beaming expression and glowing cheeks tell me the answer.

"I do. He's a doctor; actually, I invited him for dinner today. Will you be staying?"

"I would love to meet him, but Harry is going to pick me up at four o'clock."

Her eyes widen. "And who's Harry?"

"We worked together during the war in France, and he came to find me—only yesterday—at the hospital."

She squeals in excitement. "Then Harry will join us for dinner too. Is he English?"

"Yes, but his mother was born and raised in Poland. He grew up in London, as his father is English."

She gives me a knowing look. "I don't have to ask if you're in love. I see it all in your eyes."

I answer with a soft laugh. "You know me well. So, you aren't coming back to Warsaw?"

She shakes her head. "No. Waldek had to go on business a week ago; he said there was nothing but piles of ruins, all the old buildings reduced to rubble. I'd asked him to look for our old tenement and couldn't believe it when he found it, one of the very few untouched ones. He said our flat is still in good condition; if you wanted to, you could go back."

"I'm leaving for England, Joanna," I tell her. "If I'm able to cross the border. Harry has a flat in London, so you could sell our old Warsaw home and keep any money you manage to get for it."

She narrows her brows. "Are you sure you don't want your half?"

"Yes, we're leaving tomorrow. I want to be with Harry and I think things will be easier in England than here. I just hope we get there with no problems. Harry assured me that he has it all under control, and I trust him. But, to be honest, as long as we are together, it doesn't matter where we live. If we are unable to leave Poland, we will stay here."

"Thank you, then. I truly appreciate your generosity." She wipes her tears.

I give her hand a squeeze. "It's the least I can do for you. Is that abbey on the hill still abandoned?"

She smiles. "In 1939, eleven Belgian monks moved in, but we don't really see them. They occupy the area that survived the fire in 1831, you know, the part of the monastery hill called the castle."

I nod. At some point long ago, we both went to the local library and researched the history of the monastery. I still remember the motto of St. Benedict: *Ora et labora*. Pray and work. "Do you remember how we used to sit over there talking for hours while watching the river?"

Her face beams. "I do. My mother always got so upset when she found out that we spent time in that abbey."

"I would love to take a walk there, if you're up for it, of course."

"Why don't you go now? I have a few chores to do. I need to boil some nettles to feed the pigs? And my parents and Waldek should be here in an hour."

I feel a dropping sensation in my stomach. It's what we sometimes ate in the camp—boiled nettles.

She must notice my distress because she says, "Are you all right?"

I can't tell her the reason for my nervousness. "Yes, I'm just tired, but a walk along the Vistula will do me good."

"You'll enjoy it; it's even more beautiful now. Make sure to be back in time so we can eat as soon as Harry arrives." She smiles. "It will be great to spend more time together before you leave. I've missed you so much, my friend."

"I've missed you too."

SIXTY-ONE

BEATA

June 1945, Tyniec, a village near Kraków

I walk along the Vistula River while inhaling the air rich with scents of wet dirt and algae. Water trickles gentle as a bird takes flight flapping its wings. The Benedictine abbey and church, which was founded in the eleventh century by one of our kings, perch on a white limestone rock above the river, surrounded by greenery.

I stop at the foot of the monastery that looks like a majestic medieval fortress and enjoy kisses of sun on my skin. I splash cold water between my hands, appreciating its refreshing feel.

After a long, peaceful moment, I climb uphill to the monastery entrance. I lose myself in the stunning view of the valley with the river flowing through it and the fields all around.

I pass through an archway and follow a path to an open courtyard surrounded by the stone and brick walls of the church and monastery. Throughout the centuries the abbey has been ruined and rebuilt many times, and for over a hundred years it was abandoned. Consequently, different styles, like

Romanesque, baroque and gothic, are all mixed into its architecture.

I head toward the Church of St. Peter and St. Paul. During my previous visits, I have always found it peaceful and easy to pray in there. I want to thank God that I am still alive, despite so many traumatic events in my life.

Upon entering, the familiar iron latch in the shape of a fish brings a wry smile to my face. I think of my favorite novel, *Quo Vadis* by Henryk Sienkiewicz, and of Ligia drawing a fish symbol in the dirt while Marcus has no idea what it represents.

The air is cool and intensified by the fragrance of fresh-cut flowers, but above all, I'm surprised by the monks who are gathered near the altar chanting in Latin, all oblivious to the world around them.

Not wanting to bother them, I kneel in the back of the church with its linden-wood stalls and black marble décor. I admire the gothic chancel, baroque nave, and high altar of black marble. It's so good to be here again.

I find it reassuring to know that this church hasn't changed at all and wasn't ruined by the German military. On my every visit here before, I was always alone, as Joanna waited for me outside. Now, with the monks here, this place seems alive, while still offering a secluded place for prayer.

Peaceful feelings envelop my heart, while my life plays out before my eyes. When I was little, I often thought that God didn't care about me because he didn't give me a mother or father who would love me. I found it difficult to pray and just recited the prayers when asked, without any real understanding. But with time, I realized that the honest thoughts I sent to God made me feel less lonely.

When Felka died, I succumbed to an inner pain and couldn't talk to anyone about it. I never stopped praying and that brought me moments of relief. Harry helped me to believe that it all doesn't in fact end when our bodies die. Soul and spirit don't die. He's always felt his mother's presence, first as a boy, and later as a grown man.

I embraced things that before I knew nothing of or hadn't thought of. Harry gave me a wonderful gift by deepening our conversations to these aspects of life and death. It helped me to keep hope in the worst times—the years I spent in the camp in Brzezinka.

God never left me alone. He sent good people my way, people like Halina.

I thank Him for letting me survive that hell, my sicknesses; for bringing back Harry to me; for Joanna's survival. I pray for Halina, that she is fine and one day will find her way back home.

I pray for all those souls who perished in that horrible camp. I pray for all of them without words, knowing that God understands. I still can't find the right words to talk about it. I can't express the horrors I went through or witnessed, not even to Harry. Some things must stay in silence, until the right words come.

Maybe, with time, I will be able to open myself to those memories, but right now it's all too fresh, too painful, too traumatizing. Only my dreams reveal the truth of it all, tormenting my mind and soul.

Then I pray for Jerzy and for his beautiful family, that they find the strength to go on in this life without him. I remember Marian and Henryk, and my other Polish friends from the Cipher Bureau, and pray for their lives now.

I pray for the good people I met in France. I thank God for putting them in my path, so that I could continue believing in the goodness of humanity.

When I'm done, I walk out and perch beside the old well in the southeastern part of the courtyard. It's where I often sat with Joanna enjoying the tranquility of this place. I have a few more minutes before getting back to my friend, as I promised to help her prepare our dinner.

It doesn't seem real that tomorrow I will be leaving with Harry for England. When he said it yesterday, I felt no restraint, no anxiety; it was music to my ears after all the times of such loneliness. Besides, I've no plan when comes to staying in Poland. I could not remain in the hospital, because soon there will be fewer patients from the camps, and they won't need me anymore. It's not *my place* anyway. I'm not sure about my life in England, but as long as I'm with Harry, nothing else matters.

I sit for a few more minutes until a voice interrupts my thoughts.

"Here you are," Harry says, and I look up to see him walking toward me, so handsome and smiling that my heart skips a beat.

When he puts his arms around me, the entire world comes to a standstill. He deserves to have my honesty.

I turn his way and look into his darkish gray eyes. "There's something I must tell you."

He wrinkles his forehead. "Is everything all right?"

"Yes," I quickly assure him. "I want to be honest with you. I need you to know something."

He takes my face between his hands. "If this is about leaving Poland, I'm convinced that we can have a better life in England. But if your heart tells you to stay here, I will stay with you. I want you to know this."

His words touch my soul and bring tears to my eyes. "I want to leave with you," I say with a gulp, "but I don't deserve you." I can't stop sobbing.

"Please, don't—"

"No, I need to tell you this before it's too late. I couldn't stand to lose your trust." I have to tell him, and so I do—about Halina's dire situation and the night spent with Georg.

He listens, the whole time holding my hands. "Why would

you think I could reject you for this? Is that how little you think of me? What matters is that you survived. Nothing else."

Once more, Harry proves his love. "It's important that we build our relationship on honesty," I say.

"I'm so sorry you had to go through this, darling. I'm so sorry I couldn't do anything to save you. I'll never forgive myself for not getting you out of that horrible camp. But you need to know that there wasn't a second in my life when you weren't on my mind. I hated feeling so powerless and hopeless. I prayed every day for you to have enough strength to survive. I asked my mother to watch over you, and I know she did."

"Oh, Harry," I cry. "You couldn't have taken me out from there. That wasn't possible. Don't berate yourself for it. I love you."

"I love you too, my princess."

SIXTY-TWO

BEATA

August 1945, London

"Darling, what is it?" Harry asks as he enters the high-ceilinged drawing room of his apartment. It is located in one of London's richest districts, and it was only upon our arrival here in the summer that I realized Harry's wealth. It still makes me uncomfortable, but to my relief, his father and the rest of the family treat me with respect.

I smile, pushing aside my thoughts. "How was your meeting?"

"Come here," he says. I oblige and we engage in the sweetest kiss. For a moment I forget about my worries. When he holds me like this, it's as if the entire world stops.

"Don't drift away from me," he whispers. "Tell me what's been bothering you."

"I will never drift away from you. But you're busy at your father's firm, so I want you to relax when you're back home, instead of listening to my worries."

"I'm obviously failing at making you happy." His gray eyes

meet mine, as if trying to read my mind. "I've been noticing your sadness when you think that I don't look."

"Don't even say this. You make me the happiest woman in the world." I rub my thumb on his cheek. "You're my everything."

He takes my hand in his and kisses my knuckles. "Tell me all, then, so I can understand your sadness. Are you homesick?"

"Homesick? No! My home is where you are." I look around. "Though I admit it's not easy to get used to this luxury after the camp years, I do feel so happy here."

"If you want, we can move to the cheapest apartment in London. Whatever brings peace to you, princess." He winks at me and kisses my forehead.

I laugh. "Stop this. Our home is here, and I shouldn't be so whiny. I truly appreciate all of this. It's just that I can't stop thinking of Halina." I sigh, finally telling him my trouble.

"I'm sure she is fine. You said she was sent to Germany, so she might be still there, or maybe she's back in Poland."

"That's what Georg said, but who knows? Back then, I thought I saw in his eyes that he was truthful, but I don't know anymore." I swallow hard. "Maybe she is dead."

He shakes his head. "If that was the case, you would've known. You said they were executing escapees in front of other prisoners."

"I hope you're right and she's still alive." I nod and wipe my tears. "I feel like I abandoned her."

"You risked everything to save her. Everything." His face takes on that determined look I know so well. "We will not stop until we find her. I promise you this, princess."

Toward the end of August, we have our wedding, but we only invite Harry's closest family and relatives. After the terrible deprivations of war, having a huge, extravagant wedding doesn't sit well with us.

I only invite my Polish friends, the ones who stayed in England after the war and with whom I once worked at the Cipher Bureau. Those times seem so far away now. But sharing our happy moment with them brings so much peace and makes our wedding even more special.

Then we enjoy our short honeymoon in his enchanted castle outside of London where we forget the entire world.

SIXTY-THREE

BEATA

Five years later: January 1950, Warsaw

An old, stained tenement glowers at me through the snow-flurry. I bury my face in the softness of my cashmere scarf and cross the cobbled street. Once more, I curse myself for not wearing a warmer coat on this trip. I have been spoiled by London life. Winters in Poland can be brutal.

When I get inside, the stench of urine hits me first, followed by the odor of mold. I shake off the snow from my coat and boots, feeling bad for creating a puddle on the cement floor.

The cries of a baby fills the space while I hear a woman's voice shouting at someone to get out. I shrug and massage my hands to bring circulation back to them. The commotion must be in the other part of the building because I can't see anyone.

It seems I picked the worst day for my visit. We arrived this morning from London, and I couldn't wait any longer before coming here to see Halina. If she is even here.

We've been searching for her for many years, but it was only last month that I received information from the Red Cross that she lives in this building.

I lumber forward in search of door with the number eight on it, unable to shake off the misery of this place. Cigarette butts and empty glass bottles are strewn around the filthy corridor and vulgar words are scrawled on the paint-peeling walls. The building is in quite a rough neighborhood of Warsaw, so I shouldn't be surprised.

As I go further along, the crying baby and raised voices grow louder. I spot number six, then seven, and the next door is wide open. It must be eight. It's where the noises are coming from.

After double checking that it's the right number, I peek in without knocking. No one would hear it in such tumult.

A pretty woman with black curls holds a crying baby in her arms while a little boy clings to her legs. The woman winces every time a heavy-set lady in an apron and headscarf throws insults at her.

"You either pay the rent or there is no room here for a loafer like you," she says and spits to the floor.

"Please, give me another week. I will get the money," the woman holding the baby says, her eyes feverish and over-bright.

I freeze. It's Halina's voice. I didn't recognize her right away because I remember her as gaunt and with her head shaved. This stunning woman with beautiful hair and healthy skin is my dear friend.

My elation at recognizing her fades quickly once I realize the situation Halina and her children are in. The woman-predator pushes Halina in the direction of the door, like she wants to throw her to the curb right this moment.

"What's happening here?" I say and glare at the woman with deep wrinkles on her face.

She scowls back at me while running her small eyes over me, then her features soften a fraction. "I apologize for the noise. Are you visiting one of the tenants?" She folds her thin lips into an awkward smile.

I straighten up. "Yes, I am here to see this nice woman," I say and point to Halina who stares at me incredulously, her mouth falling open. She has recognized me.

The lady wrinkles her nose, as a harsh expression returns to her face. "You must find another place for chatting because this *nice* woman doesn't live here anymore." Her voice is stern.

My pulse speeds up. "And you must have no heart to be throwing her little children out into the blizzard."

Her eyes bulge and she breaths heavily. "It's not your business unless you pay for her," she retorts. "Or I'm calling the *milicja*."

I want to shake her, but I summon all my restraint and maintain my calmness. Telling her what I really think will make things much worse, and I don't need the authorities here.

"I will pay," I say, my skin tightening. "How much does she owe you?"

She instantly beams. "Follow me." She walks smartly out of the flat.

"Beata, please, no," Halina says shyly. "You don't have to."

"Yes, I do." I smile reassuringly at her. "It's all good. I will be back in a minute."

The woman leads me to her own apartment. It reeks of boiled cabbage.

When she tells me how much Halina owes, I can't resist laughing in her face. "That's all? You want to evict her for such a little amount?"

She doesn't even look ashamed. "Yes, because it will just keep adding up from month to month; she won't be able to pay, not now when her husband is dead."

"Her husband died?"

"In the UB prison. He was a threat to public security." She smirks. "Because of that, she won't get any help from the government, and it's not like she can find a job. I told her to chuck the children in the orphanage, so she can support herself, but she is stubborn."

I can't comprehend the lack of compassion this woman shows, but I don't comment any further. I pay what Halina owes and without another word or gesture, I walk back to my friend.

The door is still open, but Halina isn't standing there anymore, and the baby is not crying. I go inside and close the door gently behind me.

The little baby girl sleeps peacefully in a tiny cradle while her brother sits beside her, on a beat-up but clean rug, playing with a wooden toy car. Everything here seems old but clean and taken care of.

The flat smells of baby powder and baking soda. I kneel beside Halina's son. "What's your name?"

His big brown eyes look up. "Jurek. Are you Mama's friend?"

I smile gently. "Yes. She's lucky to have such a good helper like you. Are you watching your baby sister?"

"I always do when Mama is busy," he says with pride. "Papa told me to when the bad men came for him."

My heart sinks and I think immediately of Samuel's innocent bravery; how is it that these poor children have to bear such responsibility?

"I can't believe it's you," Halina says wiping her hands on the faded floral apron she's wearing now.

Tears spring to my eyes as we hug each other for a very long time, without any words.

"Mama, is everything okay?" Jurek's tentative voice brings us back to reality.

"Yes, darling. This is your aunt Beata. Do you remember I told you about her?"

He scratches his head but nods. "I thought she looked different."

Our eyes meet and we chuckle in understanding. "I looked different too, sweetheart," Halina says. "Why don't you go on playing and watching your sister while I talk to your aunt?"

Once we settle at a round table painted dark brown, Halina serves coffee and puts out a plate with two chunks of home-made apple cake.

"There is so much I want to tell you, but I don't know where to start," I say. "I'm glad I finally found you."

She looks away. "I'm so sorry for before. I will give you back what you paid that witch." She sighs. "She only plays harsh, but she wouldn't throw us out."

I take her hand in mine. "Don't worry about it. She told me about your husband. I'm so sorry."

She stifles a sob. "Stalin's puppets murdered him. He was a partisan throughout and after the war." She sniffs. "We met after the war. I begged him to settle down and stop fighting communists, so we could have a normal life." A tear trickles down the side of her nose. "When I got pregnant with Jurek, Robert agreed to leave the partisan life in forests. He found a job as electrician, and we were happy." She sniffs again and wipes more tears away. "Until last month, when they charged into our home in the middle of the night and arrested him." Her voice is devoid of emotion now, as if she gives up to the feeling of powerlessness. "Last week they informed me about his death. They wouldn't release his body, so I can't even bury him."

I squeeze her hand. "My heart goes out to you."

"I'm cursed. First, I lost Antek and now Robert."

"You must go on for the children. They are your blessings."

She nods. "If not for them, I'd have ended my misery a long time ago."

"They are beautiful children," I tell her. "How old is the little one?"

"Amelia is four months."

"I will help you. I will find a good place for you and the children."

She shakes her head. "I can't even afford a single room now." She laughs nervously. "I'm the only one left of my family." Silence speaks volumes for a long moment. "I will have to see if Robert's brother out east can help me."

"You don't need to. Harry and I will take care of you and your children, Halina."

"Harry?" She smiles. "I remember that when you talked about him, your eyes always sparkled just like now. You wanted to survive that place for him. I'm so happy for you, my friend."

"Thank you." I smile at her. "He found me after the war."

"Do you have children?"

A feeling of heaviness sets in my heart. "No. We've been trying, but with no luck."

"Stop trying and it will happen," she says and grins cheekily at me. "You're fretting too much, let Nature take her course."

"You're probably right." I take a sip of my coffee, a little embarrassed. "I mean it, we will take care of you and the children, Halina. Since the war ended, Harry helps his father to manage the family business and it's flourishing. We've the means to help you, and we will. You'll not worry ever again about money."

More tears run down her cheeks as she realizes my sincerity. "I can't accept this."

"If not for you, I wouldn't have survived the camp. You took me under your wing from the very first day, and I will never forget that. What I'm doing now is nothing compared to what you did for me."

"Oh Beata," she says, reaching for my hands. "You'd have survived without me because you're strong. Besides, if not for you, I wouldn't even be here." Her serious gaze finds mine. "One of the nights when I was dumped into a rotten cell without any food or water, after being beaten almost to unconsciousness, I was visited by a man. I don't remember what he looked like because I was in such awful condition. But I will never forget what he told me. He said that my friend Beata asked him to help me. He gently told me to stay strong for another few days, and that then the misery would end. He let me drink water from his tin and left a sweet roll for me to eat. Two days later, I was sent on a transport to Germany. You asked him to rescue me, though I don't know how you accomplished it."

Georg might have shown signs of kindness, but he also committed so many murders during the war. "I will tell you more about this man, Georg, tomorrow. Now I better go back to Harry before he alarms the whole of Warsaw."

"Before you go, there's something else I need to inform you of," she says, staring down at her hands.

I grow still and forget to breathe. "What is it?"

She clears her throat. "I was diagnosed with breast cancer last month." Her voice breaks and she falls into my arms when I reach out for her.

On my way back to Harry, I can't stop weeping. The ferocious wind blowing snow into my face makes it even more unbearable. Thankfully, our hotel is only ten minutes from Halina's flat. Once I knew her address, I made sure to stay close to her neighborhood.

My heart bleeds for Halina and the hardship she's going through. She managed to put her life together after the war and the terror in the camp, but then fate knocked her down again. I will do everything in my power to help her defeat this terrible disease that's taken hold of her body.

When I enter our hotel room, Harry pulls me into his

embrace. "I started worrying, princess. The weather is bad, and you didn't tell me where exactly your friend lives."

"Oh, Harry," I say, cherishing the warmth of his body. Words can't describe my love and affection for him. I hungrily drink every moment with him, yet I can never have enough of him. "Halina and her little children are in terrible circumstances."

He orders hot tea with honey, and I tell him Halina's story.

"I'm so sorry your friend has to endure this." He presses his lips to my forehead. "We will find a way to help her. We must try to get her to England, but this won't be easy. Stalin's secret police might be still watching her because of her husband." He rubs his chin, deep in thought. "But it's worth trying, as she would receive much better treatment in London. If she stays here, we will pay for the doctors and take care of her children until she regains her health." His smile is so soft and full of compassion.

I don't wipe away my tears. "Promise me that you will not die before me. I want to go first," I say as I kiss his mouth. Then, a moment and many kisses later, "I love you," I breathe. "My Harry."

EPILOGUE

BEATA

Harry and the children build sandcastles while their laughter rings out, bringing a surge of emotion to my heart. It's the middle of the week and we are on the private beach that belongs to our property, so we are alone here.

The crash of waves against the shore is like the lost moments of my life. I inhale the briny sea air, enjoying its salty taste on my tongue. Life has proved over and over that it can be sour.

Thanks to Harry's connections in the British embassy, we were able to bring Halina and her children to London where she received the best possible treatment to cure her cancer. She fought for over a year, before she finally succumbed, taking her last breath on the fifth day of March 1952.

She was a true warrior right to the end, but that terrible disease turned out to have the ferocity of a wolf. Losing her was so hard for her children. They still wake up at night in tears. If only I could bring back their beautiful mother...

Harry and I adopted both children and love them as our

own. I often ask God why he took so much away from Halina and gave it to us. I will always keep my friend's memory alive, so her children remember and cherish her. And to help with this, I've set up a foundation in her name, which helps women with breast cancer.

And so, Halina lives on this earth still, even though she has already crossed to the other side. She lives in her children, in our memories, in her foundation and all the women to whom it will give hope.

We talked a lot throughout the last year of her life. Besides Harry, she was the only person with whom I was able to speak about the camp. She understood my nightmares and fears, because she endured it herself.

She confessed that her entire family had been killed in the gas chambers. She couldn't share that with me when we were still in the camp, because words failed her whenever she tried.

The war took so much from all of us, and so many paid the ultimate price. My Felka will always stay in my heart, and there's not an hour in a day that she doesn't come to my mind. I will meet her again one day.

Camille, Leon and Marcel were killed in an air raid in their bakery. I will never forget them; they were the sweetest people who made the highest sacrifices.

We also found out that Georg was diagnosed with schizophrenia and admitted to a mental institution in Berlin. He had a trial and was sentenced to prison for life, but he'll never be released from the institution.

We visit Joanna on our every trip to Poland. She has a loving husband and three spirited children. The flirtatious girl is gone, replaced by a mature and independent woman—who hasn't lost the mischievous glint in her eye.

Last year, I visited Mrs. Moreau, who adores her grandchildren. Her son returned in 1945, after working throughout the war for the French Resistance. In the end, he proved to be worthy of his wonderful mother.

Once Marian Rejewski and Henryk Zygalski came to England in 1943, they were placed in the Polish armed forces, where they worked on cracking ciphers. They never got to work at Bletchley Park, though. There had been such significant advances with Enigma by this point that the British didn't need them anymore. Besides, people such as Knox, Denniston and Turing, who knew the Polish cryptologists and how critical they were to the war achievements, were no longer at Bletchley. After the war, Marian Rejewski returned to his family in Poland while Henryk Zygalski stayed in England.

I hope that one day the world will learn that if not for my dearest friends, Marian Rejewski, Jerzy Różycki and Henryk Zygalski, the Enigma secret wouldn't have been cracked in time to alter the course of the Second World War. The entire war would have lasted longer, with many more lives needlessly wasted. Our Polish cryptologists deserve their prominence in the history books.

A LETTER FROM GOSIA

Dear reader,

I want to say a huge thank you for choosing to read *The Codebreaker Girl*. If you enjoyed it, and want to keep up-to-date with all my latest releases, just sign up at the following link. Your email address will never be shared and you can unsubscribe at any time.

www.bookouture.com/gosia-nealon

The Codebreaker Girl is historical fiction, but the facts behind it are very real. Marian Rejewski was a Polish mathematician and cryptologist who was the first in the world to solve the unseen German military Enigma cipher machine. Later, along with two other mathematicians and cryptologists Henryk Zygalski and Jerzy Różycki, they developed methods and equipment for cracking the Enigma ciphers. There are also many other great people whom I mention in this novel, like Gustave Bertrand and Gwido Langer.

But in this book, fiction and reality mix. My protagonists, Beata and Harry, are fictional characters who go on the journey with the cryptologists. For example, the meeting in Pyry did truly happen, and the cryptologists traveled to France to keep working on their Enigma mission. So the book is heavy on historical facts, and it's only until Beata ends up in Perpignan when fiction overtakes, though the war background still stays true to facts.

This book tells the story of Beata and Harry, two people falling in love in the midst of war. But it also shows the true story of the Polish mathematicians and cryptologists who deserve an honorable place in the history books thanks to their genius accomplishments.

I hope you loved *The Codebreaker Girl* and if you did, I would be very grateful if you could write a review. I'd love to hear what you think, and it makes such a difference helping new readers to discover one of my books for the first time.

I love hearing from my readers – you can get in touch through my social media or my website.

Thanks,

Gosia Nealon

www.gosianealon.com

facebook.com/GosiaNealonHistoricalFiction

x.com/GosiaNealon

BIBLIOGRAPHY

Robert Gawłowski, *Jestem tym, który rozszyfrował Enigmę. Nieznana historia Mariana Rejewskiego*, Episteme Wydawnictwo, Lublin, 2022.

Andrzej Krzysztof Kunert (Opracowanie), *Polacy – Żydzi, Polen – Juden, Poles – Jews 1939-1945 Wybór źródeł.*

Quellenauswahl. Selection of Documents. Rada Ochrony Pamięci Walk i Męczeństwa. Instytut Dziedzictwa Narodowego. Oficyna Wydawnicza RYTM, Warszawa, 2001.

Marian Rejewski, *Memories of my work at the Cipher Bureau of the General Staff Second Department 1930–1945*, Adam Mickiewicz University Press, Poznań, 2021.

Stanisław Strumph Wojtkiewicz, *Sekret Enigmy*, Iskry, Warszawa, 1978.

Dermot Turing, *XY&Z: The real story of how Enigma was broken*, The History Press, Great Britain, 2021.

Dermot Turing, *The Enigma Story. The truth behind the 'unbreakable' World War II cipher*, Arcturus Publishing Limited, Great Britain, 2022.

ACKNOWLEDGMENTS

Special thanks to Natalie Edwards for inspiring me to write this novel. When she came up with this wonderful idea, I loved it right away. Thank you, Natalie! I'm so lucky to be working with such an amazing editor. And huge thanks to the entire team at Bookouture for your brilliant work, and to Emma Hargrave for her awesome job on line editing.

I'm very thankful to my husband Jim Nealon and my sons Jacob, Jack and Jordan. You are my everything. I dedicate this book especially to you because every day you inspire me and bring me true happiness. I'm very proud of you and love you so much.

I will be always thankful to my sister Kasia Pasfield for her unconditional support while here on Earth, and now from Heaven. I think of you every day and I feel your presence. I know you keep watching over your beautiful sons, Matthew and Ryan, whom I cherish to have in my life. I love you forever.

My gratitude goes to my beloved parents Elżbieta and Zdzisław Szmitko; my brother Tomek Szmitko who always researches interesting historical facts for me; my brother Mariusz Szmitko and his gorgeous family; my parents-in-law Jane and Francis Nealon; my sister-in-law Stephanie Nealon for always sharing about my books on social media.

Warmest thanks to my friends Iza Pszeniczny, Mary Ann Cinque, Ania Albrecht, Ania Pierwocha, Asia and Rafał Kudzia for their amazing support; to Shari Ryan whose incredible talent and determination inspire me; to Aga Chaberek for always reading my books and sharing her thoughts with me; to Izabela Wójcicki, Marta Wesołowski and Polonia of Long Island for organizing my first book signing party; and to the rest of my family and friends in Poland and United States.

Special thanks to Jack's teacher, Ms. Annie Warm, whose passion for teaching and nurturing our children is inspiring and beautiful; to Jacob's teacher, Mrs. Jill Firmbach, for her dedication to teaching our children and for being a remarkable teacher; and to all the other teachers for their hard work and guidance. I'm beyond grateful.

Huge thanks to all my readers for your wonderful reviews, comments on social media, emails, messages. And most of all, thank you for reading my books and inspiring me to keep writing.

PUBLISHING TEAM

Turning a manuscript into a book requires the efforts of many people. The publishing team at Bookouture would like to acknowledge everyone who contributed to this publication.

Commercial
Lauren Morrissette
Hannah Richmond
Imogen Allport

Data and analysis
Mark Alder
Mohamed Bussuri

Cover design
Eileen Carey

Editorial
Natalie Edwards
Charlotte Hegley

Copyeditor
Dushi Horti

Proofreader
Claire Rushbrook

Marketing
Alex Crow
Melanie Price
Occy Carr
Cíara Rosney
Martyna Młynarska

Operations and distribution
Marina Valles
Stephanie Straub

Production
Hannah Snetsinger
Mandy Kullar
Jen Shannon
Ria Clare

Publicity
Kim Nash
Noelle Holten
Jess Readett
Sarah Hardy

Rights and contracts
Peta Nightingale
Richard King
Saidah Graham